VANILLA

by

Mona Kabbani

MONA KABBANI

VANILLA

Vanilla

Mona Kabbani

Copyright 2021 by Mona Kabbani

This is a work of fiction. Names, characters, places, businesses, events, and incidents are the product of the author's imagination or are used fictitiously and are not to be construed as real. Any resemblance to actual events, locales, organizations, or persons, living or dead, is entirely coincidental.

All rights reserved. No part of this book may be used or reproduced in any manner whatsoever without written permission from the author except in the case of brief quotations embodied in critical articles and reviews.

ISBN-13: 9798712816507

First Edition, March 2021

Edited by Spencer Hamilton

www.spencerhamiltonbooks.com

www.nerdywordsmith.com

Graphic Design by Mitch Green

Instagram @mitch_grn

www.radpublishing.co

Illustration by Andi Brotten

Instagram @andibrotten

www.unbearablescares.com

VANILLA

PROLOGUE

Page 10

PART ONE

Page 28

PART TWO

Page 137

PART THREE

Page 267

EPILOGUE

Page 375

"Love has no age, no limit; and no death."

John Galsworthy

"Love does not claim possession, but gives freedom."

Rabindranath Tagore

"Let me tell you that the children from their very birth are born to evil. Satan seems to have control of them. He seems to take possession of their young minds, and they are corrupted. Why do fathers and mothers act as though a lethargy was upon them? They do not mistrust that Satan is sowing evil seed in their families."

Ellen G. White

VANILLA

To unconditional love.

To my Teta Mona.

MONA KABBANI

VANILLA

by
Mona Kabbani

PROLOGUE

The diner's atmosphere breeds silence. The kind of silence your mind draws after being caught red-handed in a dark alleyway with a dirty needle: tense, and apprehensive, and, above all, wishing you could escape.

Tiffany is craned over, morphed into some rusty yet galvanized machine; the miniskirt of her waitress uniform fights to reveal her bottom as she bends over. It's the same song and dance night after night. *Bend. Wipe. Tug. Bend. Wipe.*

And still, she persists. Above all, she persists.

The diner's owner, Tony, suggested she write "stubborn" on her résumé under *Special Skills*. At the time she'd been cleaning the grout in the kitchen with a toothbrush, hacking up a lung as her body fought her mind to collapse. He insisted she take the day to rest, but she refused.

"Tiff, you sure you don't wanna just go home and get some shuteye?"

"No. Being alone in that room is a nightmare. I'd rather be here."

"Ain't you stubborn, eh? Add that to your résumé! Ha!"

Not that he'd ever want her to leave the diner. He'd be devastated if she did. The two years she's worked under him have been the best years for the joint.

In this case, rather than a nasty cough leeching her energy, what dares stand against her stubbornness is a stain, taunting her, its dirty little mouth open and laughing. She has been struggling to remove the stain from the dessert display case, exhausting her muscle strength and threatening to break the glass every second the grime remains. But her opponent is stubborn as well. No matter how long she rubs or which unlabeled chemical solution she attempts to drown it in, the stain refuses to budge, testing her resilience. But, as always, she persists.

Above all, she persists.

Ness stands behind the register. Her blood-red nails fly across the keyboard of her phone like a fevered pianist as she chomps down on a piece of bubblegum. She, too, wears the same yellow polo and red miniskirt of their waitress uniform, though she rarely steps out from behind the counter, shielding her lower body from the eyes of passersby through the diner's windows.

Ness never offers to help clean and Tiffany never asks her to—an unspoken agreement between them Tiffany finds mutually beneficial.

Absentmindedly, Ness pops her gum. Tiffany flinches, a spike of frustration bursting through her spine, but she resolves to ignore it. They've already had this argument several times before; going through it again would be insanity.

"Why do you have to fucking pop your gum so often, Ness? In fact, why do you have to pop it at all? Doesn't it taste the same either way?"

"Jeez, Tiff! I'm sooo sorry it bothers ya so much! But ain't nobody else complaining."

"That's because nobody else is here, Vanessa! It's three o'clock in the morning! It's just you, me, and Tony, and he's in the back so he can't hear the damn popping!"

"Well. Maybe ya should wear some headphones then."

"Oh, right. Real fucking professional. I'll wear headphones so I can't hear when the customers come in. Let me do just that to make your life more conveniently annoying. Is it really that hard for you to just not fucking pop the damn gum?"

"Yes, it is. All right, fine, fine! I'll stop poppin' the damn gum. Two years ya been workin' here, Tiff, and you're really crampin' my style."

A toddler would be easier to argue with. At least you could punish them with a smack on the back of the hand or simply force them to stop. Maybe lock them away in the wooden prison walls of their crib without any gum. But with Ness, that isn't possible. She's too old for that kind of training. Too old and too set in her ways. You can't condition behavior anymore. And no matter how many times they've argued, she'll never stop poppin' the damn gum.

It's no use. I don't know what else I could do.

Tiffany glances over at Ness, watching her click away at her phone, her eyes glued to the screen. She hesitates for a moment, thinking that the longer she watches, the longer the want, that annoying tic, will stay at bay. After a few clicks, Tiffany returns to the stain.

Blissful silence . . .

Pop!

Tiffany jerks. She is about to open her mouth into a scream when the bell above the door chimes. Her attention is pulled from the damn poppin' to the diner's front door, where two men hobble in. They nearly fall flat on their faces as they stumble over the leveled black-and-white tiling.

The bell chimes again as the door shuts out the night behind them.

Tiffany stands and places the dirty rag behind the counter, brushing the imaginary dust from her uniform. Before she takes a step toward them, Ness from behind the register hisses, "Hey. Be careful, will ya? These guys look no good. Like trouble. I've seen before on the news, guys like this pretending to be drunk. They walk into empty joints at night and start fights. Some even try to rob the place! Ya don't wanna get caught up in that mess. Bad news, I tell ya. Bad, bad news."

"What, those two drunks?" Tiffany glances over then turns back to that mess of fire-engine hair. "I appreciate it, Ness, but I wouldn't worry."

Blood-red nails fiddle nervously with phone keys.

Tiffany's brow furrows and she continues in jest, "Besides, this *is* a twenty-four-seven diner. Isn't it our job to take care of these idiots?"

"Yeah, yeah. Sure. But if I ain't worrying, then who is? Who's watching out for you then, huh?" Ness rolls her eyes into the back of her head, the whites looking purple under the neon lighting of the diner. "No worries. You know me. I'll watch out for ya even if ya mock me. I'll be back here with my phone ready to dial nine-one-one."

Vanessa's face, with those green eyes that stare so beggingly outward, disappears as she returns to the comfort of her phone screen. The clicking of keys continues. The constant *tap-tap-tap* sound reminds Tiffany of a time when she found Ness staring out the window, tapping her nails against the register and biting her lips so hard, Tiffany thought she might pop one open.

"No gum today, Ness?" Tiffany had asked in a passing joke.

Ness's eyes met hers instantly, like a wind-up toy with springs strung so tight, the slightest breeze from saying hello would trigger it like a whip. Tiffany backed her weight onto her heels, shocked by that hollowed and pale face. She recognized the depth of that fear immediately. It was like looking into a mirror.

Tiffany's lungs inflated and she broke the fear-filled silence. "Are you okay?" She placed her hand on top of Ness's, stopping her from scratching ugly designs into the plastic register keys.

Ness shuddered, then relaxed and smiled. "Yeah, I'm fine. Thought I saw a guy I knew pass by. Was scared he was gonna walk in here."

But that's how Ness is with every guy who walks into the diner. The bell chimes, a man enters through the door, and Ness is as stiff as a board. Like her body might seize into paralysis if he takes a step too close to her.

It's no wonder she's never had a serious boyfriend.

But then again, Tiffany isn't one to talk.

Tiffany watches the screen's light shift back and forth ever so slightly across Ness's face. She shakes her head, annoyed by how quickly Ness's moods change, then walks over to the two men as they loudly complain about the lack of service.

"Hello and welcome to Big Daddy's Burger, where we always feed you right! Will that be a table for two?" Tiffany strains a smile as she greets them.

The two men turn to her with tight, quivering lips. They look her over, their eyes traveling up her legs, her stomach, taking a pit stop at her chest, and finally settling on her face. As they attempt to take in steady breaths, they burst into laughter. Droplets of spit land on Tiffany's cheekbones. She flinches, frowns, and wipes the saliva from her skin.

"Aw, man! Ain't you the most gorgeous thing?"

"See? I told yous this place was good! Service, and with such a beautiful smile!"

"You're damn right! I'm sorry I ever doubted you!"

They cackle at each other like hyenas, the stench of alcohol shooting from their mouths like untimely fireworks. They have already forgotten about Tiffany, the object of their enjoyment, who remains standing right in front of them. She waits with a hand on her hip until she realizes their attention is long gone.

She clears her throat. "I'm sorry. Excu— ... Excuse me, gentlemen!"

They look back at her, wonder filling their eyes as though they are just seeing her for the first time.

"Hey there, gorgeous!"

"What's up, cutie?"

"Yeah! Whatcha need, doll?"

"Hey, you got a boyfriend?"

"I asked if you would like a table for two," Tiffany repeats.

"Huh?"

"We's in a food establishment, man."

"We is? Oh, shit! I remember now. I was hungry!"

"So was I!"

"So a table for two?" Her throat tenses up.

A scoff. "Well, duh!"

She ignores their resumed cackles, her discomfort swelling as she walks them over to a table. She hopes they are still following her—she doesn't want to have to re-collect their attention. She would probably just abandon them if so.

But probably not.

They are a few staggering steps away but trailing. She guides them to a booth. They catch up and each takes an opposing seat.

"Alrighty, what can I start you two off with to—"

"Look, doll, we already knows what we wants."

"Yeah, gimme a milkshake. Chocolate." A sloppy wink.

"Ooh, yeah. Get me one a them too!"

They pick up their menus from the table, squinting as if they were written in a foreign language. Tiffany stands with her pen still pressed against her pad in anticipation.

"And to eat?" she asks.

"Just come back to us with those shakes. We'll tell yous after." A hand waves, dismissing her.

Tiffany clicks her pen and slides it and the pad back into her skirt apron. She hesitates, watching the men struggle incredulously before turning away.

Fucking morons.

She walks back behind the counter to the milkshake machine and flicks the switch on—one of the few pieces of machinery that isn't covered in rust or dust. It greets her with a soporific whir, its resonating hum putting her into a trance. She welcomes the sound into her ears, letting it drown out the customers' words. She plays it like an instrument, thinking about all the cleaning the kitchen could still use. All of that deep scrubbing, trying to reach the grime that managed to sink so far into the grout. Beyond reach if not for maybe—

"Hey," Ness whispers, having quietly stepped up behind her.

"Jesus! Ness!" Tiffany reacts, nearly knocking over a glass. "Don't sneak up on me like that!"

"Sorry, sorry. But keep ya voice down. Ya so damn loud."

"Well? What the hell do you want?"

"Are you okay? They seem like pricks."

Tiffany looks behind at the two, watching them turn their

menus in circles. She turns back to the machine. "Pricks, yes. Paying customers, also yes. They're fine, Ness. They're not going to rob the place. They can't even hurt a fly."

"Ya sure? They ain't fakin'?" Her eyes nearly bulge out of her head and quickly dart back and forth between Tiffany and the table.

"I highly doubt they're faking." Tiffany chuckles to herself. "Aw, shit!" She flicks her finger. A glob of chocolate milkshake spits out onto the counter. "Dammit! It overflowed. Get me a rag, will you?"

Tiffany blindly holds out her hand. *Plop!* A heavy, wet substance falls into her palm. From its dripping ick, she knows it smells rancid and will dirty more than it can clean.

"Jesus, Ness. A *clean* rag! I can't wipe down the glasses with this rat!"

"Okay, okay!" Ness responds defensively. She bends over and pulls out a clean rag from the bottom drawer, handing it off.

Tiffany nods. "Thanks." She polishes up the overflowing glasses, making sure not to miss a spot.

A gruff voice behind them calls: "Hey! Where're the milkshakes, ladies? I can see yous both bickering back there! What kinda customer service is this?"

"Tiff! You said they was harmless," Ness whispers, her body shaking like a traumatized chihuahua.

Tiffany freezes for a moment, Ness's anxiety pouring into her. "They are. Just don't respond."

With steady hands, Tiffany stakes a plump cherry and a straw into each shake. She places the glasses on a black tray and walks them over to the table.

There, she stumbles and nearly drops everything to the floor.

They're watching me.

But when she looks up from her blunder, she sees that they aren't. That they're laughing to each other like brainless animals.

So why does she feel so unnerved?

She regains her balance and makes it the rest of the way, her stomach descending with every step.

"Here you go."

She sets their milkshakes in front of them and they drag them to their chests to take a sip.

"Damn, that's a good shake." Lips smack.

"Are yous surprised? Look who made it!"

The men turn to her simultaneously and grin.

The room is dark, but at this angle, the dim neon lights highlight their swollen, red faces as they try to keep their eyes uncrossed long enough to look at her. Their upper bodies sway back and forth. Tiffany grows nauseous from the motion.

No, these grins aren't what's making her uncomfortable. She's faced grins like these before.

She averts her eyes and pulls her pad and pen from her skirt apron. They watch her, then turn to each other and roar laughter onto their drinks—as if this diner wasn't covered in enough of their saliva. She scrunches her face in disgust as the glasses sweat spit.

"Doll, what's a gorgeous girl like you doing waitressing in a rundown place like this?"

She clicks her pen and presses the ballpoint to the page. The yellow pad drinks in the black ink. "Taking your order, sweetheart." She flashes them a sweet smile, holding back the itch in her throat that begs to tear wide open into a shriek. "Now, is there anything else I can get you two?"

"Yeah." The other snickers. "Let's get a bottle a syrup and yous on a plate!"

"'Ey! What an idea!"

They both throw their hands up in victory, nearly smacking knuckles into their milkshakes. Tiffany flinches as the glasses teetertotter on their bases, threatening to fall over and crack. When they finally roll back into stability, she lets out a weak chuckle.

"Ooh, aren't you two funny?"

They continue on, but she doesn't hear their next few comments. Their voices muffle in her ears like the *whomp-whomp* of a large air-conditioning unit. A high-pitched tone follows. She no longer hears the customers and she no longer sees them. In fact, she's not even sure if she can feel herself, the pulse in her chest having suddenly petrified and the pad and pen in her hands growing weightless.

Her eyes are caught on something through the diner's dark windows. Something that siphons the life from her body like a straw plunged into a milkshake.

An apparition stands on the other side of the street, watching her from the shadows of a dark alley. She could feel it before, the eyes on her like an anxious tug in the pit of her stomach. Only now does she realize it wasn't coming from the two drunks at the table—it was coming from something far worse.

This is it.

She stares and it stares back. Its unwavering body is barely definable beneath the black trench coat, but hauntingly tall. Its blue eyes and silver hair shine like scales even through the thin streaks of streetlight. Its presence sets her nervous system on fire.

She gulps.

Shit.

Her hands start to shake, scribbling black lines of distraught lace across the pad. An image of blood-stained steel flashes into her mind. The itch in her throat nearly causes her to squeak. She presses her fingernails into the palm of her hand, digging red crescent moons into her skin, forcing herself to control her tremors.

Cautiously, she puts the pad and pen back into her apron. She doesn't want to look away nor make any sudden movements. She doesn't want to set it off.

"Hey, lady! Aren't ya listening?" Fingers snap at her.

"Yes," she says. "Yes, yes. If you'll excuse me . . ." She backs away from the table toward the diner counter, ignoring their now irate complaints. She doesn't break eye contact with the figure across the street. Not until it turns and walks up the road.

"Fuck, fuck, *fuck* . . ." she murmurs under her breath.

It's coming for me. Whether it has to walk through those doors or not, it's coming.

She spins around and lifts the partition, stepping behind the counter toward the kitchen.

Tony, a stubby man with a scruffy beard wearing a dirty chef's hat, the stench of wet food and sewage forever leaking from his moist pores, steps out and blocks her path.

"Hey! You okay? Ness keeps botherin' me. Those boys givin' you trouble?" A concerned look stretches across his large face. "'Cause I'll kick 'em out if they are."

Tiffany waves her hand. "No, no, Tony! They're fine. I just don't feel well is all. I need to leave." She grabs her coat and purse from under the counter. "I only have one table. Let Ness take it over. She can do it. She can have the tip. I don't mind."

"You sure?" he calls out after her.

But she is already gone.

If I leave from the back door, she thinks, *I might have a chance.*

Ness is in the kitchen, clicking away on her phone. She *pops* her gum—Tiffany doesn't flinch this time—then notices her coworker. "Hey! What's the matter? Where ya goin'?"

"I think I'm gonna vomit—" is the only answer Tiffany can muster before her throat seizes up.

"Well, if ya gonna vomit then—"

Tiffany pushes open the back door and steps out into the damp night. She looks to either side but sees no one. The streets are nearly empty at this time.

With her arms wrapped around herself for warmth—or for some semblance of a shield—she walks out onto the road. If she stays under the streetlights, they'll keep her safe. They'll keep it at bay. She knows the thought is silly. Still, she thinks it, if anything, for the strength in comfort.

If I turn down the next road, it might not see me. It might have walked into the diner. It might already be looking for me there. I might have escaped.

Even so, she can't help but search. It would be better, she thinks, for her to know where it is than to deal with the uncertainty. With the anxiety building in her chest, ready to pop at any movement as if it is here and all around, just a slight, chilling touch away. It would be better to know it is near than to not know and to find out too late. She searches as she walks and scares herself when a group of late-night partiers turns down the street. Their jovial screams cause her body to stutter.

"Shit!" An embarrassed moan escapes her as she shakes her head and looks down at the ground.

You're going to give yourself a heart attack. You're going to scare yourself to death.

She laughs. *To death. Ha!* At first, it's a low chuckle meant only for herself. For herself to feel the hearty bounce in her belly. But it latches onto her throat and soon that itch she'd been feeling before finally explodes into the air, the force of it so strong it throws her head back not into screams but into laughter. Unstoppable, untamable laughter.

Why are you so afraid? It won't ever leave you alone! Might as well face it! You're stuck with it forever as long as you live! And maybe even longer than that! Maybe even in death! But keep your chin up! You already know that dying is pain!

There's a cold breath on the back of her neck. A breath that comes from the lungs of the Devil himself. Her skin prickles and she stumbles forward. She turns around, but there is nothing there. Only empty space.

Still, the prickle never settles. She feels the needles pierce her skin. Sharp, steel needles. Needles stained with blood.

You're stuck with it . . .

Her knees wobble beneath her hips and her stomach fills with thousands of centipedes. Her bladder weakens and she grows nauseous. She wants to kneel over and hurl, but a spike of adrenaline like a dormant flight instinct awakens through her system.

Without true rationality, she charges into a sprint.

"Fuck, fuck, fuck!" she cries, because she can sense it now. She can sense it approaching and she is not ready to face it again. She never will be.

She runs down the empty road like a wild animal hunted, her limbs flailing about. Only a few flickering streetlights shine down on her; otherwise, she is mostly hidden in the darkness. The yellow halos have all gone out. Her arms and legs pump desperately. She nearly trips from her uncontrolled speed.

"Fucking fuck! Someone fucking help me!" she screams, trying to get someone's attention, anyone, but no answers come. Looming bystanders witness through the windows of their safe homes a crazy girl running from nothing.

But it's not nothing. She knows it's there behind her. She can feel it like she can feel the blood pumping through her veins.

Reluctantly, she looks back. The road is empty.

"Fuck!" she screams out one final time. Her body begs for rest, fighting with her emotions over the fact that no one is chasing her so she no longer needs to run.

But just because she can't see it doesn't mean it's not there.

Her legs are about to give. She whimpers from exhaustion and turns down a dark alley, unwilling to rest, an easy target, in the middle of the open street.

She slows and spins, staring at the gaping lit entrance of the alley as she walks backward, deeper into the shadows.

It's coming.

But nothing appears.

Her final step leads her into a wall. She stops and presses against it, taking a moment to catch her breath. As she exhales, the fog from her frozen breath obscures her vision of the entrance and she waves her hand to make it disperse. She wants to make sure she can see it when it comes.

And it always comes. One way or another, it comes and gets what it wants. Like how it used to come through that dark metal door all those years.

There's a flutter against her spine. Her heart stops.

The wall she has crushed herself against begins to move.

She yelps and whips around.

A foot above her, two blue eyes glare through the darkness.

It's here.

Her vocal cords freeze. She can feel her heart pick up speed in her chest. She takes a step back, but her foot lands in a pothole. Her ankle twists and she falls into a puddle. She's disoriented but a hand clamps down around her neck, instantly yanking her back into focus. She is choking, her esophagus squeezed like a nearly empty tube of toothpaste. The hand lifts her off the ground, brings her to its raging blue eyes. She grabs the hand with her own and tries to pry the cold, dead fingers from her neck, but it's too strong.

She struggles with a few more kicks before hanging limp like the prey she has already accepted herself to be.

Possessed.

Keep your chin up. You already know . . .

Its eyes smile. A grin filled with sharp teeth appears inches from her face.

"Why must you always run from me? You know it is no use by now," the grin says through a sinister voice. Its tongue snakes out from between its lips as it speaks. "Ever since you were young, you would always try to run. Oh, don't look at me like that. Don't look at me with those bulging eyes, so surprised to see me!"

Tiffany can feel herself fainting. The slow loss of consciousness. Darkness coils around the edges of her vision.

. . . you've always known . . .

"Hush, hush, foolish girl. I know it has been a while since I've come to visit. And look how much better you are doing! No one could ever tell you were so sick! Hmm? What is that? Oh, yes. I have missed you too. But let's not waste time on such glib emotions."

. . . that dying . . .

Tiffany gargles on the clump of thick mucus and terror building in the back of her throat.

"Now, listen. Do your dear life-saving doctor a favor, will you? I need you to find someone for me. This is very important, so listen carefully. Are you listening?"

Tiffany's body jerks for life.

"I need you to find someone for me, someone very specific. I need you to find her and I need you to kill her."

. . . that dying is pain.

Those fangs glisten and Tiffany blacks out.

PART ONE

CHAPTER I

Fourteen years earlier

A little girl with golden-blond pigtails wearing nothing but a dirty white dress sits on a cold concrete floor. Her toys are scattered in front of her: a stuffed blue dog, a stethoscope, and a syringe. She picks up the stethoscope, wraps the black rubber cord around her neck, and picks up the dog. She places the eartips in her ears, wincing at the icy touch of the metal bars against her collarbones, and presses the steel drum against the dog's chest.

She hears nothing.

She lets the drum drop from her hand and picks up the syringe. It feels heavy and rough but not as cold as the stethoscope. It's the same temperature as the palm of her hand. She guides the needle to the stuffed blue dog's neck and pierces it deep through the fabric.

The stuffed blue dog does not protest or cry out in pain and she knows it never will. She presses on the plunger, injecting a dose of air into its cotton-filled body, her own body shaking with anticipation. She slides the needle out, places the syringe back down, and re-collects the drum in her tiny, porcelain fingers. She presses the drum once again to the dog's chest.

Still, nothing.

She sighs, lets the drum drop, and picks the syringe back up, repeating the same steps over and over again. *Press,* nothing, *inject, press,* nothing. It is the only thing she has to do in this concrete room. There are no windows for her to look through to admire the scenery, no clock for her to watch, no television, and no book for her to read—if she could read. In this room are only a lumpy mattress shoved into the corner—complete with a lumpy pillow and a lumpy blanket—her three toys to play with, and a heavy, dark metal door. On that door is a deadbolt lock.

She pulls the syringe out of the dog's neck and checks its chest.

Nothing.

She sighs again and places the stuffed blue dog back on the floor. She takes care to rest it nicely on its side so that it's comfortable. Even if it does not thump like her, she believes it deserves to be comfortable.

She fiddles with her thumbs, rolling them around each other, and turns to the gray walls that form her room. Her eyes find the large stain she once thought of as a horrifying creature trying to slither its way in. Trying to open its jagged teeth to birth her nightmares. Only to learn that the stain is nothing but an inanimate pattern she can study and trace and love just like the cracks she finds along the walls. A stain that kisses her fingertips with brown water. Brown water that tastes the way her metal door smells. Dirty and metallic. A stain she plays with until boredom takes over and she hopes for a new stain to appear.

But the walls all look exactly the same. There is no new stain.

She lies down, her hair spreading out on the floor around her like a crown, and stares up at the ceiling. It's lined with a few familiar cracks she has already gawked at until she yawned. One of the cracks leads up to the single lightbulb in the room that hangs from the center of the ceiling. It's held up by a piece of silver duct tape that keeps the bulb from dipping close enough to the floor for her to reach. She watches it cast a flickering, sterile white light across the cracks.

She frowns and closes her eyes so she can rest her vision behind the cool darkness of her lids. She pats her hand around her body and around the floor, eventually finding the drum in her tiny fingers. She picks it up and brings it to her chest to listen.

Thump-thump. Thump-thump. Thump-thump.

It is a while before anything else happens.

Thump-thump. Thump-thump. Thump-thump.

There is a knock on the door. She does not move when she hears it. She is too busy listening to the sound of her chest to be bothered.

"My sweet?" a voice like thick liquid says from behind the

metal frame.

She doesn't respond.

"My sweet, I'm coming in. Daddy has a present for you," the voice sings.

The lock snaps and the door creaks open. Heavy footsteps. The door shuts and the lock snaps again.

"Now, what are you doing on the floor?"

His footsteps approach and she opens her eyes. His shadow blankets her. Big, white hands reach down and scoop her up off the floor. They carry her to the mattress and lay her on their lap.

His face is above hers but the details of it are darkened by a shadow. All she can see is the shiny silver hair, the bright blue eyes, and the glistening grin.

"Daddy?" she whispers.

"Yes, my sweet. Daddy is here," he hums as he brushes her hair back with his long, boney fingers.

He pets her and she purrs softly at the frigid touch. When he lifts his hand to the top of her head, she can see the familiar tattoo on his wrist and stares—two black dots, which always seem to painfully throb, decorated by curvy black lines like a lace painting. She wishes she could trace the lines, but she has always been too afraid to ask.

"Daddy has a gift for you," he coos.

His hands shift, placing her down in a seated position on the mattress next to him. She can see him a little more clearly now that the light shines directly onto the profile of his face. His skin is pale white and smooth, without a blemish or wrinkle—the complete opposite of these cracked and stained walls. Not even a vein pops from beneath his skin, besides the veins beneath his tattoo; in some lighting, she can see them there, like deep blue snakes. The snakes he's described to her that the creatures keep as pets and feed pieces of flesh and bone to. His eyebrows nearly match the color of his skin but are thick enough to be visible. Thick enough that she can almost always read his emotions from a distance. When they aren't furrowed, they are calm, flat lines. His hair is gray, a shade lighter than these concrete walls, and he wears it slicked into a perfectly neat do. So neat that she thinks if she were to tap on it with her knuckles, it would sing a metallic song to her like the metal door does. His eyes are piercing; they look at her with hunger. His sharp and wide jawline complements those eyes, making it seem like he could actually eat her if he wished to; when he smiles, his teeth sparkle. He is almost always smiling at her. Even right now, as he reaches into the back pocket of his pants and pulls out a lollipop.

"Would my sweet like a sweet?" he asks, holding the candy up in front of her.

She smiles and nods. Her cheeks nearly eclipse her eyes from how happy she is to see the gift.

He unwraps the lollipop for her slowly, carefully peeling back the paper to reveal the bright red candy. He opens his mouth; she mimics him. He places the lollipop on her tongue and closes his mouth. She copies and instantly feels the euphoria from the sugar shoot into her brain.

She is always excited by the taste of sweets.

A grin spreads across his lips and he leans in to kiss her

forehead, his hand against the back of her head. He scooches down the mattress and lies, resting his head on the hard pillow. He pats the space next to his body and she lies with him, nuzzling into the crevice between his arm and ribcage. They stare at the ceiling together.

A few silent beats pass before he whispers the question he has asked her many times over:

"Are you my sweet little girl, Vanilla?"

She removes the lollipop from her mouth and answers as she always does:

"Yes, Daddy!"

"Good."

She sleeps.

As her daddy slowly rises to leave her, the pipes creak and groan behind the thick layers of concrete, though their sounds are not loud enough to be heard by innocent ears. They carry with them, through the rusty slides that traverse the building, the thick concoction of blood and chemicals that have been poured down their drains by the Devil calling himself Daddy. The pipes drink it in—they will drink anything in—and flush the liquid through the pull of gravity until their contents are deposited into the sewage system, relieving the pipes of their aching and swelling.

It has been some time since they have visited the girl's room and stopped to say hello. It has been some time since they've paused to watch her, leaving her a present, a seed of their brown water concoction that would expand into the stains she so loves. It has been some time and they have found interest in other rooms, leaving their kiss of blood-filled stains in parts unreachable to her.

CHAPTER II

She had fallen asleep without being conscious of it. She dreamt of playing with her stuffed blue dog, sitting in the middle of her room with the dim lightbulb dangling just above her head, that sterile white flicker spreading a sore itch across her skin even in her dreams. She had just picked up the syringe after hearing no thumping when there came a scratching against the metal door. She looked up and called for her daddy, thinking he was the one causing the noise from behind the door. Thinking he was standing there, teasing the signal to his entrance. *Just come in already, Daddy!* But his comforting voice was not what answered. Instead, the scratch grew louder and louder until it became a blood-curdling screech, as if something were viciously digging, engraving tortured marks as it peeled away silver ribbons of metal. Then it became pounding. Desperate pounding and distorted screams like something needed urgently to get inside. To get inside and get to her. She screamed for her daddy, but the pounding only grew worse and worse until she thought the door might burst open.

Don't come in, don't come in, DON'T COME IN! STAY OUTSIDE!

She jerks awake, her eyes wide in horror, aimed directly at the entrance. But there is no pounding. Not anymore.

Just a dream? she wonders. She stares vacantly around the room, caught in a trance between two worlds, her mind struggling to make sense of just one.

As her senses reassemble into reality, clicking back together like puzzle pieces until there is a solid picture of gray, they pick up the delicate sound of scratching struggling to be heard from the wall behind her. This time the scratching is real, but her skin does not pucker.

She looks around. Her daddy is no longer here. The bare stem of her lollipop lays on the mattress in his place as if to take his role. As if to tell her, *It's okay! It's okay that Daddy is gone. I'm here. I'm here with you!* The top of the stem has been chewed up and crushed to a point like the tip of the syringe. She picks it up and pops it back into her mouth, savoring the last bit of flavor still trapped within the paper stem. Her muscles decompress.

The scratch continues, demanding attention. She can hear the uninterrupted *ktch-ktch-ktch* as if it is right next to her ear. She turns to the wall behind her mattress, places one nail against the concrete, and digs, welcoming in the familiar sound. The *ktch-ktch-ktch* scratches back at a heightened speed, excited by her response.

It—whatever *it* is behind the wall *(or maybe within the wall)*—has visited her many times before. It calls her at random, she supposes when it can, starting off slow then growing irate when not acknowledged. The first time she heard it, she had a similar experience to that of her first meeting with the stain. She cowered, grew curious, grew brave, and then tested the threat. And just like the stain, the scratch did not hurt her. It did not yank her into its dark clutches through its grip on her finger. It did not drag her into the Outside for her to be preyed and feasted upon by creatures alike. (It has passed her mind many times before that the scratch might be a creature from the Outside, waiting behind the wall, gaining her trust, tempting her closer, stripping away at her defenses, until one day . . .)

She knows it would probably be safest for her to ignore the scratch. Then she could forgo her fears altogether. But it would only scratch longer and louder, stealing away her sleep. And although this reason is enough, there is still another reason why she chooses to entertain the scratch: to take her chance at being face to face with a hungry, panting creature on the other side. It is a reason she only vaguely understands because she has never known a life where she is not lonely. And time passes effortlessly when they are together.

So she scratches back.

Eventually the scratching stops, and so does the passage of time, jolting her back into the claustrophobic present. She tries to get its attention back so that it will play with her for a little while longer, wanting so badly to be distracted from her loneliness. She scratches harder and harder, nearly ripping her nail right off its bed in the process, but she hears nothing in return. She bangs her fist against the wall and lets out a groan, daringly near to a scream but not daring enough. There is still only silence.

Silence, which means she is once again alone.

She sighs and turns her back to the wall. She looks around for something else to do, a bubbling frustration filling her chest. On the floor in the center of the room are her toys. Her three toys that are all she ever has to play with. That are supposed to provide her endless fun without ever changing. That often make her feel suffocated in the monotony.

But at least they never leave me.

Her frustration rises a degree in temperature, cooking into anger.

She is reluctant, but after staring at her toys for a few more moments—the stuffed blue dog lying on its side, its black beady eyes fixated on her—she gets up and walks to them. She takes a seat in the center of the spotlight where the lightbulb dangles several feet above her head. She can feel its light pouring down her back, the burning sensation searing across her skin as it bakes her. It's an itch. An itch she cannot and will never be able to scratch.

The light spreads to the floor in front of her, flashing on and off, making it difficult for her to play without being distracted by its flicker. Her cooked anger begins to boil. Not only is she alone, but the only other animated thing in this room is that sickening white light.

Foolishly, she looks up, forgetting that she is now seated directly beneath it, and is painfully surprised. She almost screams, the stamp of light blinding her even after she looks away, but she is able to hold back the sound in a muffled squeal. She covers her eyes with her arms, curling over and burying her head in her lap. The backs of her lids are bright and burning. She presses into them with the palms of her hands to soothe the discomfort.

Her boiling anger overflows into her throat.

Even after the burning stops, she remains with her head in her lap. The darkness feels cool against her eyes, though she can still see traces of light seared into the backs of her lids. Blazing spots that follow her irises wherever they go. It hurts to see, but it is better than looking at that white light again.

Warm tears wet her legs. She cries, trying not to make a sound—she doesn't want Daddy to know. Her body convulses from forcing back the wails begging to burst from the top of her throat. She chokes on her own screams and swallows, shedding tears until there are no more tears left in her to shed.

When she is done crying, she stands and wipes her face of snot with the backs of her hands. She re-collects herself, calming her whimpers and palpitating chest, and grits her teeth.

The boiling anger has turned into steam and risen.

She glares up at the lightbulb and plucks the lollipop stem from her mouth. Her hands are curled into tight fists, knuckles impossibly white, tendons bulging. She is determined to put an end to the flickering white light. She jumps toward it, swinging at it with the lollipop stem like a maniac writhing for sanity. But this maniac never reaches sanity. Not even close. She is far too small and it is far too high.

Staring too fixedly at the light for so long has only blinded her more. She collapses to the concrete floor in defeat. The backs of her lids are on fire, marking her sight with bright spots of failure. Her eyes melt into puddles that leak back into her skull. She feels humiliated. No matter how hard she tries, she cannot win against it. It will always flicker, never allowing her eyes a bit of rest, taunting her with the emptiness of her room, showing her just how alone she truly is.

It will always tickle that unreachable spot on her back.

JUST GO AWAY!

The thought roils, bouncing back and forth in her skull like a violent echo.

JUST GO AWAY! JUST GO AWAY!

Without looking up, only wanting to hurt what hurts her, she grabs her stuffed blue dog and chucks it into the air. She hears a *woosh*, a *bang*, and then the pitch of glass exploding. Shards fall, cutting at her skin, and she screams from the shock—a scream so uncaringly tortured, it scorches her lungs.

Footsteps approach. The lock snaps and the door is thrown open. She can hear him, but she can't see him. She refuses to open her eyes.

"Vanilla? My sweet? What happened?" His voice exudes worry but tamps down on a hint of undirected rage. Caring yet predatorial.

She doesn't move nor answer, her pain leeching on her

insides, rendering her a nonsensical screaming machine.

She feels him scoop her up and cradle her convulsing body in his arms. He bounces her up and down with soft shushes, attempting to quiet her. But she does not stop. She does not know how to. She couldn't control the light, and now she has forgotten how to control herself.

What makes her finally stop is a shriek. A shriek that bursts into the room with the intensity of a light burning your eyes or your daddy's worried rage. She instantly quiets to listen, making sure it's not herself she's mistakenly hearing. But though she stops, the shriek does not. Her ears perk and she opens her eyes to look toward the sound, the afterimage distorting her vision. In his haste, her daddy had forgotten to shut the metal door behind him and now a strange cry has entered the room with them. A high-pitched shriek so emotionally familiar yet so distant. Her daddy grunts and marches over to the door, kicking it shut with a fierce snap. The shriek asphyxiates into silence.

It will be many years until she hears that shriek again.

Her daddy growls under his breath.

She whimpers at the closed door, then buries her head back into her daddy's chest, fatigued from her tantrum and too tired to wonder. He presses his hand against the base of her skull so that she remains blinded by his body. When she tries to lift her head, he keeps her forced against him.

"There, there, my sweet," he sings, the sour tang of his anger only just dissolving from his voice. "I am here. I will protect you. You are safe."

She feels him sit down. When he removes his hand from the back of her head so she can lift herself from his chest, the room is dark.

I won? She won! She finally won against that awful white light!

A wave of joy surges through her. But then a feeling of dread crawls in and tugs on the pit of her stomach, reminding her of her new dark reality. Now she realizes that winning is not synonymous with happiness. That the two don't always come hand in hand. But it can be synonymous with fear. With anticipatory terror. A fear of what's to come.

"Daddy?" she asks, unable to see him, though she can feel him there.

"Yes, my sweet."

He takes her arm in his hand. A soft rub and a painful prick.

She yelps. "Daddy, I'm scared!"

He shushes her. "You are fine, Vanilla. I am here."

Another rub. Another painful prick.

"Daddy, it hurts!"

"I know, I know," he says.

The painful prick slips out from beneath her skin. Her vein throbs after its removal. *Isn't it that veins throb?* she thinks. *Isn't that what Daddy told me?*

He says, "But it is over now. You are safe, my sweet."

I can't remember . . . The blue snakes . . . don't they throb?

He lies her down carefully on the mattress and hums to her until his hums sound like long, distant echoes. She feels the sleepiness slowly creep across her body, slithering through her veins until it reaches her every limb. It climbs up her spine and eats away at the new memories that are working so hard to store themselves in her brain; instead, save for a few, they are consumed. Soon, she can no longer keep her eyes open. The difference between them open and shut is barely discernible.

The last thought she has before she falls into a heavy sleep is if this is what her stuffed blue dog feels like.

CHAPTER III

When she wakes, the room is bright again.

She shields her eyes with her tiny hand, controlling the slow increase of light flooding back to her senses as she adjusts. Apprehensively, she removes her hand and faces the light in full. She would have thrown another tantrum, enraged at thinking she had won only to be fooled by the light's return, if not for the fact that the light is different. No longer white and flickering, but yellow and warm. The new hue makes the room look calmer and brand new. She likes the way it gives a new shade to the walls and to the floor. She looks up. Now, instead of a dangling lightbulb that taunts her by being just a few jeering, unreachable feet above her head, a long, glowing tube is glued flat to the ceiling.

She smiles.

Everything has been returned to its place, the room

immaculate. But she remembers what it looked like before. She remembers her tantrum and how it covered everything in shadow and glass, even if her memory of it feels woozy.

It happened, didn't it?

Even if her memory feels woozy ... and groggy ... and so distant from her, like the long echo of a doorway where *(a shriek?)* darkness finds infinity.

A shallow red mark lines her arm just below her shoulder, slight but still there. She touches it and winces.

It wasn't just a dream ... was it?

A moment before, she was so certain. Now, as time sets in, her mind churns her memories.

She gets up and tiptoes over to the center of her room, careful not to step on any glass, real or imagined, and sits by her toys. She meets nothing sharp along the way.

Nothing?

But—wasn't it?!

Settled, she eyes the dog and notes a gash where white fluff struggles to break free. *It must have been cut by the glass when it broke the lightbulb.* Proof. She tries to push the white stuffing back inside but only makes the gash wider and causes a chunk more to fall out. She places the dog back down, afraid of gutting it any further.

It was.

She picks up the syringe and holds it to the light. The barrel shines bright, refracting and intensifying under the new glow. The glass absorbs the yellow shine and she thinks it almost matches the color of her hair.

She smiles, feeling light and fluttery, the sight of it injecting a more pleasant memory into her brain—one that she is certain, without a doubt, happened. She remembers when her daddy first let her have the syringe. It was the third and final toy she was allowed to keep. He had walked into her room, standing tall just before the metal door, and she saw it in his coat pocket, the plunger just peeking out.

"Daddy, what is that?" she asked.

"What, this little thing?" he responded, pressing his hand to his pocket. He pulled it out and showed it to her. She thought it was beautiful, the way the light shone through the glass like a vision into a brighter realm. "This is called a syringe. It's a handy tool I use in the Outside."

"The Outside?"

"Yes. The Outside beyond these walls. Don't you remember, Vanilla? Where the creatures are."

"Yes, Daddy. I do! The Outside is beyond these walls where the bad creatures are and I can't go! But that's not what I'm asking." She stomped her foot after reciting the engrained information. He smiled at that, a deeply content smile. "I'm asking what do you *use* it for!"

"I will show you." He took her stethoscope and placed the eartips in her ears. She shifted them properly into place. He picked up the dog and pressed the drum against it. "Do you hear anything?"

She fidgeted and shook her head. "No. I never do!"

He removed the plastic cover from the syringe, the needle new, still lubricated. She watched it gleam, enchanted by how it sparkled—and by how much she wanted to touch it. She followed it with her eyes, not realizing where it was being led. Then she saw the dog, saw the needle tap the dog's neck, saw it sink inside.

She yelped as her daddy pressed the plunger down. "You're hurting him! You're hurting him!" She thought the whole scene looked so awful. Maybe the dog couldn't express its pain, but she could tell. She could feel it.

"No, I am helping him."

He removed the needle. She could almost hear the *shing* as it sliced out from the fabric.

"Now. Do you hear anything?"

She hesitated, then listened. At first, she heard nothing. But then there came a faint *thump*. And then ... there it was again! Louder and louder, falling into a rhythm!

"Yes!" she exclaimed through giggling teeth. The pain, so horrifyingly excruciating, morphed into life.

He smiled, held the dog up to tickle her nose, then dropped the stuffed animal back into her hand like dead weight. She frantically pressed the drum against it, excited by the new sound she could listen to for eternity. But the thumping had already stopped.

"And that is how this is used," her daddy said with pride, jiggling the syringe between his fingertips.

She looked up from the dog, her eyes wet with wonder. For a moment, as the syringe teetered between his fingers, it looked fluid. Like its form was far beyond anything she could ever comprehend.

"Daddy?" she began, never removing her eyes from the glass barrel.

"Yes?"

"Can I have it? Please?"

He paused in thought. "I don't know if that would be such a—"

"Please, please, please, Daddy! I promise I'll take good care of it!"

"I'm not worried about that," he said. "I'm worried about you hurting yourself."

"I promise I won't! I'll be super careful! Super, super, SUPER careful!"

His eyebrows tensed in thought. But her pouting lips made his face softened. "All right. I suppose you are big enough now to—"

"Thank you, Daddy!" she shouted.

He laughed and handed the syringe to her like a creature bestowing a flower. "Remember to be careful," he told her. "This is my gift to you, but if you hurt yourself, I will take it away. Not only will I take it away, I will punish you for it as well."

Her excitement eclipsed the threat. "I won't hurt myself! I promise!"

And she has gratefully kept that promise. The more careful she is, the longer she will get to keep the syringe. She hopes that it will remain with her forever, so that one day she might hear the dog thump again when the magic strikes just right.

Thump-thump. Just like her own chest. *Thump-thump!*

Now, as she turns the syringe around in her fingers, staring at the edges, she sees something new. She brings the glass barrel to her face and squints.

Hidden against the inside seam of the barrel is a dark red smudge, pooled and winking. *It must be new,* she thinks. She spends too much time carefully inspecting her toys for her to miss a thing like that.

She frowns, wanting to know more about the smudge, and resolves to take the syringe apart. Two fingers squeeze the needle while the other hand grips the plunger. She bends these parts downward until she hears a *snap*. The syringe disassembles easily into three pieces: the needle, the glass barrel, and the plunger. She picks up the glass barrel, wiping the smudge off with the tip of her index finger. She brings it to her nose and inhales. It is wet and sticky and smells like the metal door.

Blood?

There is a knock.

"Vanilla, my sweet?"

With gasping breath, she picks up the pieces of the syringe to assemble them back together. *Be careful, be careful, be CAREFUL!* She collects the plunger and the glass barrel and as she reaches for the needle, it kisses her with a prick. She jerks her hand back from the sting and smacks her other palm over her mouth to snuff out her yelp. A circle of blood forms where the needle met her. She whimpers and holds her finger up, wanting to get a closer look at her own blood, seeing how it's the same color as the smudge. She has never seen her blood before, though she knows she is filled with it. Knows it's the color of one of her daddy's favorite shirts.

Her brow furrows in thought—

Did I get my own blood in the barrel?

—and the yellow light shines across her view.

If it weren't for the new light, she would never have seen them: two tiny purple dots on her wrist. She brushes them with her thumb, feeling slight bumps, and shudders.

The lock snaps and the metal door swings open. She sticks her bleeding finger in her mouth and looks helplessly at the doorway, her eyes growing sleek as glass. The blood drips onto her tongue. It tastes like brown water.

"How is my little— Oh! What happened here?" Her daddy stands in the doorway, staring down at the disassembled syringe. He shuts the door behind himself and takes a step toward her, picking up the pieces. "Did you do this?"

"No, Dah'dy! I di'n'! I wo'h up and i'h wa'h like tha'!"

His jaw tightens despite the ridiculous sight he might have found adorable on any other occasion. But not now. He doesn't like it when she lies to him.

"Are you telling the truth?" he asks, his voice hardening into a blunt shell, and then asks again: "Vanilla, are you telling the truth?"

She doesn't answer at first, but he can sense the change in her body language. He can feel the increase in her heart rate as she turns her eyes away from him like a cowering dog who knows it's done something wrong.

Slowly, she shakes her head.

No. It was a lie.

The corners of his mouth curl into a forced smile and his voice melts into warmth. "That is all right, my sweet."

He fiddles with the syringe pieces, scolding himself silently as he does, not letting the expression reveal on his face. He can smell the blood dissipating from inside the glass barrel. He'd switched the needles incorrectly.

Foolish.

Without needing to watch the mechanics of his hands, wanting instead to relish in her reaction, he balances and twists the pieces in his fingertips. He snaps them back together and the syringe is once again whole. Her eyes watch him like a charmed snake. Awe fills her, nearly overflowing beyond the brim of her lids. Her skin faintly glows and a tentative smile curls across her slim lips. A smile just for him.

His dead heart flutters more than usual at that look of lovingly dependent gratitude. An exhilarating tingle spreads across his normally numb skin. Only she can do this to him, and now, he wants to be closer to her, like she's a magnet intensifying that feeling of being alive.

He sits down cross-legged in front of her and holds out the syringe. She reaches out to grab it, but he yanks it away before she can, her skin grazing his cold knuckles, leaving her kiss of warmth. She jerks back in fear and he smiles.

"That is all right. But do not lie to me again. Do you understand? How can I keep you safe? How can I protect you if you lie to me?"

Her eyebrows scrunch together, vulnerable eyes peeking into his. "I whon' lie aga'h, Dah'dy," she promises.

"Good."

He returns his open hand to her and she plucks the syringe from his palm, the pads of her fingertips leaving rivers of heat where she touches. He inhales and exhales, the effects of her just setting in. He wants to grab her, rip her off the floor, curl her into his arms, but he might kill her in the process. So, instead, he watches her from this short distance and eventually asks:

"Now, why is your finger still in your mouth? Aren't you over this childish phase by now?"

But she doesn't hear him. Her attention is directed at something else.

She squints critically at the syringe, turning it over and over again in her free hand. But the barrel is clear. The red smudge is completely gone.

That's because I wiped it off, she thinks to herself.

She places the syringe down on the floor and looks at her index finger, expecting to see the red smudge smeared across her skin. But it is bare. This is not the hand she used. This is not the index finger she used to curiously wipe away the smudge.

By process of elimination, the finger she used is the one that is in her mouth right now. The one that is bleeding—that she has touched with her tongue multiple times, licking away the red smudge with it. That wet, sticky, winking smudge.

A nauseating feeling lurches in her stomach.

"My sweet, are you okay?"

He presses his hand to her forehead. Her skin is drenched with sweat and he grows worried by the sudden onset. *I just dosed her.* He tries to pick her up to place her on his lap, but she shakes him off and averts her gaze to the floor, refusing to budge from her now statuelike position. Her finger sinks deeper into her mouth.

He recoils from her and his voice descends. "Vanilla, what is going on?"

She doesn't respond. Her face now drips with guilt.

His eyes sharpen. He doesn't ask again. Instead, he reaches his hand out, palm open, upright and waiting. A silent yet demanding gesture with power that breaks the air where he moves.

Reluctantly, she removes her finger from her mouth and gives it to his grip. Over and over again she thinks, *Don't tremble, don't tremble, don't tremble.* And, amazingly enough, she doesn't. In his large, boney hand, her baby finger is still and bloodless, barely even a dot from the puncture wound to show for the mess. She lets out a sigh of relief, her heart rate dropping. She looks at him and giggles, but his eyes are still peering down at her finger, watching and waiting.

And then his eyebrows furrow.

She shifts her gaze back just in time to see the balloon of blood that swells at her fingertip. Her heart rate spikes. He can sense it. The blood drips down the side of her finger and falls onto his hand with a quiet yet deafening *plop*. The contrast between her dark red blood and his pale skin is striking. She wouldn't know it, but it reminds him of red roses caught in a fresh winter's snow back when he hadn't been this way. When he had been innocent like her.

"I'm sorry," she whispers shamefully under her breath.

Her daddy doesn't say anything at first. Silently, he stares at the blood, thoughts churning through his head. What he must do. How he must react. What would maintain his code of conduct. Decidedly, he leans his head so that her view of her hand in his is obstructed. But she can feel his breath inch toward her and then . . . a harsh kiss. When he lifts his head, the balloon of blood is gone and does not reappear.

"No need to be sorry, my sweet. Accidents happen. I only want to make sure you're okay." He forces a smile, hunger roiling within him all the while like a winter's storm. *I will not become angry. She will feel safe with me.*

He reaches into his suit jacket pocket and pulls out a small square package and a bandage.

Magic, she thinks.

He tears apart the package and removes a towelette that smells like sharp stink. She scrunches her nose and gags, but then becomes obediently still at his glare. He grips her hand and wipes down her finger with the towelette, keeping her hand forcefully in place when she flinches from the wet sting.

But she does not protest. No matter how much it hurts, she does not protest.

He peels away the protective layer of the bandage and wraps it around her finger tight enough that she can feel her blood pulse in place beneath. The wound is hidden.

"There!" he says when the fix is done. "Do you feel better?"

She nods.

"Good! Now, let's replace that finger with something sweeter."

From his back pocket, he conjures a lollipop, new and perfectly encased. He peels off the wrapping and her lips part without thought.

He grins.

He holds the lollipop near her mouth, but not near enough. When she leans in for a bite, he clicks his tongue and shakes his head. She hesitates, understands, and returns to her original position.

"Will you lie to me again?"

"No."

"Are you my sweet little girl?"

She brightens and answers, "Yes!"

"Good."

He places the lollipop on her tongue and she chomps down on it with glee. As the sugar seeps in and the euphoria chews on her brain, she forgets about the pain from her finger. She forgets about the two purple dots below her wrist and the horrible red smudge she sucked down into her stomach. She forgets her curiosity over any of it, because she no longer wants to know.

I will only know what Daddy tells me because he will keep me safe, she thinks. *He will keep me safe and happy.*

And in this moment, as her daddy picks her up and she drinks down the melted sugar, she no longer feels painful loneliness. She no longer feels the want to tear out of her skin and run around, just muscles and tendons, in circles forever. She doesn't feel suffocated by claustrophobia or strangled by impossibly untamed outbursts. Instead, she feels elevated happiness, gushing gratitude, complete ecstasy.

It's all right, it's all right. Daddy is here! He is here, holding you in his lap! Holding you so close. Don't you see? There's no reason to be sad! You are his!

His fingers wrap around her waist, his touch calculatedly gentle. She looks up at him with joy in her eyes and he kisses her forehead. From so close in this steady yellow light, she thinks she can see through his skin. She thinks she can see the blue veins behind that paper flesh.

They giggle and laugh *(forever!)* while her daddy bounces her on his knee. His eyes scan her body, his gaze following his fingers as he traces the lace of her dress.

"Oh, Vanilla . . ." he says, suddenly disappointed.

"What?" *I'm sorry!* she instinctively cries out in her head, the vein of throbbing guilt slithering back into her.

"You tore your pretty dress."

He holds up the dirty white fabric. She can see the tear in it grinning back at her. She hadn't noticed it before because of all the ruffles that overlap the skirt. It hid from her. Hid until the perfect moment. And of course he noticed. He notices everything.

"I'm sorry," she whimpers, out loud this time. *Please fix it! I have my lollipop and we were so happy!*

"That is all right, my sweet." He looks over the rest of her dress, a twitch of disgust winking across his expression. "This dress was growing dirtier and dirtier. It needed to be replaced either way."

He places her down on the mattress, her body writhing slightly, refusing to let go. She wishes she could coil around him, be a part of him like those twisted veins beneath his skin. When he tries to stand, she is clutching onto the edges of his jacket, holding him down like an anchor. He smiles softly, a patient curl across his lips, and nods to her as if to say, *It's time to let go.* His hands find hers and he kindly peels her fingers from his jacket one by one, standing when she is detached.

We were so happy...

She watches him as the muscle in her chest throbs with pain. Without another word, he opens the door *(Please don't!)* and leaves the room.

Don't go! she begs silently.

But the lock has already snapped shut.

She sits, staring at the door, waiting for him to come back.

We were so happy. What happened? What did I do?

But the door doesn't reopen.

It's my fault.

CHAPTER IV

What if the pounding begins and it's not Daddy? What if the creatures are the ones pounding on the door? With their big fists and—and ... Oh, no! I'm so scared ... Bang, bang, BANG! Please don't let it bang. But then again, I can't open the door to let them in. Only Daddy could let them in, and surely he would never. Surely, if he saw them banging on my door, he would stop them!

By now, her muscles have come near to atrophying. She has no way to tell the time, but it has been what feels like an eternity since her daddy left, and he has yet to return. An eternity that she has spent sitting, staring at the metal door, paralyzed by a fear of moving. Of moving from where her daddy last touched her.

She has grown tired of looking at the door, but a part of her is scared to look elsewhere. If she were to look elsewhere, everything may come crashing down on her frail soul. She doesn't want to pay attention to the tugging feeling in the pit of her stomach that feverishly begs to be acknowledged. She doesn't want to think about the cut on her arm, the wound on her finger, the red smudge from the syringe, the dots below her wrist, or her empty room. Her loneliness. The sound of her daddy slamming the door. It is all too much. She is too vulnerable. Too filled with pure, untainted emotion to deal with the circumstances. If she tries to make sense of it all at once, she is afraid that her insides will break. She is afraid to know what it would feel like if that tugging in the pit of her stomach finally got to rip. So instead, she thinks about the bandage and her daddy and how he fixes her and . . . and . . . the green pill!

Ah, yes! The green pill!

The green pill that fixed the banging in her head that once came, maybe even similar to how the creatures bang. The banging that crept into her head so subtly, she could barely sense it coming until it climaxed in her brain. How it kept her from sleep and crunched her thoughts, making her skull feel as though it were shrinking. (Although she knows skulls can't shrink, bones don't shrink!)

And the big green pill her daddy handed to her.

In the midst of her pain, she still managed to laugh at him and at that pill. She thought it was so silly. No way a weirdly shaped ball that fit so easily between her teeth could help her. It was so small! What could it possibly do? But he demanded she swallow it. So she did.

It felt like a lump caught in her throat that would never go down. He assured her she would not choke on it, and she struggled to keep from gagging it back up so she wouldn't upset him. She managed to get it down and keep it down, but it did nothing to fix the banging.

She laughed some more.

"I knew it wouldn't work, Daddy!" she declared.

"Give it time."

So she did. She waited. And waited. And he was right.

"What did we learn from this, Vanilla?"

"To never doubt Daddy!"

He always knows how to fix her. How to stop the banging. Does he ever get the banging? Is he ever in pain? If he were, she would fix him. She would be glad to fix him. It would be like magic, doing something herself she never thought possible. But he never needs fixing, at least from what she can tell. There never seems to be a banging in his skull. Never an eruption in his body that makes him curl over in pain. He is always standing tall and proud, filled with invincible power. But she wishes she could fix him all the same, if just to return the favor. Just to show him how much she would do for him.

But I have my blue dog! she thinks. *I can fix it! I can make it thump again! And then Daddy will be proud that I fixed something like he fixes me!*

She leaps up, the excitement detonating in her chest, and hurries back over to her toys in the center of the room. With giddy hands, she curls the stethoscope around her neck and in her ears, picks up her stuffed blue dog, almost drops it, and presses the drum against its chest.

Nothing.

Inject. Press.

Nothing.

Nothing?! Her body slumps over in defeat. She moans with sadness, her mouth curling downward into a large frown. *I can't fix it. I can't fix it like Daddy fixes me. I can't do it . . . I can't show him . . .*

As she wails, her mouth opens a little too wide, her tongue undulating between her gums. The lollipop she'd forgotten about clings on for a few beats before slipping out and onto the floor. She freezes, smacking her lips together, only tasting bland saliva now *(loneliness)*, and stares in horror. Pieces of dirt stick to the bright red ball, making it inedible.

Without realizing it, she has started to scream. A flood of pain escapes through her throat that she cannot stop. She screams and screams, screams for her daddy, his title exploding out of her mouth, knowing he would come and fix it. Wanting so badly for him to fix it.

But she screams and he does not come. For the first time, he does not come.

She shoves her head into her lap, trying to curl up into a tight ball. She does not want to look at her room, its awful emptiness. She screams for him as loud as her lungs allow until her throat is raw and sizzling and she can't scream anymore. So instead she breaks down into tears, wheezing out droplets of salt. But still she calls for him, even if they are just sob-filled whimpers that cannot be heard through that thick metal door.

She hears the lock turn slowly within the door and snap into place. Her head whips up and her neck pops. Her daddy walks in through the doorway, his steps lethargic, a sheet of white fabric draped across his forearm. He closes the door behind himself *(snap!)* and looks at her, his expression blank and apathetic.

"Daddy!" she yelps and grabs onto his leg.

"What is going on, my sweet?" he questions, his voice calm.

She can only remember her pain.

"Please, fix it," she mumbles into his leg.

"What are you— Ah ... I see," he responds, eyeing the lollipop on the floor, feeling her body tighten like a tourniquet around him. "I see the problem. And, of course, Daddy will fix it. That is an easy fix, my sweet. Do not worry. But first, I must fix something else." He bends down and her body turns into a bear trap. He pinches her lightly. "Vanilla, I need you to let go and stand up. Be a good girl for Daddy."

With heavy reluctance, she abides and her muscles release. He peels her off and props her up onto her feet, but she remains staring down at the floor. He frowns and places the back of his hand under her chin, forcing her little head to look at him. The way her facial muscles tense shows him confused sorrow.

"Look what I have for you!" he sings with a smile. *Let me turn that frown upside down.*

He holds out the white fabric by its shoulders and lets it unravel before her. It waterfalls down into a new white dress.

She smiles at it with glee, instantly feeling her pain leave her chest.

"Do you like it?"

"Yes!"

"Good! I am glad. Only the best for my sweet." He reaches out and squeezes her cheek between his thumb and finger, leaving a cold kiss. "Now, lift your arms."

She obeys, lifting her arms high into the air and arching her back like the most beautiful ballerina. He reaches for her, this image pulling a memory from his mind. The first time he'd ever brought her a real dress. She was so excited to wear it that she nearly tore out of her old dress, if that sack of fabric could have even been called a dress. But it was all he had for her at the time. He hadn't thought about getting her something nicer since she rarely ever saw herself. But foolish him, he realized. It wasn't what she saw but what she felt.

He had spent so much time trying to pick it out, eyeing each design and pattern, his head growing fuzzy with the worry that she might hate it. That she would throw it back at him with heated anger. After all, this was the age of tantrums. But did it matter if she did? Was she even capable of hating anything he brought her? What else did she know?

Still, he figured it would save him the trip if he just asked, knowing he wouldn't be able to stand her disappointment; it would only ruin him. He brought the dresses to her in the only convenient way he saw possible. In the only way he would ever show her anything from the Outside.

She was sitting in the corner on the mattress, giving the

stuffed blue dog a physical, when he walked in with a grand smile printed across his face.

"My sweet, I have a question for you," he began, nearly bursting with excitement through the seam of his lips.

"Yes, Daddy?"

He sat next to her and tugged teasingly on one of her pigtails. "You know Daddy only ever wants the best for you? You know that, right, my sweet?"

She nodded, smiling reassuringly.

He whipped out his hidden trick from his back pocket. What he revealed to her was a deck of thick, square papers, each one printed in muted colors. Photographs. He spread the deck out for her so that she could view each individually then asked, "Which do you prefer?"

She squinted at them, seeing small versions of different dresses, all so very beautiful to her.

"I don't understand, Daddy. What are these?"

"Why, they are dresses, Vanilla!" It was her first time seeing photographs, so he was not surprised by the confusion. But a little agitated by the apathy. He wanted a more energetic response, filled with awe and wonder.

"Yes, I know, Daddy! I know what a dress is! I'm wearing one right now, silly! But why are they so small?"

"Small?" He laughed and rolled his eyes. "They are not small, my sweet. They are photographs of real, life-size dresses. They only look small here because they are printed on small paper."

"Photographs?"

"Yes. For example, I can take a photograph of your stuffed animal here and it would appear on one of these pieces of paper. It would be a photograph of your stuffed animal, only it would look small in relation to the size of the paper."

She thought for a second, processing this. He knew she wasn't stupid, so he let her think with patience.

"So . . . these are real dresses?" she clarified.

"Yes."

"Real dresses that would fit me?"

"Yes, Vanilla. You see, I go to the Outside with a machine called a camera and I point the camera at real dresses. I snap a button and the camera prints a photograph of the dress on this small paper. It's all relative."

"Relative?"

"Yes. Like how from this distance"—he picked a photograph and held it an arm's length away—"this photograph looks smaller than from this distance." He brought the photograph close, right up to her face so that it doubled in her vision. "The photograph is still the same size, just at varying distances. And the camera takes an image of the dress, which remains the same size. This is just a different presentation of it."

"So . . . the photographs . . . it's almost like taking a piece from the Outside?"

Anger sizzled in his chest. He glared at her with impatience, but then his eyes softened and he smirked. "Yes. Like taking a piece from the Outside."

"Could I have a photograph to take a piece of you?"

"No . . . no, you could not, my sweet. Now! Which dress will it be?"

She looked at the assortment and placed her finger on the most intricate of them all.

"I like that one!"

"Very well. I will bring it to you."

"Daddy?"

"Yes, Vanilla?"

"Can you bring me more photographs? They're nice to look at."

He frowned at first. And then he grinned. He grinned a devilish grin and, oh, did he realize all the fabricated lessons he could teach her about the Outside she would never see: the awful snakes, some reaching one hundred feet long, that the creatures kept as loyal pets; the hazardous deep chasms at random in the streets that would so easily swallow her whole, never to be seen again; the sticks and stones the creatures used to bash each other into mush. *All terrifyingly available to you right outside your door, my sweet!*

"Yes. I will bring you more photographs."

But he never did show her a picture of a creature. When she asked if he had any, he told her they were so horrifying she might never be able to sleep again.

That was arguably true.

"Are you going to put the dress on me or not, Daddy?"

He falls out of his thoughts and back into the present. "Yes. Don't move," he orders as he grips the bottom of her old dress and lifts it off her, revealing her bare body. He tosses the old dress to the side and slides the new one on over her arms, glancing at her bare, unscathed skin before covering her. *She looks perfect.* He tugs on the skirt, making sure it's properly snug. "Much better! Beautiful! Now, give Daddy a twirl!"

She squirms and feels the dress slide across her skin. The fabric feels cool like water. She spins around, obliging him, feeling the dress flow up and around her. Giggles burst from her lungs. The sadness dries from her face. Her daddy laughs and claps for her as she dances for him in blissful amnesia, each step pirouetting her deeper into oblivion. He reaches for her and sweeps her off her feet, joining the dance with her in his arms. They float around the room in gracious motions, their joined laughter emulating music that she has yet to hear. She feels the air slip through her pigtails, cooling her down into a form of raw happiness.

When the laughter quiets, her daddy takes a seat on the mattress and lies her down.

"Now, close your eyes and open your mouth," he orders.

She obeys.

He grins and places a fresh lollipop on her tongue. She smiles, her eyes still closed as she relishes in the taste, swirling the lollipop around the insides of her cheeks. The sugar shoots into her brain, encouraging her indifference. She lets it.

He wraps her up in his embrace, adjusting her dress, and holds her bandaged hand in his. He sees the two puncture wounds below her wrist and sighs. He runs his hands through her hair and hums softly for her while she rests. She looks at peace now, that confused sorrow having finally unlatched itself from her small body. Her tears are dry, her heartbeat once again calm. No longer palpitating. He has taken care of all her troubles. He has made her happy. All except for these two troubling marks. But they should heal soon.

They *will* heal soon.

He leans down, kisses her forehead, and whispers, "You are fixed."

He hates to leave her, especially when she so sweetly rests within his arms. So vulnerably available. Bare, supple skin peeks out beneath the ruffled fabric. The temptation is delicious. He is afraid that if he stays any longer, he might tear her apart. He might kill what he loves so dearly. So he forces himself to pry away from her innocent body and he leaves the room, locking the door behind himself.

He is hungry.

CHAPTER V

She is alone.

The room is once again empty and she once again has to deal with the loneliness, although she feels better primed for it now that her daddy has fixed her. The light no longer strains her eyes, her dress is no longer dirty, and the wounds on her upper arm and finger no longer hurt. In fact, the cut on her upper arm has already healed completely, pure white skin left in its cure.

She doesn't know at what point in her sleep her daddy left her—he rarely ever stays until she wakes—but he has been gone for a while now. Long enough for her to have taken several naps. Long enough for her to have forgotten what he feels like. She knows he will return—he always does; it is just a matter of when.

So she waits. She waits and she thinks of him and it hurts her stomach when she thinks of him so she tries to distract herself. But despite the hurt, she can't help but wonder when he will return. It could be any moment now that the lock snaps and he enters. The anticipation keeps her on edge, her eyes magnetically drawn to the metal door. Sometimes she doesn't even realize she is looking at the door until she falls out of that blurred zone where her mind becomes a blank, empty space. Then she returns to reality, the metal appearing in clear straight lines before her rather than in blotches of silver and gray.

The part of her that no longer wants to feel the pain of missing her daddy begs for a distraction. It begs for her to take her mind off him so that the tugging will stop itching her insides. Stop making her feel like something is crawling around inside of her. If she doesn't force herself to turn away, who knows how long she will let the tugging hurt her stomach while she stares at nothing?

If the door doesn't move . . . if it does nothing for long enough . . . does it become nothing? Does it become nothing like the stuffed blue dog?

She tears her eyes away from the door and looks down at her dress instead, feeling the outline of every seam. She thinks about how beautiful the dress is and how comfortably it drapes over her body. How its smell doesn't make her nose scrunch and how flawlessly white it is. It reminds her of her daddy's skin . . .

Her stomach protests and she shakes her head, refocusing her thoughts.

It really is beautiful.

When she grows tired of studying the details, she stands and twirls, trying to see how high she can make the skirt fly. She runs around the room, jumping and laughing when her skirt flies high enough to encase her in a momentary cocoon, her bare thighs feeling the rush of a self-made breeze.

"Daddy, Daddy! Do you see me? Look how high I can jump!" she giggles out with glee.

And then she halts. *Stop thinking of him or else I'll yank harder! Or else I'll rip!* She winces and sighs and walks over to her mattress, dragging her feet across the concrete floor. She collapses down onto the stiff padding and leans against the wall, rolling her thumbs around each other. Her body is exhausted and her mind is bored.

She stares at the door and zones out, receding into the strange comfort of the silver and gray blotches, trying to think of anything else but her daddy.

For how long she rests in that blurred zone she does not know, but she can tell it has been a while because her thumbs ache and her vision takes longer than usual to realign. She stops rolling her thumbs and reaches her arms out in front of her, stretching her limbs back to life. The stretch in her muscles feels energizing; with each muted crack she feels more and more revitalized. She yawns, blinks a few times, then turns to the wall behind her. She bites her lip and places her hand out in front of her. Her fingernail scratches the concrete slowly at first and then more confidently, hoping for a response, almost certain one will come. But there is no scratch in return. She tries knocking a few times to get the scratch's attention, but it's no use. There is nothing.

She grunts at the wall and crosses her arms, turning away from the vacant disappointment. Her vision slingshots around, automatically pulled toward the metal door. The tugging creeps back into her stomach and she quickly looks away to the center of the room. She sees her toys and gets up, shuffling over to them and sitting with her back to the door. At least this way she can avoid the temptation to look.

She ignores her spine's want to rotate on its hinge and wraps the stethoscope around her neck. She picks up the stuffed blue dog and checks its chest.

Nothing.

She frowns and squishes the dog in her hands, shaking it lightly as though she might be able to force the *thump* out of it.

Still, nothing.

Sighing, she picks up the syringe. Despite the beginnings of learned futility, it still feels heavy and magical in her hands. She is about to stick it in the dog's neck, puncture it with the tip of the needle, when her mind coils around a new thought. The holes she found on her own body. On her wrist. The two purple dots that seemed to have appeared out of nowhere, inexplicably popping out from beneath her skin.

She turns her arm over, but it's bare. The dots must have healed—or, at this point in her state of mind, she wonders if they were ever even there. Wonders if she simply imagined the veins and the blood rising to the surface of her skin as if to say hello, climb out of her body, and play with her for a little while . . . then grow and grow until they became ten-foot-long, slithering things, dripping in her gore and suffocating her with their affection—

No. They were there. And she wants to find them again. To dig in deep and force them to resurface. Maybe this time they will come all the way out.

She holds the needle up to her arm, the steel winking under the yellow light, and presses the point to her wrist without breaking the surface. If she adds a little more pressure, maybe she can carve them out. But the more pressure she adds, the more it digs and stings and hurts. Still, she doesn't stop. Her skin trembles and grows hot. Pain shoots up her limb. She can almost hear the creak of her skin, its wailing protest, its threats to break under the steel; its defensive shrieks. The sudden rush of pain like a whip traveling up her nerves.

She winces and retracts the needle, heavy breaths controlling her chest. Her body shakes, but she does not drop the syringe. The recoil of pain sinking back into her system feels almost euphoric. Almost like sucking on a lollipop. The fearful anticipation of quick, gut-wrenching shock . . . it feels different from what she is used to, which is boredom or anxiety.

Discomfort.

Or nothing.

The slow burnout of pain's aftershock feels better than nothing.

Still holding the syringe, she places the dog down and carefully lifts the bandage from her finger. It slides off with little resistance and reveals the small red dot—the aftermath of a wound which has faded considerably. She stares at the red dot and the tugging returns, pulling at her guts like she is a puppet on strings. She lifts the needle and holds it an inch away from her finger, the anticipation making her skin tingle. Her spine shivers and she smiles slightly from the sensation. The tugging yanks and she guides the tip of the needle into the small red dot, feeling the snapping and breakage of her newly healed skin. At first, the pain is not so unbearable and she is a little disappointed. She bites her lip. Another yanking tug and she twists the needle, causing that final snap in her flesh.

The surge courses through her nerves, cruelly whiplashing through her system. She yelps and drops the syringe, crushing both of her hands against her mouth to keep herself silent. She doesn't want Daddy to know. She refuses to cry. Hasn't she already broken her promise once? *He'll be so angry if he finds out!*

When the shock simmers and her other senses return, her eyes roll back. The tugging is gone and all she can feel is the rush of adrenaline. It isn't until she notices the smell of the metal door just beneath her nostrils that she falls out of that sensation. Its overwhelming aroma is pungent, nearly making her gag. She removes her hands from her mouth and realizes her fingertips are dripping in blood. She licks her lips and can taste brown water on her tongue. Her eyes grow wide. She panics, rubbing her mouth with the back of her hand, smearing blood across her lips while her finger continues to bleed. She tries to stop the bleeding by pressing down on the wound, but it only bleeds more when she removes the pressure, like a leaking spout with a broken valve. She wipes the excess blood on her dress and whimpers as the new dress turns from pure white to dirty red.

Despite the sacrifice, the bleeding doesn't stop.

The lock snaps. She freezes in horror and watches the door slowly open. Slowly, slowly, but not all the way. No more than a foot ajar, the door stops, then closes and the lock snaps shut. She sighs in relief but sits in paralysis, not knowing what to do with all the blood pouring from the tip of her finger. How to hide the evidence for when the door finally does open. The unfathomable amount that came from just a little prick!

The lightbulb winks out with a *click*. She is blind, whimpering in the darkness. The lock snaps once again and she hears the door creak open.

She can sense his presence like the brush of steel on her skin.

"Daddy?" she cries out softly.

"Yes, my sweet. I am here."

Instinctually, or maybe involuntarily, she lifts her arms into the black nothingness and is raised off the ground. She feels him cradle her as he walks over to the mattress and lies down with her on his chest. She curls up, pressing her ear to the velvet of his suit jacket, trying to stop herself from shaking. She doesn't want to cry but being so forgivingly held by him makes it hard to hold it in.

He runs his long fingers through her pigtails, down her arms, and to her hands, feeling every bit of her. How she trembles so softly and sniffles like a lullaby. He could smell the blood the moment he opened the door. That sweet tang of violence that makes him salivate. Coming from her, it's all the more impossibly irresistible. He brings her hand to his face and kisses her fingers, careful not to bite. Careful . . . not . . . to bite . . .

"I'm sorry, Daddy," she whispers.

"That is . . . That is okay. You are safe with me now. You are safe. You are okay. You are . . ." He loves the taste of her. He would drink her forever if not for the fact that she is finite. He would drink her forever if not for the fact . . . "Vanilla, my sweet. Do you know that you are Daddy's favorite?" he asks, high off her scent.

Her ears perk up as her mind races, and for the first time there's a silence in her stomach. *Don't you see?* But she doesn't. She doesn't understand the question. She doesn't understand that there are more little girls like her in the Outside. Because the Outside is filled with creatures and the only ones capable of emotion are her and her daddy. She doesn't understand that her daddy has options, that he could possibly be with anyone but her.

She doesn't understand that love is a choice.

So, she simply answers, "Yes, Daddy. I do."

He grins as he kisses her fingers, feeling himself retreat into that delicious euphoria, making sure to keep at least a single tether of control bound in reality as he sinks into her.

While he tenderly preys upon her, she idly picks up the drum of her stethoscope and presses it against his chest, hoping for a thumping to drum her to sleep.

She searches.

And she searches.

And she finds nothing.

MONA KABBANI

CHAPTER VI

When she comes to, the room is still dark. She blinks a few times, making sure that her eyes are open, that it's not just the backs of her lids keeping her in the dark. She adjusts, her sight finding a spectrum of shadows. She wiggles and feels him. Her body freezes, feeling his arms wrapped around her, his ribcage pressed against her, his still, unmoving body curled tightly into hers. He is here, even after she wakes.

He is still here!

An urge to move, to stretch, seizes control of her; she tries to squirm into comfort without disturbing his rest, afraid that he might leave if he finds her awake. She would give anything for more moments like these. More moments where he is with her, so intimately crushed against her when she rises. But as she shifts, so does he, and she fears she may have stirred him despite her efforts.

"Daddy?" she whispers, ever so softly in case he did not wake.

"Yes, my sweet?" His deep voice cuts through the darkness.

She flinches.

"Did I wake you?" she asks hesitantly.

"No. I've been awake."

"Oh . . . okay . . ." Her thumbs twirl in circles she cannot see. "Daddy?"

"Yes?"

"Am I still bleeding?"

"No."

"What about my dress?"

She hears him sigh and thinks she can see the cloud of his breath. "The dress is ruined, Vanilla. But I will get you a new one."

"How?"

"I will buy you a new one."

"From where?"

"From the Outside."

"How?"

"With money, my sweet."

"What is money?"

He pauses, taking a moment to think of a description that would best suit her understandings. "It is a kind of paper."

Her face scrunches up with confusion. "How can you get a beautiful dress with paper?"

"It's a special kind of paper. More valuable than normal paper."

"Why is it valuable?"

He pauses again, then smirks. "Because the creatures desperately want as much of it as they can get but there is only a limited amount of it."

"Oh . . ." Her thumbs slow. "I don't think I understand."

"Hmm. Well, think about it like this." He seizes the opportunity with a grin. "There are creatures in the Outside, correct? Hundreds of them."

"Yes."

"And there is only one of you, correct?"

"Yes, Daddy."

"Which means you are valuable, correct?"

"I suppose so . . ."

"So, anyone who has you has something of value. Which means everyone wants you, but they can't all have you, correct?"

"Right . . . because there is only one of me?"

"And you can't be *split* into pieces and shared amongst the creatures." He pinches the joint of her elbow. "You wouldn't be you, and therefore you wouldn't be valuable. Correct?"

She winces at the thought of being ripped at the limbs, each piece given to a creature as a present. "Yes . . ."

"Yes. And you are mine. *Correct?*"

"Yes!"

He settles, satisfied, and continues, "So, let's say I want something that a creature owns. Because you are valuable, they may give me what I want in exchange for you."

Her face twists in horror, heart pounding hysterically against the inside of her chest. He can feel it; he hopes she truly understands that fear.

"You wouldn't give me to them, would you, Daddy?! You *wouldn't*, you *wouldn't*, *YOU*—"

"No, no, my sweet! It was only an example." He digs his fingertips into her skin, calming her with his icy touch. "I would never give you away for anything in the world. I am only explaining that you are like money. That you are valuable."

She can feel his arms constrict around her body. The corners of her mouth still from the trembling and then curl.

They lie in quiet until her fear lessens.

"Daddy?"

"Yes?"

"What's outside the door?"

His jaw tightens. "The Outside."

"Yes, I know that," she whines. "I *know* it's the Outside. But what *is* the Outside?"

He grunts, his voice turning into a low gurgle. "It's an unsafe place. Especially for valuable things."

"But . . . I think you're valuable, Daddy."

He is caught off guard. A low flow of emotion pours into his stomach—the distant, all too infrequent feeling of love. The affection builds and bursts once in his chest like a dying star, then leaves all too quickly, like a fleeting hit. Self-defeated laughter laces his response:

"Thank you, my sweet. But you are far more valuable than you can ever imagine."

She blushes, her body suddenly feeling hot where his warmthless skin rests. "So, you can go to the Outside and I can't?"

"Yes."

"Why?"

"Because I can protect myself. You are too vulnerable."

His tone is curt, but she does not notice.

"Valuable and vulnerable . . ." She hesitates over the words, their consonants uniquely rolling around in her mouth. "Well, what if we went to the Outside together? That way the creatures know I'm yours and they won't come near us!"

"That is not how the Outside works, Vanilla. The creatures will try to steal you away from me. They may fear me, but the moment they see you, they will hunt you down. Do you want that? Do you want to be taken from me? To never see me again?"

"No . . . no, I don't!" The realization escalates in her suddenly frantic words. "Daddy . . . Daddy, that's not what I meant. *No! N—*"

"Don't worry, my sweet! As long as you stay safe here with me, those creatures from the Outside won't get you. You'll stay safe here with me, right?"

"Right . . . yes, I will," she whispers, her throat quivering painfully.

"Good."

"Daddy . . . ?" To speak now feels like injecting a syringe into her esophagus and dragging the needle up and down the flesh. But she clears her throat and speaks up. "Daddy?"

"Yes?"

"What . . . what would happen to me if the creatures got me?"

His voice is blunt. "They won't."

"Yes, I know. But what if they did?"

"Then you would die."

She is quiet for a moment in expectation, the word having no real impact on her. When he does not explain further, she asks, "What is 'die'?"

He tenses, eyebrows furrowing at the realization of what he's just done.

"Death," he says softly.

"Huh?"

"The correct phrasing is 'What is death?'"

"Oh. Okay. What is death?"

Now he feels pain. He feels anguish for foolishly spitting out a concept that never needed to be discussed. He hates to acknowledge it, but what can he do now? She cannot see him struggling, but his body language changes. If he holds on, she will never die. If he holds on, she will never die—

(. . . despite the fact that she will.)

The thought repulses him, jerks him back in disgust; it reminds him that he is not the only one who has control over her. He is not the sole determiner of her fate. Death is as well. As long as he lets it, Death has its say. Both he and it are in her veins.

And he allows Death to be a part of her. The conflict enrages him.

"Do you wish for the creatures to get you?" he growls, poking at her ribs and enticing her to stir, wanting her to feel the fear of her curiosity he no longer wishes to entertain.

"No! *No*, I don't!" The sudden change in his temperament horrifies her. She can't help but giggle under his prodding, but her fluttery breaths are filled with anxiety.

"Then don't ask such questions you shouldn't be concerned with! Or else I'll toss you into the pit of creatures myself!"

"No, no, NO, Daddy, please, no! I'm sorry! I—"

He stops and she silences. His grip tightens around her, the arches of her ribcage fitting perfectly into the palms of his hands. He presses into her. "Don't you see, my sweet? You need not ask such questions, because I am here. And as long as I am here, you need not worry. You are safe."

"Okay," she gasps, her heart racing in her throat. *I am safe.* "Okay."

He sits up on the mattress and places her on his lap. She wraps her arms around his neck and nuzzles her face into its crevice. He pulls her away from him. She whines. He grabs the sides of her face, digging his fingers into her jaw, and presses his lips against hers. His breath tastes like brown water, metallic, and her teeth feel like they could pop out of her gums from the pressure.

She smiles against his mouth.

He pries her off and his lips disappear from her senses. She can't feel him anymore, loneliness taking its place inside of her once again. She suddenly feels so cold.

The light turns on. Her eyes squint from discomfort; when they adjust to the brightness, she sees that the concrete room is empty. The door lock snaps. She bends her legs into her shivering body and hugs them, her knees wrapped in red-spotted fabric. She rests her chin and stares at the door.

Bang-bang-BANG!

She gasps.

They're trying to get in!

She wiggles away until her back presses against the opposing wall. Her mind plays tricks on her, making the doorway seem like a vacuum that wishes to suck her into the Outside. Distorted gurgles escape from the walls. *Creatures.* She whimpers, afraid to be taken. Afraid to be stolen and never seen again. *Afraid to die.* But that won't happen. She will stay in this room forever. He will protect her. He will keep her safe.

She is his.

CHAPTER VII

It isn't long until her daddy returns. Her body didn't even get the chance to cramp in its strained position: legs curled into chest and chin resting on knees. The lock snaps. She instantly stands against the wall at attention.

The door opens slightly and then shakes as though it were laughing at its own weight. Her daddy stands pressed against it, struggling to balance a large metal bucket of water and a brick of soap in his hands. Slung across one shoulder is a towel and across the other is a new white dress, the lace glittering against the yellow light. She eyes it and runs to help him, but he shoos her away with a hiss. She takes a staggering step back, nearly tripping over her bare feet.

You've frightened her, he thinks, and in an attempt to heal the fright he sings, "Vanilla, my sweet, sweet Vanilla. Go stand over by the bed for Daddy, please."

He doesn't like her being so close to the open door.

She obeys and steps away. He places the bucket of water in the middle of the room and quickly turns to close the door and snap the lock shut. He twists back around toward the bucket and drops the bar of soap in. It makes a distinct *plop* when it hits the water and sinks to the bottom. He places the towel and dress carefully to the side, rolls up the sleeves of his white button-down shirt, and dips his hands into the water. His arms pump viciously in and out of the bucket; she watches as droplets splatter across the floor. The droplets turn into hundreds of mini stains that disappear into the concrete as quickly as they appeared.

Like the strange dots . . .

"Come over here now," he demands in mid-thrust. The tattoo of lace on his wrist shows momentarily when it breaches the surface. She thinks she can see the vein beneath throbbing.

She skips to him and leans her body against his side, feeling the vibration from his arms plunging in and out of the bucket. She looks down into the water, her reflection muddled by a layer of clean bubbles forming at the surface.

He stops and pulls his hands out. His skin glistens as droplets fall and spot his black pants.

"Vanilla, test the water."

She obeys, recognizing the usual command, and dips the tip of her finger into the surface. The water feels cool but not unbearable.

"How is that? Does it feel good?" he asks.

She presses her lips together but smiles and nods her head.

The water is never the right temperature. In fact, it is always just a little too cold but tolerable, like a frigid tease on her sense of touch. Yet he always asks as though they might have a different internal gauge for frost. And she never tells him otherwise.

"Are you sure?" he asks.

"Yes, Daddy."

"Good. Go. Take off your dress."

She takes a few steps back, giving herself enough space, and clumsily begins to remove her dress. She is able to lift the fabric halfway up her ribcage before she hits the limit of rotation in her arms and can't lift any higher. She tries to jerk her shoulders up, bound by the skirt, but the dress won't budge. Like an animal in confusion, she writhes to break free but only stumbles in circles. She grows frantic. She can't see, but she can hear her daddy's laughter; her skin heats up in a blush. She squirms, her spine twisting like a trapped snake, desperate to remove the dress. He laughs some more and she begins to feel lightheaded. Still, he laughs and she wants to scream. Before she falls over to helplessly flop on the floor, the dress is tugged off her with ease.

Her daddy's face is suddenly a breath away from her own.

Her face scrunches up, but when he kisses her hand, she releases her anger.

"Hi, Daddy," she says forgivingly.

"Hello, my sweet." He smiles, his pearly white fangs shining through. "Are you okay?" Laughter lingers on his lips.

"Yes."

"Good."

He puts the damaged dress down and picks up her naked body, walking her over to the bucket. "Are you ready?"

She gives a sharp nod and a toothy smile. "Daddy, look! I have teeth like you!"

He laughs. "No, my sweet." A moment's pause. He looks at her vacantly, and then with awful caring. "But maybe one day."

Before she can respond, he dips her into the water. The drastic drop in temperature makes her skin freeze. She almost yelps, but gulps it down.

"Are you all right?" he asks. He can sense the spike of her heartbeat through his palms.

"Yes, Daddy!" She forces out the response, a load of shuddering breath escaping her lungs with it.

He stares at her curiously but says no more. *If she chooses to suffer, that is her own freedom.*

Submerged from her neck down, she acclimates to the cold. Her skin loses its want to shiver. She exhales and lets the muscles in her body relax, descending to rest against the wall of the metal bucket.

Sitting behind her now, her daddy tugs on her pigtail. Satisfaction bursts from one side of her scalp when he pulls out the band, like there was an itch in her skin she didn't realize needed to be scratched. Her hair cascades down onto her shoulders. He pulls out the band to her other pigtail and runs his fingers through her golden waves. She purrs. After a few strokes, he grabs her hair in his fist and lays it like a rope across her collarbone.

"All right. I need you to hold your breath now." He places his hand on the top of her head. His long fingers drip around her skull, clutching onto her so perfectly.

She takes a deep breath in and puffs out her cheeks, caging the exhale.

He smiles at her and the last thing she sees are his teeth before he forces her head down under. She hears the calming hush of water pass over and suddenly, she is in a new world. A world where she does not have to worry about control. Her body feels suspended, though her limbs are restricted within the walls of the metal bucket and her spine is pressed against the bottom. Everything within her is muted yet heightened, and overall, it is peaceful. She lets the breath slowly seep from her and feels the bubbles tickle her nose as they float away. Even from down under, she can hear them pop at the surface.

She wheezes out the last bubble and her lungs request a refill. Fear prickles her skin. The water instantly distorts into unwelcoming ice, yet at her center she feels warm. Her chest cramps and pleads to expand, but she does not try to force her way to the surface. She simply floats in acceptance.

She closes her eyes and waits.

The pressure on top of her head is released. Her daddy's hands reach into the bucket and pull her above water. When the air touches her nostrils again, she gasps and shoots out wet, mucus-filled coughs. Her daddy's eyebrows furrow with worry. He sits up on his knees, hands hovering over her shoulders, ready to pull her out entirely.

Her sputtered coughs turn into laughter.

"Ha! Ha! I tricked you, Daddy!" she teases.

He lets out a sigh of relief and chuckles. "Yes. Indeed, my sweet. You tricked me."

After her laughter settles, he dips his hands back into the water and presses down on her stomach, feeling it recede beneath his touch without objection. Satisfied, he fishes the bar of soap out from under her—she feels his fingers trickle across her vertebrae down to her tailbone as he does—and rapidly rubs the bar between his palms. The waves excite her and she attacks the rising bubbles, popping them to reveal the surface. As he brushes the bar of soap across her skin, blood and dirt lift from her paleness and turn the water brown. But her eyes are on him, watching as he bathes her with such intense focus. He takes extra care to make sure that no spot on her body goes untouched. A smile accompanies the flutter in her chest, but she quickly looks away when that flutter turns sour.

Her attention shifts to her hair. It snakes down her neck, over her shoulder, and dives under the water like a golden waterfall. She looks at her arms, tracing her skin with her gaze, following through to where his skin meets hers. To his wrist. To that throbbing vein that bumps to a dot.

Then she remembers.

"Daddy?"

"Yes?"

"Sometimes I get dots on my arm."

"Dots?" he asks, but as soon as the word leaves his mouth, his eyes twitch toward her wrist.

"Yes. They kind of look like holes that bump up under my skin. Kind of like yours. Like your tattoo."

"Ah, I see . . ."

"Where are they from?"

He stops scrubbing but doesn't look up from the water. He takes a few moments before he answers. "They're happy freckles, my sweet." He continues to scrub.

"What does that mean?"

"It means that whenever we are happy, the dots appear."

"Oh!" She glances over at his tattoo. "Well, if that's the case, then . . ." She looks down at her bare wrist, the healed flesh staring back at her. "Shouldn't there be more dots?"

She turns to him with a smile and he grins at her in return, his body covering hers in shadow.

"Yes, Vanilla. I suppose you're right."

CHAPTER VIII

Eight years later

He kneels next to the large porcelain bathtub, the top buttons of his dress shirt undone and humidity trickling down his chest. His hands are in the water, gliding a sponge across her sleek skin. When he is done, he presses his hands into his knees and uses the leverage to stand.

She stares up at him. A chunk of his petrified silver hair became unglued and has fallen over his painfully blue eyes. Eyes that are so unlike her own dark ones. But she can still see him clearly. His face is stone. Without a crack in his now settled expression, he holds his hand out to her, his long fingers unfurling toward her chest. She takes it, eyeing the smooth skin stretched across his ribcage beneath the buttons, and uses his anchoring strength to stand with him. He guides her out of the bathtub and watches her naked body balance over the ledge to reach him. Ice water drips down her bare skin and she shivers from the cool air touching her, freezing her into stiffness. He feels her body tremble and pulls her in close, concealing her within himself so that her nose presses into his chest. But still she trembles.

Because he is none the warmer.

(And she is only growing colder.)

He plucks the towel from the sink and wraps it across her shoulders. She grabs the edges and tightens the towel around herself, her legs still shaking because the towel no longer reaches down to her feet.

Gradually, her body stops shivering.

"Are you still cold?"

"No."

"Good."

He rips the towel off her and wraps it around her head. His hands press and rub into her skull, soaking up excess water and wringing droplets from her hair.

The aggressive motion warms her scalp and she purrs.

He removes the towel from her head and lets it fall to the floor like a used-up carcass. His eyes travel up her body, calculating, until they make contact with hers. A film of greenish-yellow light coats his face. But he still looks as pale as porcelain.

He picks up her dress from the sink ledge and flicks his fingers upward, motioning for her to raise her arms. She obeys and feels the fabric and his hands compress down her length as he slips the dress over her body.

"Daddy?"

"Yes?"

"I think I need a new dress."

He furrows his eyebrows and takes a step back to look at her entirety. The dress fits snug, the hem of the skirt barely reaching halfway down her thighs. Her chest seems stuffed into the fabric. Overall, her body looks rigid and uncomfortable.

She is growing too fast, he thinks.

"Yes . . . yes, yes, you are right, my sweet. I'll see what I can do."

He steps back toward her, placing his hands on her arms. He presses his fingers into her skin, feeling how she has aged, and sighs. He leans into her and kisses her forehead, inhaling her scent.

He is still taller than her, but she has grown enough to the point where she can rest her forehead on the center of his chest while they both stand. She does that now, and he grabs the brush off the sink to run it through her hair. She closes her eyes and feels the bristles glide down her back. His chest feels like a still wall against her unstable body.

He places the brush back and pulls her off his chest. She stands upright and looks at him as he parts her hair down the middle with his fingertips. Around his wrist are two black hairbands. He twists half of her hair in his palm, tugging at her scalp, and ties it into place with one band. He removes the second band to tie the other half of her hair, and when he does, she can see the tattoo. The black lace crawling across his skin. It looks painful.

A swollen dot and a vein throbbing and bulging from beneath like a purple snake hunting for escape.

"Daddy?"

"Yes, my sweet?" he answers just as he finishes tying the second pigtail.

"What happened to your wrist?"

She reaches out to touch it; he lets her despite his flinch. She traces her finger across the swollen vein, careful not to press down. Afraid she might hurt him by busting it wide open and letting the snake rip his skin apart in order to breathe.

He smiles to himself, watching her fascination as he reaches into his pocket and pulls out a thin strip of black fabric. "Well, you see, Vanilla, I was so excited to see you that my happy freckle nearly exploded."

She makes eye contact with him, the sparkle in his stare consuming her. She scrunches up her nose and giggles, but his face grows solid and hungry and she eats her giggles down.

"Da—"

But before she can start, the black fabric is tied across her eyes. She is led out of the bathroom, her steps staggered. She hears the bathroom door shut behind them, and that's when she begins to count.

One, two, three, four . . .

. . . ninety-three, ninety-four, ninety-five—

And on the ninety-sixth step, they stop. He spins her around and she feels his hand under her chin. He squeezes his fingertips gently into the muscles that connect her jaw. Her mouth promptly falls open. A moment later, she tastes sweetness pressed on her tongue. His fingers remain on her mouth. They glide along her jawline and down her neck until they hit her collarbone and the touch disappears entirely. She stands there, cautious to move without him directing her, until she hears the lock snap. She rips the fabric from her face and finds herself back in the concrete room all alone.

CHAPTER IX

She lies on the floor of her room, lollipop in mouth, listening to her chest through the drum of the stethoscope. The successive thumps sound weaker than usual, less pronounced, verging on undetectable. Panic settles into her—not enough to spike her heart rate, but enough to make it known that she fears the inevitable nothing in her chest. But she finds a trick. A way to fix it. If she presses the drum deep and sucks down a sharp inhale, her chest bursts with momentary vitality. Enough to satisfy her. So she does it again and again, feeling solace in the thumps, until she feels light-headed and so lets her chest settle before restarting.

Her hair is nearly dry now but still cold, plastered across the concrete floor instead of laying against her back to freeze her spine. She touches a wet strand, separating it, then traces her fingers down to her wrist, feeling how flat and smooth the skin is—besides the tendons, which stick out like ropes. But no bumps or throbbing veins. No happy freckles. Not like Daddy's.

She frowns and fidgets in her dress, trying to find comfort despite feeling strangled. Her thighs are bare, leaving much of her lower half exposed, the skirt recoiling from its place every time she tugs it down. She crosses her legs and inhales deeply.

Thump-thump. Thump-thump.

The lollipop clicks between her teeth at the same rate as the thumps, until the thumps grow quiet once again and she drops the drum entirely. She removes the lollipop from her mouth and holds it up to the light, shutting one eye as if looking through a microscope. As she twirls the stem between her fingertips, she admires the chaotic bubble formations trapped inside the red shell. She stares in wonder, then sticks her tongue back out in a pout.

She already misses the taste of sweet.

She places the lollipop between her teeth and crunches down hard, shattering the candy—the full force of an explosion within her cheeks. Her mouth drools as she chews, the lollipop shards dissolving completely across her tongue. She exhales into contentment, not caring now that the thumping has probably returned against her ribcage. All she cares about is the ignition within her skull.

Biting down on the stem like a dog with a used-up chew toy, she gets up and walks over to her mattress. Her body drops like dead weight onto the lumpy cushion and falls against the wall, her face resting on the cold concrete. She uses her fingertips to scan the wall, brushing them across the gray grooves and crevices and subtle parallel cuts. A piece of concrete crumbles under her touch. She runs her fingernails over it and scratches downward, deepening the grooves.

A faint scratch sounds from the other side.

A smile creeps across her lips. She curls her hand into a fist and knocks.

There is a moment of pause and she worries that she only imagined the sound. But soon after, a knock returns to her from the other side.

She bounces and giggles, settles herself down, and knocks twice.

Two knocks return to her from the other side.

Entertained by the distraction from her lack of lollipop, she plays: knock once, knock twice, knock twice, and then knock three times; a scratch here and a scratch there. Without fail, her sound is returned. A few times, she scratches shapes into the wall, like the outline of a stuffed blue dog or a smile, and listens for the shape to be scratched back to her through the concrete. She thinks she can hear the shape of a lightbulb.

As she listens, she hears a *snap*. She tilts her head to the side and waits for more, trying to understand the sound, but now there is only silence.

The realization dawns on her that the snap did not come from the other side of the wall.

She cowers away, standing as quickly as possible.

The door opens.

The thumping picks up, pounding in her chest, and she can't

understand why she suddenly feels so sick. The anxiety in her stomach tugs at her guts.

"My sweet, I think I found a dress to—"

He stops in front of the doorway, a new white dress across his shoulder. She watches him sniff the air, his nostrils pulsating, before he asks:

"What is wrong?"

"What do you mean, Daddy?"

She acts innocent, trying to minimize the tremble in her voice. As she looks up at him, she can't help but notice the long dark hallway behind him. For a fleeting moment, she thinks about making a run for it. About bolting down the dark corridor into the Outside, escaping into the mouth of the unknown. But what would she be running from?

He steps away from the door and slams it shut behind him without taking his eyes off her.

"Why are you afraid?"

"I'm not afraid, Daddy!"

He takes a step toward her, kneels down, and motions with his hand for her to come closer. She obeys and takes a step toward him. He motions again, not happy with the fear-filled distance between them, and she steps closer and closer until she is only a few inches away from the tip of his still nose. He reaches his hand out and brushes her cheek.

"Your skin is warm," he observes, and brings his hand to her chest. "And your heart is beating fast . . . faster than usual . . ." His eyes squint into a glare. "I'll ask again. Why are you afraid?"

VANILLA

Before she can answer, there is a knock on the wall. A knock that, although distant and muted behind thick slabs of concrete, fills the room with a never-ending echo of guilt. She remains facing him, biting her lip in hope that he won't notice. But his head whips to look at the corner of the room where the mattress meets the wall. Where the scratch sometimes secretly greets her.

Only, now it is not so secret.

"What was that?" her daddy growls, his face contorted into something unprecedented. He looks threatening, ready to bare his fangs and shred a threat from the Outside into thousands of tiny pieces.

She stands, paralyzed, afraid that her insides might burst out of her. But he does not waver at her fear. He is too focused, too predatorily concentrated, to notice.

When he does not hear her answer, his rage increases. He growls again without removing his eyes from the wall.

"Vanilla. What—was—*that?*"

The fury, laced so tightly around his voice, strangles her into convulsions. Tears fill her eyes as she croaks out her answer:

"It's the scratch," she whispers, wishing she could be as small as her words.

"The *what?*"

"The scratch!" she yelps as a tear rolls down her cheek. She has no other words to describe it. She has no other information she can give him, as much as she might like to, because she herself doesn't even understand what it is. It is just a sound that sometimes comforts her, that appears from nothing and leaves with no proof of its existence. She cannot explain it. She does not understand it. So she weeps because her innocence has otherwise silenced her.

He smells the salt from her tears and turns from the wall to look back at her. The anger in his face melts and regret takes its place. He raises his fingertips to the peak of her cheek and wipes away a fresh tear. He leans in and presses his lips against each of her eyelids, licks up the salt with a kiss. "Why are you crying?" he asks, his voice sounding more like a lullaby now than a violent storm.

Through snot-congested sniffles, she answers, "I-I don't know."

"You have no reason to be afraid. You know that. You are safe with me." He places his hands on either side of her ribs.

She nods in affirmation but says nothing else. The pit of her stomach is twisted in agony and she is too frightened to meet those blue eyes. She keeps her head down and her arms behind her back.

"Come. Come with me."

He holds her hand and walks her over to the mattress. He sits down and taps the lumpy space next to him. She sits hesitantly.

"You know, this room is very old," he starts, not removing his stare from her.

She nods in reply. Cautious, she looks up at him with wide, wet eyes.

"And old things creak."

Her eyebrows raise and she tilts her head.

He continues, "They make noises like knocks and squeaks because they are slowly collapsing."

"Collapsing?"

"Yes. Falling apart."

She gasps. "Is the room going to fall apart on us?" Panic fills her at the thought of them both being crushed under a ceiling of concrete.

He laughs, and she feels his laughter like a safety blanket extending from his throat, wrapping itself around her.

"No, no, my sweet. The room will not fall on us. A room of this strength does not fall simply from being a little too old." He runs a hand through her pigtail. "This room was built to keep the Outside out, you see?" He uses his other hand to pat the concrete. "To keep the scary creatures far, far away from you. To keep you safe! Nothing can get in and steal you away unless they are me and know how to get in. Even if the creatures take huge sticks and try to bash the walls in!"

He growls with amusement as he delicately tugs on her pigtail. A whimper escapes her.

"Even if they throw gigantic rocks or pound at the walls with their hundreds of giant fists, snarling for what is inside, they cannot break this room. No matter how much they want you, no matter how much they scream and beg for you, no matter what force they use, and no matter how strong they may be, they cannot break in to get near you." He kisses her forehead and smiles. "That is why I built this for you. To keep you safe. So, no. This room will never fall on us."

She bites the inside of her mouth and twirls her thumbs, wanting to vomit up the nausea inside of her.

He leans over and knocks on the wall. A knock is returned a second later.

His smile turns sinister.

"It is simply these walls creaking back at you. A room can only be so strong and yet so perfect. I'll have this fixed right away, my sweet. You don't have to worry anymore." He squeezes her fidgeting hand. "The creaking will no longer bother you."

"The scratch," she corrects him in a whisper.

"Yes . . . the scratch will no longer bother you."

He gets up and starts to leave.

"Daddy?" she asks.

"Yes?"

"Is that dress for me?"

He stops a few feet away from the door and turns back to her. He places his fingertips on the fabric laid across his shoulder, a wink of forgetfulness flashing across his face.

"No. Not for today, Vanilla," he replies.

He turns back around and leaves, snapping the lock shut behind him.

She rests the side of her head against the wall, staring at the door, unsure of what to do next. She closes her eyes for a moment, thumbs chasing each other.

Slowly, her thumbs curl with her fingers into her palm and she knocks on the wall.

Nothing.

She scratches her fingernails against the concrete.

Nothing.

She sighs and slumps, accepting the nothingness. She looks up. The cracks in the ceiling look as though they are getting larger—or maybe it is just her imagination. Maybe it is just her thoughts wandering off into dangerous parts, wondering about possibilities other than nothingness.

Wondering what would be worse: if the ceiling collapsed and crushed her . . . or if the Outside got in.

CHAPTER X

Nothing.

She growls and picks up the syringe.

Inject. Press.

Drum to chest.

Nothing.

Nothing . . . nothing?! Nothing, nothing, nothing, nothingnothingnothingnothing!

She snarls through clenched teeth and squishes the dog down to half its size between her hands. Each muscle in her face tightens, her eyelids squeeze shut, and she directs all of her strength into her fingers, grunting with every ounce of pressure, feeling the cotton scrunch within the sack of dirty blue fabric. The dog doesn't make a sound beneath the punishment. It accepts it, adapts to it by shrinking beneath her force, although she expects at some point to hear a *pop!*

Her muscles begin to tremble with the tension. After a few more grunts reciprocated by silence, she opens one eye and glances down at the poor thing crushed within her hands, crumpled into a pulp and probably suffering while she stares on in awful wonder. A wave of distress overcomes her. She lessens her grip, drops the dog to the floor, and frantically presses the drum against it, readjusting the steel multiple times across its chest.

Nothing.

With clumsy movements, she picks up the syringe and places the tip of the needle against the dog's neck. Before she pierces it through, her thumb slips and she prematurely presses on the plunger. The needle wheezes out a stressed hiss. Her ears perk at the sound of it, her sense of urgency diminishing. She looks at the empty glass barrel.

It's just air.

There is a moment of contemplative pause before she spins, searching. Searching for something else she can use to fill the barrel with, some substance other than air and hope that might be the magical cure hidden in the cracks of her room. But there is nothing within the barren concrete besides her mattress, and surely she can't shove fabric and foam down the needle.

She frowns, her mouth drooling at the sudden thought of a lollipop: that sweet red candy. Wishing she could melt one down in her mouth and use the liquid as a cure. Knowing how lollipops make her feel: deliciously energized. Maybe the stuffed blue dog would enjoy that. Because she enjoys it. Maybe it would make the dog finally thump. Because it makes her go wild. But it has been a while since she was given a lollipop, and she isn't sure that if she had one now she would waste its sweet taste on the dog.

On nothing.

She presses her lips together, swishing her tongue inside her mouth, stirring saliva between her cheeks.

A second idea seeps into her head.

She bites down on her tongue. Rivers of saliva pull from the back of her jaw and pool in the center of her mouth. She turns the tip of the needle toward herself and spreads her lips, doing so while keeping the drool from dripping down her chin. She inserts the needle carefully between her lips and pulls on the plunger, allowing the void to suck out her mouth's contents. A mixture of spit and bubbles fills the barrel with a crackling ooze.

She removes the needle from her mouth. A string of mucus frowns between the syringe and her face then snaps in half. She wipes and redirects her attention to the dog. She sticks the needle in its neck and presses on the plunger. That crackling ooze follows. Gradually, the fabric surrounding the needle darkens. Sticky water leaks from the fibers.

She pulls the needle out, places the syringe down, and presses the drum against it.

Nothing.

She drops the dog with a huff and rests her chin on her hands in thought.

There must be something else. Something must work. How did Daddy get it to thump?

VANILLA

She glares at the syringe and picks it up by the plunger with two fingers. She peers into the barrel, squinting her eyes as if the closer she looks, the more likely she will understand what to do. Understand the intricacy behind the emptiness. There are clusters of bubbly foam clinging to the inside of the barrel. They remind her of the smudge.

The blood.

Her eyebrows lift. She holds out her finger and pauses to weigh the possible consequences. To think about what would happen if she . . .

But her thoughts don't go far. Not further than the thought of that thumping.

(The thumping she herself is slowly losing.)

She grits her teeth and pricks herself with the syringe. She winces as a roll of blood forms, a stark contrast against her pale skin.

Like Daddy's when . . .

An emotional flashback of fear and confusion seizes her. She gasps and quickly shuts her eyes, holding her breath. Behind her lids, she sees darkness, nothingness. But she can feel the sting on the tip of her finger. That familiar, hedonic sting. An elated pain lurches up her throat, but she traps it before it can get any further.

It's all right. Daddy won't let anything bad happen to me. He said so! I'm safe. I'm safe. Behind these walls, I'm safe.

She opens her eyes and lets out a sharp exhale. She feels her body settle and blinks a few times to dry the water from her lids.

With numb expression, she dips the tip of the needle into the ball of blood and pulls the plunger. A few drops of red climb into the needle, but not nearly enough to fill the barrel. In her mind, the empty transparency of the glass should be glowing red by now. She squeezes the tip of her finger over and over again, harder and harder. Blood drips down her knuckles toward her palm. She tries to collect it all in one place and tediously vacuums every bit she can, growing frustrated when a spot dries too quickly, clogging the syringe.

A cluster of thick, red bubbles is now formed at the top of the needle.

Her finger still bleeds, but she does not need any more. Staring at the snakes of red slithering down her wrist makes her sick. She frowns and looks at the skirt of her dress. Fabric she can ruin with the color of heat. She wipes her finger across her thigh instead and rubs the excess red into her skin until it disappears.

She picks the dog back up.

Inject. Press.

The needle spits.

As she pulls out the syringe, a wad of stuffing falls from the dog. A twisted clump partially dyed the color of her insides. Her bottom lid twitches at the sight.

She checks the dog's chest, still holding the syringe in her hand.

Nothing.

Her eyebrows furrow with anger and just as she is about to throw the dog across the room, the lock snaps.

"How is my sweet doing today?" her daddy's voice joyously

bursts through the opening metal.

"Daddy!" she shouts excitedly. A bit of residual anger tumbles off her tongue like a breaking dam.

"What are you doing, Vanilla?" he asks sternly, the door now fully open.

He looks down at her, seeing her leg covered in a film of pink and the syringe peeling specks of blood in her hand. His nose scrunches up. His stomach growls. He takes a deep breath in. *She's losing it.*

"Am I having déjà vu? Haven't we gone through this already?"

His abdomen weeps with hunger.

"But, Daddy! I'm trying to fix the dog! Just like you!" she cries.

He chuckles, the laughter concealing his concern. "And what is it that you are trying to fix?"

She waves for him to come sit down with her, a pleading expression stamped across her face. He grins, shuts and locks the door, and sits cross-legged in front of her, holding his breath. Together they sit on the floor like two children sharing secrets.

"Look," she says as she sets the stethoscope's eartips inside his ears. She presses the drum against her chest. "Can you hear it?"

He nods. "Yes, my sweet. Of course I can."

"Now, look." She moves the drum to the dog's chest. "Can you hear it? Can you hear it, Daddy?" Her frustration overflows into her words.

He shakes his head, amused by her impatience. "No! I can't!"

He takes the dog from her and turns it over in his hand. It's filthy. His stomach whines at the sight of it: bloody and ripped open like the beginnings of a botched surgery.

"So, you are trying to make it like you?" he asks.

"Yes!"

"And why is that?"

He watches as the conviction in her eyes dims.

"Look." He mimics her, setting the stethoscope's eartips back into her ears. He presses the drum against the dog. "Do you hear anything?"

"No, I don't. That's what I'm trying to tell you!"

"Ah, yes. But now . . ." He moves the drum to his chest. "Do you hear anything?"

His chest is silent. A cage of emptiness. Concrete and still.

Nothing.

She shakes her head softly.

"Right. And do you think *I* need fixing?"

She shakes her head again. *Never.*

"So. Maybe the dog is not the one who needs fixing." He raises an eyebrow at her, then looks down at the stuffed thing. His face grimaces. "Actually, maybe this dog does need fixing . . ." Another clump of bloody stuffing falls from its open wound. It might as well have fallen onto his surgical table. He would have stuffed it back in and sown it shut with its dirty insides swelling. Too damaged to be worth the fix. "Perhaps I should get you a new one . . ."

"No!" she yelps, and reaches to snatch the dog from his hand, afraid of it being taken away from her forever. As she does, she lets go of the syringe. It falls in slow motion, twirling through the air until it lands. But there is no *clink* of glass against concrete.

Because it lands in her daddy's leg.

The room suffocates in silence. Her hands are wrapped around his, the dog still gripped between his five fingers, trapped in a cage of flesh. She is frozen, staring directly into his eyes. She tries not to look at the needle, afraid that if she does, her insides will jump out of her throat.

Nothing in his facial expression changes. Neither before nor after being pierced—as if only a slight breeze passed between them. Without taking his eyes off her, without even a twitch beneath his skin, he grasps his other hand around the syringe and slowly pulls, creating the illusory sound of friction between steel and flesh. The silver is now blanketed in dark red. A drop slips from the steel and lands somewhere below her periphery.

Her eyes cautiously migrate and she sees only the slightest hole where the needle fell—no darkened fabric around it like the bloodied, darkened fabric surrounding the puncture wound on the stuffed blue dog. His pants look dry apart from a solitary dot a few inches up his thigh where the drop from the needle presumably landed.

She returns her stare to him, afraid that if she does not maintain eye contact, she'll be defenseless.

Against what? She isn't sure.

His expression is flat and lifeless, like the expression on the dog even after being repeatedly stabbed. *Nothing.* He opens his fist, releasing each finger in mechanical succession. The dog falls into her hands and she brings it back to her lap. It feels light and weak laid across her thighs, almost nonexistent, like its previous weight evaporated from fear. She tries to sit up straight but feels too weak. So she watches and waits.

Moments pass and he grins. His fangs shine beneath his pale lips. A dark lullaby of a voice leaks from his mouth. "I think you need a new syringe, my sweet. This one is old and"—he looks inside the glass barrel, eyeing the blood and spit—"filthy."

She swallows but is unable to quench her throat enough to speak.

He places the syringe down on the floor and stands. She watches helplessly as he turns, snaps the lock, and leaves, the door left gaping as he does.

Left open . . .

The hairs on the back of her neck shoot up as though a thousand volts surged through her blood. Seeing the door wide, a dark tunnel leading to more darkness, and not hearing that second snap of the lock after his departure, makes her skin crawl. She is too frightened to move, paralyzed by discomfort like sludge weighing down on her skin.

If circumstances were different, she would have at least walked to the entrance, maybe even taken a few steps too close to peer into the Outside. To take a gander at the never-before-seen. Maybe seeing would put to rest her nightmares of the Outside and the creatures and their big fists and their hungry mouths . . . Maybe she wouldn't fear the petrifying clamp of their thieving touch any longer. But she fears that if she moves, her daddy will charge back into the room, his rage trailing behind him like spikes of cold steel.

And that fear trumps the other.

The light goes out. The room is dark except for the pale glow that crawls in through the open doorway. She hears his footsteps return and sees his shadow enter the room moments before his body does. He closes the door and she hears a snap. Her nerves calm.

The room is now completely dark. A few moments pass before she feels his cold fingertips under her chin. She naturally drops her jaw. A ball of sugar and happiness is placed on her tongue. An ever-too-long craving of satisfied euphoria explodes within her skull.

Her body, numbing through her taste buds as her eyes roll like loose marbles in her skull, is lifted off the floor and carried over to the mattress. Even before she is placed back down, she begins to feel drowsy, the fireworks in her mind settling into twinkling stars. His icy skin turns into a warm blanket. His stillness levitates her, undisturbed and safe, removing any fear of falling. Her insides relax in suspension. She is tired. Ready to lose control of her consciousness.

She barely notices the sting in her arm nor the suction beneath her skin. The long, dragging pull from her veins. The sound of gentle slurping.

When she wakes, she is alone.

The light is back on, yellow and blazing. A new freckle has popped up under the supple, pale skin of her arm.

In the center of the room, waiting for her, is a brand new syringe.

CHAPTER XI

Despite how beautiful and golden the new syringe is, it does not fix the dog. There is still nothing in its chest, and she has grown less and less afraid of that nothing with each passing moment, realizing there are possibilities other than that *thump-thump* thumping.

In the lonely moments after waking, she whispers in weak breaths to the dog:

"There, there, my sweet . . . you are here with me now. You are safe. The creatures didn't take you from me while I was asleep. They didn't take you to the Outside and shred your stuffing to pieces. You are safe with me . . ."

And then her mind loses track of its stream of thought and she falters into exhausted unconsciousness. Or she stares at the happy freckles across her arm that have resurfaced and loses herself in how they double and float above her skin.

The scratching and the freckles and the thump-thump thumping.

The nothing.

The lock snaps.

She lifts her head up toward the door and smiles lethargically as it creeps open.

"Who is ready for their new dress?" Daddy pops his head out from behind the metal frame like a jack-in-the-box, a delighted grin smeared across his delighted face.

She giggles at his goofiness.

He frowns.

"I *said*, who's ready?" A dark tint in his voice.

"Oh. Me!" she attempts to shout, raising her arms up into the air, feeling her heartbeat momentarily spike before dying down. Her arms drop with fatigue.

"Good!" Half his mouth curls into a smile. The other half remains behind in its former wilt.

He brings the dress to her and she questions why it's so large when he helps her into it. He tells her she is growing too fast and he doesn't want her to be uncomfortable every time she needs a new dress. That she will grow into this one over a longer period of time.

"I don't want to grow any more. I like the way I am."

He doesn't want her to grow either, but he doesn't tell her that.

"You'll be a beautiful woman, happy in your skin before you know it."

"But I want to be your little Vanilla forever."

He chuckles. "That is nice to hear."

And then they both fall silent, something melancholic creeping between them.

He plants a kiss on her forehead and stands. "Now, I must go take—"

"*Don't!* Don't go, Daddy!"

"But I must, my sweet. Don't worry. I will be back soon."

His loving tug on one of her pigtails silences her. She waves goodbye as he turns around and leaves, knowing there is no way to stop him from going and no way to know when he will be back. The door swings to a close but does not shut all the way—and the lock does not snap.

But her daddy is gone.

She stands paralyzed, her hand frozen in mid-wave, her eyes glued to the door. This is the second time he has left the door open, and she does not understand if he is becoming forgetful or careless. Or perhaps it is on purpose.

Perhaps it is a test.

She gathers her strength and stands, takes a step forward, stops. Takes another step forward and stops again. She continues this way, a broken wind-up toy inching toward its destination, until she is right at the edge of the doorway. Breath stilled, she peers around the frame and looks across the threshold. There is a long, dark hallway, the same of which she has caught glimpses of before. A deep path with an end that dissolves into darkness.

Where the creatures may come from.

But now, for the first time, she notices something new. Along the walls of the concrete hallway are doors that look just like hers. Rows of them on either side.

She cautiously steps into the space between the door and its frame, her nose just barely touching the Outside. She inches her toes forward until her big toe is past the threshold, touching the icy floor beyond her room.

The cold causes her to jerk back in fear. As she does, she steps on the skirt of her overly large dress and falls with a hard *thump*, smacking her tailbone into the concrete. Her throat hiccups from the shock and her heart palpitates in her ribcage. She whines. Using her foot, she slams the door shut and crawls backward, eyes wide and filled with horror. Through her mind runs thoughts of creatures emerging from that deep hallway to bang on her door.

Her hand falls on something. She flinches but looks down to see that it is only the syringe. She picks it up and returns to her mattress, curling her legs into her chest.

Still, she stares at the door. Her fingers frantically tap along the glass barrel as she attempts to calm herself, afraid that the Outside might get in. That perhaps the creatures will now freely enter her room with their big fists and hungry mouths.

Is the door still unlocked? What if they start banging . . . ?

Her imagination runs wild as she grows faint, trying to define what the creatures from the Outside might look like.

Thick skin and concrete bones . . .

The tip of the needle rests against the palm of her hand; as she shivers, it carves her movements into her skin. She yelps in pain and shock, redirecting her attention to the syringe. To the shallow red scratch it left where it grazed her, the tip now pointed toward her forearm. Her happy freckles. A fresh one throbs like a hungry mouth, gaping for nourishment. It has turned purple and so has the vein beneath it, an angry, pulsating snake.

Just like Daddy's . . .

She scratches at it with the tip of the needle, relishing in the stinging relief, creeping closer and closer to that snake's mouth.

And she is horrified when the silver point easily slides in.

CHAPTER XII

Six years later

She wakes up screaming, clutching onto her stomach to keep her insides from tearing out of her abdomen. Her eyelids are clenched together as she grinds her teeth with enamel-shattering force, trying to redirect the hurt somewhere else. Somewhere she can better compartmentalize and deal with.

But the affliction will not leave her stomach. Her heart has solidified into concrete, lying dead like a clot in the center of her chest.

Her skin is drenched in sweat, pigtails matted to her face and neck like glue. She kicks her legs. Her heels smack into the concrete floor—for she is much too tall now for the length of the mattress. The pain in her heels makes her scream louder until she coughs into silence.

This is what it feels like when the tugging finally rips!

The door's lock snaps. She doesn't open her eyes, but she can hear his footsteps running toward her.

"Daddy?" she whimpers through gut-wrenching tears.

"Yes, yes, Vanilla. I am here." There is a crack in his voice where the worry pours in. Where it fills him to the brim.

She hears him gasp and feels him lie down next to her. His arms wrap around her shoulders.

"Help me . . . it *hurts!*" she cries out.

Her stomach eats at itself, shredding her apart.

"I am trying, my sweet."

She feels a sting in her arm. Something is pushed into her jaw, placed on her tongue, only it is not sweet. She hasn't tasted sweetness in a while—or perhaps she has lost the ability to.

It's a pill.

"Drink," he orders.

A cool glass is pressed against her lips and she takes the gulp of water, swallowing down the pill.

"This will make you feel better," he says. An empty promise.

He clenches his teeth together, muscles protruding from his jaw. His fingers run through the strands of her golden waves.

Hearing his words and feeling his body pressed against hers lessens the torment twisting inside of her. Or perhaps she swallowed some of it down. She takes deep breaths, trying to manage the agony. He holds her, rests her head on his chest, and dabs the sweat from her forehead with a towel. He pays no mind to the fact that contact with her skin soaks his nice silk shirt. That her sweat drenches the mattress and seeps into the foam, ruining her bed. That the blood spilling from between her legs stains his pants and sets his stomach on fire.

Of all the possible worries in the moment, he only wants her pain to stop. He wants her to be okay. He wants to fix her. But she is crumbling in his hands.

All of his work . . . his love . . . *crumbling*.

He traces his fingers down her neck and shoulders but feels no further movement, her heartbeat slow and her breath steady. Her skin is yellow, reminding him of a jaundice patient in a ward. She has been sick for a while now, rotting from the inside out before his very eyes.

(Because her body is rejecting you.)

He curses himself. *And the signs were all there.* Despite the onset—the slow heart rate, the wet, heavy breathing, the cramps *(the damn cramps)*—he thought the symptoms would abate. That continuing his treatment would eventually cure her. His *damn hubris*. It didn't. She hasn't been getting better. Only devastatingly worse, as if she is relapsing, collapsing into herself like a dying star, her health now far out of his reach, shriveling away inwardly to a place he cannot go.

And he can't fix what he does not understand: How she can be cured from her original ailment only to self-destruct years later.

(Because her body couldn't grow with you inside.)

The sickness began as a slight cough, the ones that harbor in the depths of your chest, scratching at your throat when it is just a

VANILLA

bit too cold outside.

"Daddy?" she started one day as they were sitting together, him fixing her hair back up into pigtails, her sucking on a lollipop. Her golden locks had become so long and unruly, these appointments were doubled to twice a week.

"Yes, my sweet?" he replied, focusing his eyes on the part of her scalp.

Her hands were gliding over her stuffed blue dog, her fingers ripping ever so slightly into the fabric.

"I don't feel too well." She coughed.

"What do you mean?"

He finished and dropped the brush, alarmed that she could feel ill at all.

"I feel . . . cold."

As if on cue, she turned pale, her blue veins brightening beneath her skin. He pressed the back of his hand against her forehead, but his desensitized touch could only feel the barest note of fevered heat. Trained to know that it was not enough to cause panic. Yet.

She shivered, the convulsion stronger than her heartbeat.

"I will bring you an extra blanket tonight and turn up the heat." He smiled and kissed her forehead, his lips feeling her heat inch a degree higher.

He let her be, thinking her body would overcome it with ease. *It is only a cold,* he thought. *Nothing to worry about. It is still possible for her to get a cold. She is human.* He'd seen all too many simple colds in his line of work and all too many overreactions to nonexistent medical threats. All those anxious parents who came to his office to make a fuss out of a little cough . . .

"No, Mrs. Johnson. Your son is not filled with disease, nor is he terminally ill."

"Are you sure? But look at him! He's so pale! And that cough! It sounds like there's a monster in his lungs!"

"The only monster is the probable cigarettes he is inhaling without your knowledge. The cough sounds worse for smokers. Come back in a week after you've kept him hydrated and have better locked away your own vice."

She never did come back. He had been right. He was always right about these things. *Is* always right about these things. The human body is like a first-grade textbook and he the teacher.

No, it is only a cold. It will pass and it will only make her stronger.

But soon after, she claimed she couldn't sleep.

"Daddy?!" she would cry as she jerked herself awake.

"You are fine, Vanilla. I am here. You are safe," he'd whisper as he stroked her boiling head. He imagined her brain roasting inside of her skull like a turkey in an oven.

(So much roasting.)

The coughs were keeping her up at night, and her shakes were too violent to allow a moment's rest. He felt the tremors suffocating her muscles. She couldn't control her body from wrenching itself out of sleep, and no matter how high he turned up the heat, she wouldn't stop shivering. She wouldn't just sweat it out.

"Daddy?" she whispered, the dryness in her throat causing her voice to crack so pitifully, like her lungs were filled with unquenchable desert sand.

"Yes?" he replied, his voice cracking as well.

"Why can't I stop shaking?"

"Because you are cold, my sweet."

"But my skin feels like it's on *fire*."

He didn't want to scare her. To tell her that she was sick or that such things as sickness existed. To have to explain to her that not only creatures but diseases can cause death.

And, apparently, so can he.

"Your body is just trying to grow into the beautiful, strong woman you are becoming."

She didn't respond. Maybe she didn't understand. She just coughed and twitched some more. She couldn't even close her eyes. She stared up at the ceiling, past him, as though he weren't there right beside her. As though he were the ghost.

He stayed with her through the nights, trying to stop the shakes. He had no body heat to give, and the heating system wasn't enough, so he covered her in layer after layer of blankets, trying to force her to sweat out the sick.

She sweat out pounds, but just not the sick.

Helplessly, he watched her grow weaker as time passed, seeing her wither further away with every snap of the lock. She no longer had the energy to stand and greet him when he entered her room; soon after, she didn't even have the energy to sit up on her mattress.

"Daddy . . . ?" she croaked when he opened the door.

He could hear the strain in her voice when she tried to speak. She coughed every other breath. He only wished she wouldn't try so hard for him.

"Hello, my sweet. How are you today?"

When he stepped inside, he nearly choked on his horror. He thought she was a cadaver, lying on the mattress like Death was already inside of her (resting so comfortably, too!), nothing moving except for her jaw and the droplets of sweat crawling down her skin.

He could smell the rot.

"Daddy . . . it hurts . . ." she struggled to express. "It hurts so bad. What . . . what is happening to me?"

"You're fine, Vanilla . . . you are okay. I am here. You are safe," he answered, his sorrow strangling his voice. For a fleeting moment, he thought about turning around and closing the door, snapping the lock shut once and forever. He knew what would happen if he didn't. The awful climax of his actions if he didn't turn around right then. But his chest lurched toward her.

Because he knew he was incapable of leaving her. Even in this incoming eternity.

(Fool.)

He walked to her body and saw how it was nearly dissolving into the puddle around her, immersed in its own perspiration. She was drowning in her own heat.

"Come on, my sweet. Let's give you a nice bath."

"O-okay, Daddy."

He bent over and lifted her off the bed carefully. He didn't bother to blindfold her. She wouldn't remember much and he'd be grateful if she did. He carried her down the hallway and to the bath, placing her in the tub and running water over her. She purred for a few seconds when the wet touched her skin, cleansing the top layer of grime, but then grew silent. She didn't have the energy to react any further. He had to keep her from slipping under.

She lay in the porcelain, head slumped back and mouth agape toward the ceiling, lips curved around a black hole where Death could enter freely. Where Death was already beginning to make a home.

(And what a nice home!)

"You are okay, my sweet," he whispered to her over and over again, hoping she could hear him. Hoping he was reassuring her . . . or was it really just for himself? "You are okay."

She couldn't hear him. Her sickness had pulled her in too deep for her to hear. Like trying to listen to the surface when you're ten feet under. He continued to speak to her anyway, tears swelling beneath his eyes but never spilling over.

My blood isn't working. It's only destroying her now.

He diagnosed her over and over again to find a better treatment for what he tried so hard to explain. But he'd never seen anything like what had coiled itself around her. Whatever was digging into her organs with thick spikes, killing her, somehow surpassed his skills and knowledge.

Death was taunting him. (Haha!) He understood that much. It

was taking what it wanted and leaving him weak. It laughed at him while he struggled, egging him to just do it. To just pull the trigger or say goodbye to her forever. But he wouldn't give in to it. He wouldn't pull anything. Not yet.

He spent hours upon hours in his office, fiddling with steam and fire, producing pills and tonics. He treated her with the best medicines he had to offer, the best medicines he could find or create. But nothing worked. The sickness only grew all the more vengeful the more he attempted to heal her.

"Here, Vanilla. Open your mouth. Try this."

It was so difficult to get her to swallow it all down. Her throat was too dry, even with rivers of water to help her drink the pills. So many different drugs to fill her, and still nothing worked. Nothing even relieved her of her pain.

(Just let her go.)

He took her bloodwork every day rather than once a month, thinking he would find a cell quickly mutating under the microscope that would explain something. Anything. It was easier to extract samples now that he didn't have to turn off the light to distract her when he stuck her with the needle. She was too weak to see or feel anything, and he could no longer spare the time to keep her in the dark.

(Just . . . let . . . her . . . go.)

He took her bloodwork and continued transfusing his own, as he had been doing for the past twenty years since she was brought to him, sick and dying, as a baby. The treatment that had cured her and others both before and after, but was failing him now. He hoped that if he upped the dosage, maybe increased the frequency, it would make her better. But Death was too strong and now he was the one killing her. But he was scared that if he stopped altogether, she might die instantly.

Her weight and muscle mass wouldn't stop dropping until he could see the deep outline of her ribcage and spine. He'd run his fingers along her skin, feeling the bumps and ridges of her skeletal system—it would be fascinating under any other circumstance, but he didn't want to feel her dying core. *Anyone but her.* She grew skinnier, frailer, paler, until she finally withered away into the yellow skeleton he holds in his hands now.

(And what a sad skeleton at that.)

He looks down at the stains on her dress. At the disfigured fabric, once pure, now so tainted with all the putrid colors of the sickly rainbow. After years of wear, she finally grew into it, only to soak it in filth, sweat, saliva, and blood. (So much blood.) It pains him to feel disgusted, guilty for this conflicted revulsion toward her. He loves her dearly. More than he ever thought possible.

Even if her insides are pouring out of her.

"My sweet . . ." he hums in her ear.

Her shriveled lips smack and her lungs wheeze out a dusty breath. Her lids are open but her pupils are rolled into the back of her head, showing the whites of her eyes.

As he holds her half-dead body, a tear manages to escape from his dry soul. He hasn't cried in decades. The memory of her finally causes him to overflow. Of the sweet little girl who jumped from excitement at the sound of his footsteps. The one he bathed and changed and showed photographs to and fell asleep with while she provided him with more than she could ever know. The one he vowed to keep safe. To protect. But it is far too late for that now and she is far too sick.

Death won. It knew he would pull the trigger.

(What are you doing?)

He bends down and presses his head against hers, biting his lower lip as water streams down his cheeks, soaking her face. Her beautiful, beautiful face. His teeth break skin and drops of his blood fall onto her pale lips; buds of life on rotten soil. He smells the thick iron scent and brings his mouth to hers, giving her a cold, lifeless kiss. She tastes like decay. He holds still there against her, waiting to hear her swallow all of him that has trickled into her throat. Every last drop. His blood that would save her, if not from the former way, then from this. *This damned way.*

(Stop this.)

As he does, he rests the palm of his hand on her chest, feeling her faint heartbeat.

It is the last time he'll ever hear it.

It is going to give out either way. Then we'll both be dead.

(This isn't right.)

Slowly, as if this is the way the world ends, he drags his mouth to her neck. He takes a quick glance at her arm and observes what he has done to her. The recent puncture wounds of a failed revival that are no longer healing at the rate they should be. That are resurfacing from failure. The detailed treatment, now a sadistic stick-and-poke.

He dips his hand between her legs and pulls out a bloody palm, shining with brilliant red life—the only life left in her trying to make its escape—melting into his shirt sleeve with sludge-like tempo.

His chest ignites.

(Don't.)

He bites, his teeth piercing her neck. Her skin leaks and the moldy taste of her slides down his tongue in exchange for venom. He remains, refusing to recoil away. She sputters out a cough. Her chest jerks upward as if trying to shake him off. He maintains his hold on her as he cries and she sinks back into the mattress with defeat.

A tug awakens in the pit of his stomach, a low growl that shoots rage through his system. His pupils dilate. His mouth salivates like a rabid dog's. He knows he must let go soon, but it has been years of this torturous temptation and, finally, he is giving in. Finally pulling the trigger.

A fuck-you to Death.

(You are the one who has to live with this decision.)

Her heartbeat grows fainter and fainter beneath his palm until it eventually gives like a flickering flame on its last bit of wick.

(I hope you are capable of it.)

Thump ... thump ... thum—

He must let go now. He must let go now. But he drinks and he drinks and he drinks.

And Death falls silent.

MONA KABBANI

PART TWO

CHAPTER XIII

Her eyes flutter open. The first thing she sees is her ceiling. Cracks slither like veins across the concrete. The scents of cement and dust are extremely present to her. She blinks a few times before sitting up on her mattress, her body not hesitating with weakness.

The second thing she sees is her daddy, standing in the corner of the room, one eyebrow raised over a cautious stare.

"Daddy?" she says.

"Yes?"

"What . . . what are you doing?" She searches him for some hint that would explain his strained presence. But his grip is bare.

"Nothing, my sweet." He quickly breaks eye contact. "Just watching over you. To keep you safe."

She notes his lingering awkwardness with a frown and squints down at herself, something not feeling right on her skin.

VANILLA

She is in a new dress. Only this dress is not white or covered in lace. It is black and plain, covering the length of her arms, the skirt stopping just before her knees. There is no design for her to memorize, no folds for her to flip through. Not even a wrinkle.

"How are you feeling?" her daddy asks, interrupting her wonder.

"I feel fine, Daddy . . . Why do you look so sad?"

She eyes the creases in his face: lines that curve in strange places, forming a look that makes her feel alone despite his presence . . . a look she faintly remembers seeing above her during intervals of consciousness.

The memory punches her in the gut. The torture, the feeling of sinking into a dark place while another part of her floats away. Life siphoned from her bones through the pores of her skin. Her stomach lurches from the phantom memory of her insides tearing her apart.

Wasn't she drowning in her own sweat? Wasn't she unable to breathe?

She touches her skin.

"Daddy?"

"Yes?"

"Am I dead?"

Cold shock slams into him. He jerks his head back, eyebrows furrowed but eyes sad.

"Why would you ask that, Vanilla?" he demands, but beneath the aggression his voice falters.

"I think . . ." She remembers her body losing energy until her muscles felt like stone. Until she could no longer speak, barely make a sound besides a strained cough to clear her weeping lungs. Until all she could do was lay in her daddy's arms to be poked and prodded at while she felt herself purging.

"I think . . . I think I remember being dead," she says.

A beat of silence holds suspended in the air.

"That was just a bad dream," he answers.

"A bad dream?"

"Yes. A nightmare. It wasn't real."

"So . . . I'm not dead?"

"You don't know what death is, do you?"

She pauses at this. "No."

His lips curl over his teeth. "So, how can you be something you don't understand?"

She nods slowly. "Daddy?"

"Yes?"

"Why are you so far away from me?"

"I thought I would give you some space."

"Why?"

He walks over to the mattress and sits down next to her. His breath smells pleasant and metallic, like iron laced with sugar. Her mouth waters for it—for *him*. And that is when she realizes she can smell him now, too. Smell his sickeningly sweet scent.

It's . . . *too* sweet.

She gulps down the taste and leans into him. He pulls away. He grabs her legs and swings them onto his lap. She doesn't protest. He looks down at the sample of her anatomy and presses his thumbs into her muscles, squeezing his hands around her calves and up her thighs. He shoves his hands into her stomach, digging his fingertips under her ribcage and working his staccato touch from her chest to her collarbones. He runs his hands up along the sides of her neck, placing pressure beneath her jaw.

"Open your mouth," he orders.

She obeys.

With one hand, he takes out a thin black stick from his pocket and clicks its end. Without warning, an intense white light shines out from the tip of the stick. She growls, hating it, but he ignores her. He points it down her throat then flashes it in her eyes.

She flinches, expecting it to hurt—like the day she stared so intently at that uvulal light dangling from its concrete palate—but the pain is not as bad as she remembers. It is only mildly uncomfortable, making her eyes feel like they're petals separating from her irises, like the flowers her daddy has shown her photographs of. The flowers the creatures love to destroy.

"Daddy?"

"Yes?"

"What are you—"

He presents a lollipop from his pocket and her question disappears from her throat. Her eyes grow wide and she giggles with flirtatious embarrassment.

She opens her mouth and lets her wet tongue roll out. Ribbons of saliva stretch between her pale lips. He unwraps and places it, the contact immediately triggering her taste buds. She bites down impulsively, shattering the treat to pieces.

She halts, stunned by her own force, then shrinks away with an anxious glance. But he doesn't seem to mind.

He is smiling at her. So she continues to chew.

The pieces dissolve within her mouth. The spoils feel even better than usual, as if a needle was shoved into her brain through her temple and ejaculated euphoria straight into her skull. Salivation snakes down her throat. Her stomach growls, begging for more. Embarrassed, she curls over her belly, trying to mute her hunger, but to no avail.

His smile vanishes.

"Are you happy, Vanilla?" he asks, petting her head.

She nods.

"Good."

He leans in and kisses her forehead before standing from the mattress.

"Daddy? Where are you going?"

He stops in front of the door, his hand hovering over the lock. "I have some things to do, my sweet."

Before she can stop him, he is gone. The door shuts.

But the lock does not snap.

She stares at the door. She stares and stares and stares without blinking. She stares without breathing. The door morphs in her vision, creeping farther and farther away from her the longer she stares. Her focus twists into a dark tunnel that constricts until all she sees is that metal slab. She shakes her head and rolls her eyes loose in their sockets.

Nothing feels real.

Nothing.

She is mentally floating. She stands from her mattress. Her legs feel wobbly and she holds on to the wall to stop herself from falling. She bounces up and down a few times and bends her joints and strains them until she feels her limbs are back under her control. She walks toward the door. Although far away by her vision, it is only a few steps until she is standing right in front of it. The lock's position rests in parallel to the ground. Her daddy's words echo through her head:

"This lock will keep you safe. It will remain untouched unless you wish for the creatures to come in. Do you understand?"

"Yes, Daddy! I do!"

She places her hand on the metal and carefully turns the knob, ready to stop if she hears footsteps or yelling.

Or a creature's growl.

But all is quiet.

The doorknob clicks and the door loosens from its frame. She pulls the heavy metal toward her. There is a shift in the lighting. She looks down the gaping mouth of the hallway, her skin tingling from the novelty. Freely roaming in this space seems so impossible to her—a dream, or a nightmare—yet she takes the step. The same steps her daddy takes. Her foot makes contact with the ground beyond.

She reaches the first door on her left. The first one of the hallway.

She turns toward it, a feeling of uncanniness bubbling within her. It looks like her own. Only she is on the other side of it now.

The sole difference is that where the lock should be, this door instead has a small hole.

She grabs the doorknob and turns it slightly. It gives in to the rotation. She turns the knob all the way and pushes the door, letting it swing open no more than her head's width.

She barely peers inside, only daring to stick her head in a few inches. Half of the room is obscured by the doorframe, but from what she can see, the room looks exactly like her own. It even has the same lumpy mattress shoved into the corner. A loose lightbulb dangles from its ceiling.

Here, however, the floor is bare of toys.

In the corner of the room, above the mattress, are rows of grooves dug so deep into the concrete that the hollows lose the touch of light.

Is this where Daddy sleeps?

She thinks she hears footsteps. Quickly, she jerks away and runs back into her room, slamming the door behind her. She runs to her mattress and cowers in the corner, staring at the door, waiting for it to open.

It doesn't.

She rests her hand on her mattress, feeling a solid lump under her palm. Her stethoscope. She picks it up and admires its strong structure of rubber and metal—the build she imagines her bones might look like, all wiry and joined together at the ends, breaking off into branches of functional limbs. Her daddy showed her not *photographs* of these structures but what he called "sketches." Something he drew with graphite to exhibit their insides.

"How do you know this is what we look like on the inside?" she'd asked him.

"Do you want to see the sketch or not?"

"Yes!"

"Then don't ask me silly questions."

She slips the eartips into her ears and listens to the muffled *hummm* of her surroundings. The sound reminds her of being dipped deep into a bath. Relaxing yet so full of noise.

She fiddles with the drum in her hands, tapping on it to mimic the muted beat she so loves. *Thump-thump. Thump-thump.* She lies down, staring at the ceiling for a moment before closing her eyes. She places the drum of the stethoscope on her stomach, drifting away from her thoughts. She slides the drum up to the center of her ribcage and stops tapping to allow the living thing inside of her chest to take over.

Nothing.

CHAPTER XIV

She will get hungry, he thinks. *Time will tell if left unaddressed.*

The Devil named Daddy, defeater of Death—christened name Victor—paces the room, his thoughts churning.

He can keep her hunger at bay with all the lollipops in the world—blood is a funny faculty like that, how it never ends—but it won't be enough. Though he does so wish it could be enough. Eventually, she'll need more. And more and more, until it takes her over. Until it is far too late for him to show her what will satisfy the craving and what she has to do to get there.

What the virus demands.

She'll have to figure it out for herself. How to stop the bubbling hate swelling up inside of her before it takes control. To be thrown helplessly into the void of her own desperation, only for it to dawn on her before it's too late. Before she reaches the brink.

His poor, poor girl. How she will be torn apart from what she knows and what is. How else could she understand? How else could her innocent, pure self understand what is far beyond her? What her mind could not even begin to wrap itself around?

Because that is how I created her. Blind.

Oh, his sweet pet, kept safe in that room, kept safe since infancy. Never having to deal with any kind of struggle or anxiety of free will. Never having to endure that sad, pathetic existence led beyond these walls. He cringes at the memory of clawing and digging his way through filthy streets and filthy people. What a disgusting fate. But he has protected her from that. His sweet, sweet Vanilla ... He alone is responsible for protecting her from that. She should be on her knees, begging him to accept her gratitude! Begging and begging and begging!

And yet, to continue to protect her as I do now would only mean killing us both.

He cannot keep her locked inside, caged in with this torment until she explodes within her lifeless flesh. And surely the blowout, the foggy red binge, when it comes, will be taken out on him.

He has to let her go.

But how can he? How can he when her function in the world will surpass any version of normalcy? Any grasp of the everyday. Will she need to understand normalcy in order to thrive in sin? Out there? With *them*?

Her limited knowledge ... that safe trap within her skull to which he fed such violently sweet information. What he thought was for her own good will now be her undoing.

Because, of course, fool that he is, he couldn't just let her die.

Damn his inability to foresee this! Despite his knowledge, somehow *he* was the blind one! *Hah!* From the moment he first carried her life in his arms, he knew, he *knew* he would have to accept it when the Underworld demanded her soul to collect. When she would shudder her last breath against his chest.

When Death had its way with her.

But he had to do it. He had to save her. The fool! He couldn't let her go. Not so *soon*! Not to Death, that cruel opposer. He'd be damned if he let Death have her!

But I suppose now...

He comes to a stop over the compact mold.

...now I have all of eternity.

Like a puzzle he's already figured out far too many times over, he places a white paper stick in the empty slot and fills the ball-shaped top with a healthy dose of human blood straight from his syringe. He closes the mold and waits for the metal to freeze. Once the mold issues its final *hisssss*, he pulls out the lollipop, grabbing a wrapper and neatly twirling it around the red ball. He holds the finished candy, a nightmare in confectionary disguise, at eye level and twists it between his fingertips.

These won't be enough. They won't satisfy the lust. Decades it took for him to tame his hunger into submission. His mind travels to the bags of blood resting at the bottom of his medical-grade fridge nearby, one of which he'd drained just moments before and now sits deflated in the sink like a used condom. Even so, no matter how much he drinks, he still gets the same hunger pains and adrenaline rushes of rage. No matter how much he gorges, no matter the restless nights of impossibly glutinous digestion. Still the hunger.

Always, the hunger.

He stares at the empty bag in disgust. Sometimes, even after ten or twenty or fifty, he still turns into a monster.

No, it is impossible to keep her here like this now. He needs to let her hunt.

He taps down on the metallic tabletop, letting his ideas resonate with the sound.

He could hunt with her. Teach her how to feed. Watch her humanity deconstruct into beautiful red carnage every step of the way. But then what? To be with her for every hunt thereafter would be infeasible. Without him as the constant variable to her joy, she would build up too much confidence in her independence. Suffering is a foreign concept when her daddy is always there to show her the way. He has made her life simple, easy—spoiled. Unaware of the opportunity to evolve beyond him.

He desperately fears that fate, yet still it rushes closer.

On her own thereafter, she will expand into a chaotic force, an eternal horror, a perpetual-motion machine of beauty and rage. Then she will realize that he is of no use.

And then, she will leave.

He steps out of his sterile office and takes the stairs up, veins in the concrete wall traveling with him. The lollipop twirls in front of his face, hypnotizing his rattling mind. He reaches the top of the flight and walks down the hallway toward her door.

He needs to let her hunt, yes. But he needs to know he has control. Absolute control, regardless of his presence. The times when she will have to venture on her own, he needs to make sure she will return. He must prove to her that she needs him. That without him, she will be nothing. He needs to make her permanently dependent.

He pinches the stem. His nails make indents in the paper without snapping it in half.

Such a pity. All this time and energy spent on making her life painless, wasted. Now that must all unravel like a ball of string until it is just one weak, breakable line.

And still he foresees one potential hiccup in this painful lesson:

How will he do it? How will he crush her into submission while avoiding a conditioning that will remove him from her favor, while avoiding the urge to hate him rather than depend upon him? She must fear his absence, not yearn for freedom.

She must love me unconditionally.

He stands in front of her door at the end of the hall. With a sigh, he hangs his head, fatigued from his thoughts. There is an answer to his dilemma—it is only a matter of finding it. Of digging it up from beneath the heavy gravel of one's psyche. The perfect balance between necessity and hate. Love and possession.

There is a vacancy at his side. He turns his head and sees another door, the one for the room against Vanilla's to his right, ajar. He must have been careless and forgotten to lock Vanilla's room. She must've stepped out and explored the few feet she mustered enough courage for before returning in a pang of fright. Yes—he can smell her now.

Foolish, he berates himself. *Stress is no excuse.*

That vacant space. This room has been empty for, oh, so many years. Once upon a time, it held a patient, but he released her long ago.

A harrowing child.

A thought suddenly clicks in his mind. A devious, merciful answer that curls across his lips and rests like a cradled babe in loving arms. The perfect balance. A way to cause suffering without being the causer. The method to creating control without creating fear toward the controller. A way to divert hate. The solution that will make sure his sweet Vanilla comes back.

This is his opportunity, handed to him like a gift he must accept, and it must be done now. Immediately. He might not have another chance like this.

But can I part with her so suddenly? So soon?

He has no other choice. The timing is too perfect. Her torment will increase tenfold with the incoming changes. She'll be lost and confused and desperate—they both will. But hopefully—no, for certain—she will believe this nightmare is due to his absence.

Because she left him.

He closes his eyes and carefully rests his hand on her door, giving himself a final moment to relish in her presence. To relish in her saccharine scent.

I will miss you, my sweet. But we have all of eternity now, and I must make sure to properly prepare us for it. For you and for me.

For our love.

When he's had enough time to process, to understand and accept in full the pain that is about to transpire, he lifts his wrist to his lips and bares his fangs. With quick intensity, he bites hard through his skin and tendons. Blood bursts into his mouth, filling his throat. He hears droplets of it hit the floor. The animalistic adrenaline immediately shocks his system, pounding in his ears.

Without losing a second, he swings the door, purposefully leaving it wide open, letting it smack against the concrete with a sharp thud, and storms inside.

He shouts, feeling the roar burst from the pit of his lungs, "WHAT DID YOU DO?!"

She is on her bed, playing with her stethoscope, tapping at it as though it were broken. At the sight of him looking the nightmarish way he does, she screams and cowers into the corner.

Already trapped herself, he thinks. *Such a helpless girl. If she were alive, she wouldn't last a minute in the Outside.*

He storms over to her mattress and shouts, "I ASKED, WHAT DID YOU DO?! ANSWER ME!"

Do not touch her, his weak conscious reminds himself through the black cloud of hunger filling his mind.

"Daddy?!" she yelps. Her body trembles beneath his shadow.

"GET OUT OF THAT CORNER!"

"Daddy, *please*! I can explain!" She scurries away from the wall and runs around him. In the center of the room now, she faces him, her back to the door. Nothing blocks her way to the exit.

"AFTER ALL I'VE DONE FOR YOU, YOU THINK YOU

CAN WALK AROUND THIS PLACE AS YOU PLEASE?! HAVE YOU LEARNED NOTHING OF ALL I DO TO PROTECT YOU?! TO KEEP YOU SAFE?! YOU FOOLISH, *FOOLISH* GIRL!"

"Please, *please*! *Daddy*, please!" Her voice cracks as she steps back toward the open door. "I can explain! I can—"

"HOW DARE YOU?! YOU INSOLENT, UNGRATEFUL CHILD!"

This is for your own good, my sweet.

"DO YOU THINK YOU UNDERSTAND HOW EVERYTHING WORKS?!"

He takes another step toward her.

She takes another step back toward the door.

It sickens him to see so many tears drench her face, but he forces himself to continue.

So that we can be together for all of eternity.

"DO YOU THINK YOU CAN PLAY WITH ANYTHING YOU FEEL LIKE?! OPENING DOORS AND WALKING FREELY, TAMPERING WITH WHATEVER YOU'D LIKE WITHOUT MY PERMISSION?!"

Another step forward, another step backward.

This is for you, Vanilla.

"WITHOUT MY BEING THERE TO MAKE SURE YOU ARE SAFE?! DO YOU UNDERSTAND WHAT WOULD HAPPEN TO YOU IF I WEREN'T THERE TO WATCH OVER YOUR EVERY MOVE?!"

If only you could see it, you'd understand.

A step forward, a step backward.

For your own good.

"WELL, LET ME TELL YOU, MY SWEET, *SWEET*, LITTLE VANILLA! WITHOUT ME, YOU WOULD BE HELPLESS! YOU WOULD BE NOTHING BUT A SAD, PATHETIC, LITTLE STUFFED ANIMAL LIKE YOUR PLAYTHING OVER THERE!"

He spots the stuffed blue dog just before him and crushes it, feeling no resistance against the pressure of his sole.

"JUST LI—"

A sting erupts from the side of his arm. A muted discomfort that stops him in his tracks. He halts and looks down, staring at the syringe burrowed deep into his bicep.

She picked it up from the floor and drove it into him.

He growls, although . . .

Nothing.

He does not feel the pain. And he is actually quite impressed.

She will be just fine.

He uses every ounce of rage, feeling his skin electrify as though he were covered with razor-sharp hackles. He bears toward her, his movement filled with threat. Tears waterfall down her cheeks as her body shakes. Her hands are in front of her mouth, hiding her lips that are surely bent in horror from what she's done. He'll use that horror against her.

His body shudders from the rage. In his last act, his *coup de grâce* of this sickening skit, he jumps at her.

"WITHOUT ME, YOU WOULD BE DEAD!"

She yelps, her eyes filled with anguish. With one sobbing gasp, she turns and runs out the door.

For a moment, no part of him moves except for his eyes trailing her footsteps; he remains hunched as if his prey is still beneath him. Then he exhales. Composing himself, he stands tall and watches her body disappear into the mouth of the hallway. Her little feet patter.

Victor pulls the syringe from his arm without a wince and holds it at chest level while the needle weeps his blood.

I will see you again soon, my sweet, he thinks. *Good luck.*

CHAPTER XV

Her feet pound down the hallway. She isn't sure where she's going exactly, just that she must distance herself from her room and her daddy as fast as possible. As far away from him as she can. The separation pains her more and more as it grows, but the pit in her gut settles with every step she puts between them.

Years ago, the first time she peered down this hallway, it looked like an endless cave. Like something that would swallow her whole if she traveled too far down its throat. Now, as she wipes away her tears, she can see everything so clearly, as if the hall is full of light. She can see every door spaced in parallel to either side of her, and she can see the incoming doors, and the end where they stop. If it weren't for her tears blurring her vision afresh, she would also be able to see each crack and stain that winks at her as if to say *see you soon*.

She brings herself to a careening stop so as not to slam into the concrete wall at the end of the hallway. To her right the floor becomes stacked and staggered blocks leading downward into the underneath of the world. *The underneath of the Outside?* A staircase to somewhere unprecedented, like in the photographs.

She looks back behind her. She can see the door to her room at the other end, still wide open, her daddy's distant figure small and watching. Will he come after her ... or is he waiting for her to come back? To return to him, her shoulders sunk and submission in her eyes.

No.

Either way, she is in too heightened a state of adrenaline to be motionless, and her flight instincts only push in tandem with the pull in her gut, leading her like a friend would lead a helpless puppet.

She takes the first step down into the unknown, then the second, farther than her body has ever traveled before. A couple more stairs and her feet catch on to the downward motion, dormant muscles awakened by the energizing burn.

Skipping the last few steps altogether, she leads herself to a floor that is flat and wide, more like a square than a narrow pathway. It too is lined with closed doors—not with locks like hers but rather small holes. She runs around the perimeter, looking for another exit, another hallway, but none are visible. She grabs at knobs and pushes against them. One door aggressively snaps back at her when she shoves, the metal portal glued to its frame. The others swing open, smacking into the walls of their empty concrete rooms. Rooms with nothing but blank space in grayscale. No bed, no toys—and all dead ends.

She scales the walls, a caged animal desperately searching for a way out, until she comes across a tall door made of dark wood rather than steel. She grabs the knob—made of gold rather than silver—and gives the heavy plank of wood a vicious thrust, using the side of her body as leverage.

The door gives in without objection. She nearly falls forward from the unexpected momentum.

A burst of air hits her face, carrying a scent . . . strange and complex. Fresh and dirty, almost like cold water mixed with grime. She realizes she is getting wet. Water falls from an endlessly black ceiling poked with holes that glisten, showering her. Making her dress stick to her skin. She looks about. She looks about the Outside. Everything in the Outside is dark and wet.

I'm here.

Her body twitches for motion, but she hesitates, staring at the strangely picturesque scene. The emptiness, the rivers of water weeping down an eternal path in the same direction, the concrete that bleeds out from her building onto the sidewalk and beyond.

She is in the Outside.

I'm here!

At the top of a three-step staircase, she jumps toward oblivion and lands on the sidewalk, a puddle of water exploding from beneath her bare feet. Two steps away is a black road, a bright yellow line splitting it in half through its center. The Outside is highlighted by yellow lights that shine down from tall silver poles with curved necks. She recalls a desolate street like this one—an image, printed in black and white, held between pale and boney fingers. As though her daddy had taken the photograph from where she stands now. From exactly where her feet are planted in this moment, his lingering presence radiating up through the pavement and into her soles.

"What is the street for?" she'd asked him, tapping her little finger against the glossy page.

"For the creatures to travel around," he answered.

"Why are there no creatures in this photograph?"

"Because they are all hiding."

Her head fills with noise, though the street seems to be vacant. She hears creaks and screeches and whispers in the distance as if they are only centimeters away from her ears. A loud *bang* from behind makes her jolt forward. She darts down the street, trying to run away from the racket, but it follows her.

Buildings of different shapes and sizes, ones made out of red stone and ones made out of glass rather than thick gray concrete, line the street. Some are short, shapes staring at her through their windows. Some have black silhouettes dancing behind their curtains. A feeling of uncanniness overwhelms her: a distant understanding that just hovers above comprehension.

Like the edges of a photograph that start to come into focus.

Although disoriented, she does not stop running. The adrenaline in her won't allow it, forcing her to follow the tug in the pit of her stomach. Driving her to go and go and *go* or else the fear won't stop. Or else the fear will catch her.

Until a sharpness rips through the bottom of her foot.

She screams, scraping the flesh of her throat. She skids to a halt and picks up her leg, hopping on her other foot to keep balance. Burrowed into the soft white flesh of her heel is a thick silver screw. Its flat and shiny cap reflects her terror.

It doesn't hurt. Extremely uncomfortable and visually disturbing, yes. But it doesn't hurt. Her foot bleeds, dropping globs of red onto the dark concrete which are immediately washed away by the passing stream. But it doesn't hurt. Not in the way she thinks it should.

Her fingertips grip around the cap and pull. Her skin pulls with it, but the nail doesn't slip out. She pulls harder and harder, but her skin only stretches farther out, spurting blood in reaction. She stops, watching a red snake drip down her heel and dive off its precipice, droplets falling onto the top of her standing foot. Her pale, wet skin, a sharp contrast to the now diluted pink liquid. It smells sweet but only scarcely so, a sour tang that threatens to ruin the appetite.

She sucks on her bottom lip and twists the cap, the tips of her fingers turning white from their pressure around the metal. The nail gradually unscrews from her skin. With one last twist, it pops out, leaving a gaping hole in her flesh.

She whines and hops off the street in search of a small dark corner. Her senses are overwhelmed; she just wants to get away and return to quiet comfort. Return to the enclosed elements of her room. To end the *pitter-patter* in her brain that prods at her so revoltingly. She limps down an alleyway shrouded in reassuring darkness, but her mind remains cluttered with noise. Against the deep wall is a big plastic box covered in drenched paper. She rests upon it and crosses her skewered foot over her leg. She looks underneath to reassess the damage, but her skin is bare. The wound is ... gone. Somehow healed. Only blood remains, smudged across her sole as evidence.

"How?" she questions aloud to herself.

The distinct sound of footsteps finds her senses.

She sits up, alert. "Daddy?" she calls out in a hopeful whisper.

Metal smacks into stone, a nasty *clank* diving down her ear canal and splitting her skull. She whips around to find the source.

"Now, what's a pretty young thing like yourself doing out so late at night? Isn't it a little too cold for you to be dressed like that?"

A group of four approaches her. The leader—male, based on the masculinity of his voice—holds a metal rod. He continues smashing it against the wall, emitting more nasty clanks.

Creatures from the Outside.

But they look just like her. The same build, but no skin. Only layers of loose black canvas across their forms and shadows over their faces that breathe out white smoke.

"Boys," the leader speaks again. "What do we do when we see a poor, helpless girl all alone by herself?"

"We 'elp 'er," replies one of the creatures in a strange tongue.

They all grin, ivory teeth visible beneath a dark surface. Their grins turn into chuckles; soon they're cackling like a pack of hungry monsters in disbelief of their starving luck.

She stands and faces them, every muscle in her body tense.

"Um, hello," she whispers, her voice cracking under her nerves.

The laughter stops.

"Polite little girl!" the leader declares, holding up the metal rod. He points it at her as though the action might summon her to speak. "Name, doll?"

The pack creeps toward her and she shuffles back until she is up against a wall, realizing the alleyway is a dead end. Her mind flashes to photographs of snakes and dresses, empty streets and wilting flowers, clock faces and broken bridges, trying to recall any information about the creatures other than the pieced-together nightmare of giant fists and growling mouths. But there is nothing to remember because there *were* no photographs. Not of the creatures. No lessons other than fear.

"I *asked*, what's your name?" the leader repeats.

"Vanilla," she says, fiddling with her thumbs as she tries to disappear into the wall.

"Vanilla?!" the leader shouts in humorous surprise. "What are you? Some kinda stripper? Where your heels at? Leave 'em at—"

"Please!" she cries. "My daddy will be here any minute, and he'll make sure you can't steal me away! He'll hurt you! So you better just leave me alone now, or else he'll come! Or else—"

The leader lurches toward her. His teeth are bared an inch away from her nose and he snarls. "I don't care about no sugar-daddy pimp, little girl. What, you stupid?"

A ring of bodies envelops her. A creature shoves her from the side into a puddle, dark water erupting like a fountain around her. Her elbows crash against the ground, the impact shooting up her arms and snapping her jaw shut, her tongue barely escaping the guillotine.

"Stupid bitch!" a twisted mouth yells down at her. "What stupid bitches get!"

She tastes dirt. Her teeth feel grit when she grinds them together. She tries to call out for them to stop but is silenced by the whack of the metal rod against her skull, the contact dull and fleeting. It should have knocked her out cold, but she remains conscious, lying on her side against the sharp ground as they continue to beat her. To pound down on her with their giant fists and sticks. Blows to her gut and chest light her up with fear.

Painless fear.

They grab at her arms and pin her down. One creature holds her head in place so that she can see the black void above her as it weeps into her eyes. The creature's fingers dig into her jaw and pop open her mouth. Before she can scream, the metal rod is shoved down her throat, blocking her voice. Her tongue cramps around it and her teeth threaten to shatter as the creature smacks the rod so that it vibrates against her enamel.

"Did ya sugar daddy teach you how to take it?!"

The creature pulls out the rod and lifts it over his head. He brings it down upon her shoulder and she can finally scream, curling her legs into her chest and kicking out at his stomach. Her feet make contact and the creature keels over with a grunt.

"Fucking kill the whore!" he demands through raspy breaths.

They all come down upon her, obscuring the vast ceiling and grabbing at her dress. She fends them off, yanking her arms free of their grip, kicking and punching, swatting their hands away, only to have their attacks ricochet into her ribs.

One mouth opens, revealing a circle of jagged teeth: "Bitch's strong!"

Blurred streaks of black and light disorient her as she whips her limbs about in a frenzy. Still, they come down on her, slingshotting knuckles into her jaw. The hurt is great, but the true pain comes from the discomfort. The assault on her senses—a feather made of needles tickling her system.

The stimulation fills her with rage.

"She'll tire out! Keep beating!" a different voice shouts.

"Yeah, yeah! Does she got a wallet? Purse?!"

"Ain't seen nothin' on her!"

"'Er body'll 'ave to do!"

A hand grabs onto the skirt of her dress and tugs. She hears a slight rip that instantly absorbs her attention.

A moment later, her mouth is filled with sweet iron.

"AH! FUCKING BITCH! SHE BIT ME!"

Hands pull away, leaving a trail of thick drops she can feel in a line down her center. The weight of four bodies lifts from her chest. The ceiling is still nothing but empty tears. She doesn't understand what she has done until she looks up at the group of creatures backing away from her.

One of them displays his bloody hand, three fingers missing.

She feels hard slime and knitted fabric swish in her mouth.

She spits. A succession of fingers and a clump of dark fabric shoots out from her lips. A mouthful of blood and flesh pours down her chin.

They all pause. Then one creature shrieks, setting off a domino effect as they scatter away, stumbling and tripping over themselves to escape.

"Let's get the fuck outta here!"

"Bitch ain't worth it!"

"Freak!"

They run out of the alleyway and disappear around the corner.

One final screech—

"My fuckin' *fingers*!"

—the sound of distant wet footsteps, and then silence.

She licks her lips, feeling the tacky substance cling to her skin, and whimpers. She looks down at the limp, crimson-colored foreign bits before her and gargles on the blood in her mouth. Or at least she thinks it's blood. *Do creatures bleed?* It has to be blood.

But it tastes so sweet. Like candy.

Like her lollipops.

Repulsed, she spits up as much as she can, hacking up red phlegm and wheezing until the taste of sweet iron is barely detectable. Until the taste of creatures is out of her.

She wails, covered in dirt and red stickiness, wet and disgusting, flesh stuck between her teeth. *Daddydaddydaddydaddydaddy!* She runs out of the alleyway with barely a scratch on her—but the blood smeared across her skin, drenched in her hair, and the red tears staining her face make her the poster-child for Hell.

She traces her steps, uninterrupted, until she is back home, stepping up to the tall door and swinging it open.

"Daddy?!" she shouts into the building.

Nothing.

She steps inside and runs back up the stairs. The door to her room is still open. She bolts down the hallway and bursts across the threshold.

"Daddy?"

But the room is empty. Her toys are back where they have always been, waiting with immortal patience in the center of her room. On her mattress is a pile of lollipops. Hundreds of them! Enough to last her a long while. A *very* long while, filled with sugar . . . but maybe not her daddy.

She turns around and screams back down the hallway, back down that dark throat anchored to the stomach of the Outside:

"DADDY?! DADDY, WHERE ARE YOU?!"

Nothing.

CHAPTER XVI

Her jaws click shut. A drop of black water slips from her chin and splatters against the concrete, a helpless victim dragged down by gravity. Her jaws click again. Beads of sludge melt down her body, beneath her dress, between her legs.

She looks about the empty room. Adrenaline drains from her system. A sense of security nestles in around her now that she's back in her own space. But even then, a wisp of anxiety stitches through her tendons with a thin needle, disrupting her peace.

Because her daddy is not here.

Her jaws click, trying to mitigate the bruised sensation behind her molars. The pain isn't real, but the phantom memory of it is. The disturbed irrationality of the act perplexes her.

"They'll bash against the walls with their giant fists and sticks. But don't worry, my sweet. They won't be able to get in. Not

in here."

Not in here. But out there? Out there, they'll do so much worse.

She bends over her mattress to pluck a lollipop from the pile, opting for the one that sticks out from the peak of the sweet mountain like a flag of victory. She unwraps it and lets her jaw hang loose after one final *click*, placing and replacing the lollipop on her tongue at awkward angles as though someone else were doing it for her.

It's not the same. The loving wrap of his arms around her doesn't come next like it should, but the sweet bite makes her feel a little more settled.

The sludge hardens. Her skin tightens, crackling when she moves to stand. There is a bath down the hall, just a few paces away.

I need to get clean before Daddy returns. I need to show him I can take care of myself. He doesn't need to worry about watching over me anymore. About keeping me safe. I can be careful and strong and do that for him. He can just enjoy my presence now. We can just enjoy being together, without having to worry. I just survived the Outside and the creatures without him and now I've returned unharmed! I protected myself . . . for him. And he will forgive me. He has to forgive me.

Because she doesn't know what she will do if he doesn't.

I have to get clean.

The doors on this floor all lead to rooms that look just like hers. The concrete replicas make her wonder if she's made a circle, disoriented by their proximity, going round and round and round until she grows dizzy. She leaves open the doors to what rooms she's already checked so as not to waste time looking into the same room twice or thrice, but still she double checks and triple checks. When she can't find the bath, when her efforts at being astute like her daddy are in vain, she returns to her door, thankful it sits at the head of the chain. If it were lost amongst the other doors, nestled between either row, she would surely go insane.

She turns her back to her door and faces down the hallway.

Ninety-six steps.

She closes her eyes and places one foot in front of the other, counting to that magic number in the dark, stumbling because her daddy's hands aren't on her shoulders to guide her.

Ninety-three.

Ninety-four.

Ninety-five.

Ninety-six.

She stops and opens her eyes. She's at the far end of the hall, right before the stairs. The only door nearby is to her left, hidden from the uniformity. She opens it and instantly recognizes the yellowed tile and white ceramic tub, the dirty grout and smeared mirror. She can see so clearly through the dark, she doesn't realize the light is off. It's not until she steps inside and eyes the switch, playing around with it to understand its function, that the sickly hue flashes on. She winces, stunned by how much brighter everything becomes. She adjusts and smiles at the familiarity.

Even with just one person inside, the room feels

claustrophobic, like the walls are waiting to close in around her. It must have been hard for her daddy to get her clean in such a confined space. He must have struggled to fit.

She stands in front of the mirror, brushing her fingers through her coagulated pigtails, gripping the dirty strands, twisting them, draping the golden ropes tarnished with distress and trauma over her shoulders. She adjusts the lollipop stem in her mouth.

"Look how beautiful you are, Vanilla."

His hands weaving through her roots, fingering the small of her back.

"You are the most beautiful girl to ever exist, my sweet."

His nails brushing against her cheek. Watching his fingers in the mirror waterfall down her face. Her eyebrows knitting together, innocent curiosity reflecting through grime.

"Are there others to have existed, Daddy?"

His knuckles clenching against the back of her neck.

"No."

A white towel hangs from a rail above the bath. She pulls it down and clutches it in her hands, the fibers rough and scratchy. The kind of scratchy that pleasantly satisfies an itch. She brings the towel to her nose and inhales. The smell is fresh; the faint, icy scent of her daddy lingers.

She lays the towel down on the sink and turns to the bath. From the porcelain sprout two knobs indented with ridges and a faucet like the sink. She realizes that she's never seen her daddy fill the bath—he's always had the water ready for her before the blindfold was removed.

VANILLA

She steps into the tub and crouches in front of the controls. There are two—one red, the other blue. Looking at the blue one makes her think of the cold. Of the frosty bathwater that always chilled her spine. That she put up with to be able to look into her daddy's blue eyes without interruption. That she put up with so he wouldn't leave.

She grabs the red knob and twists. A stream of water pours out from the faucet and drowns her toes. Ribbons of mist rise from the centimeter-deep surface. She tries to sense a temperature like her daddy would ask her to do, but she can't gauge it. It simply feels wet.

She twists the knob again. The stream of water turns into a blast, raising the surface level to drown her ankles. She sits against the porcelain and rests her head on the lip of the tub, feeling the distant pleasure of warmth as the water engulfs her—its barely perceptible pulse of heat makes her ache for more. As the water rises, the pressure grows. It weighs down on her, a soothing presence across her body like a heavy blanket keeping her grounded. Her fingertips travel to the hem of her dress, hesitate, then float away.

The water rises to her armpits. She uses her feet to twist the knob and the faucet stops its purging. The only noise now is the gurgle of bathwater sloshing around as she adjusts herself into comfort.

The pipes creak. She closes her eyes and listens but does not hear footsteps or scratching. She looks back into the bathwater. It's murky, darkened by brown sludge and thick blood, her legs hidden by the opacity. She rubs down her dress, squeezing out as much filth as she can from the fabric. But there's more underneath, against her skin, hiding. She can feel it touching her, rolling across her stomach, crawling down her center.

She yanks the dress off over her head and submerges it, scrubbing it against herself as the water produces black waves of filth. She rubs and rubs and rubs, refusing to give up until every inch is clean. Until even the individual stitches are free of filth. When satisfied, she lets go of the dress with a triumphant "Humph!" It lazily floats to the surface like a bloated carcass, releasing trapped bubbles of air with an ugly hiss.

She rubs down her arms and legs, her skin now an unnatural shade of bright red. Against the darkness of the water, her body looks ragingly violent. About to erupt. Alarmed, she scrubs harder and harder, but the red won't go away. It only grows brighter, angrier.

She quickly steps out of the tub. Steam rises from her body in thick clouds. Her skin splits into blisters, sprouting across her arms and legs until they open in violent bursts, vomit water, and disappear. She leans into the mirror, watching as a bubble expands across her shoulder, pops with wet revulsion, leaving shreds of skin in its wake, and absorbs back into her, petals of pink shrinking away.

The reaction carries on with indignation until it slows, bubbles taking longer to form and shorter to heal. She grabs the towel off the sink and wraps it tightly around her ribcage, knotting the corners in front of her chest, exfoliating what's left of the blisters.

Steam no longer rises from her skin, now perfectly tamed, the color and texture having returned to normal. The distant pulsation of heat vanishes to nothing.

Nothing.

"Do you think I need fixing?"

Never, Daddy.

The water in the tub is dark red. Loose hairs and flakes of dirt whirl within. She fishes her dress out, a cascade of brown falling from the fabric, and twists it at both ends delicately. Once the last possible drop is mangled from the fabric, the dress still feels wet and heavy.

She sighs and carries the dress back to her room. It leaks, dripping water along the floor of the hallway. She can hear the droplets hit the concrete behind her like sharp echoes of each footstep. When she enters her room, she immediately shuts the door and snaps the lock. The sound of it—*snap!*—sends a pleasing chill down her body, making her groin weak.

"This lock is not for you to touch. Unless you want the creatures to get in."

I think this is an exception, Daddy.

She tosses her dress onto the mattress and falls down next to it. From her impact, the lollipops shoot into the air in unison and collapse back down with hundreds of soft thuds. She crunches the last bit of candy in her mouth, tosses the stem onto the bedding, and picks up a new one. She unwraps it and places it on her tongue.

"A sweet for my sweet."

A bubbling similar to the reaction across her skin fizzes beneath the crown of her skull. She fiddles with her thumbs, glaring at the door, waiting for her daddy to walk through.

"I'm here to protect you. To keep you safe."

But he doesn't and she continues to stare, unwrapping and sucking and unwrapping as her vision fades at the edges and the metal door grows brilliantly vivid.

CHAPTER XVII

The boy chews, eyeing the silver-haired figure before him in the mist, unnerved by the stranger's complete stillness. A dark and towering statue standing just outside the streetlight's reach. The boy shifts his dirt-rimmed nails to the unregistered gun tucked between the belt of his worn-out jeans and spine.

You wanna move along, pal?

But he doesn't dare say it. A deep instinct forces him to swallow his words.

"Hello."

The boy's skin prickles at the man's voice.

"Yeah? What do you want, old man?" Frank asks, hacking up a thick loog and ejecting it out onto the sidewalk. His fingertips tremble over the handle of the gun. His skin is wet and dewy, but that's just from the aftermath of the rain, though he can taste the sweat on his lips.

"I have an offer for you."

Silence consumes the air between them. The man does not move, his body inanimate, the shadow over him concealing his mouth so that Frank can't tell if he is speaking or if the words are being injected directly into his mind.

Frank grips the gun's handle, his finger stroking the trigger. "All right . . . I'm interested."

"I know a way you can make a quick thirty thousand dollars. But you must be prepared to do something . . . egregious."

Frank lets out a thick string of laughter. "Thirty? *Thirty?!* Listen, grandpa! For thirty thou', I'll do ya anything! E-gracious or not! What's the job?"

The silver-haired man divulges.

The boy lifts an eyebrow and removes his grip from the gun, the trigger no longer a negotiation piece in this deal. "Huh, ya don't say? And what's in it for you?"

The man answers, steady and slow: "You'll be ridding me of an ever so irritating pest problem."

She reaches for another lollipop. The palm of her hand comes across mattress. She searches with spidering fingers but only finds more mattress. She looks down. The bedding is a graveyard of lollipop stems and crumpled wrappers, completely bare of delicious red candy.

How long have I been staring at the door?

Her stomach growls beneath the towel, chews on itself in complaint and demand, angry with her for leaving it empty and in want. She tries to savor the last bit of lollipop stuck on her tongue, behind her teeth, but the sugar dissolves in mere moments.

Daddy . . . ?

But she knows the request would be useless to speak. There is no one to answer her.

No one to keep me safe.

Her skin starts to vibrate, tingles like static attempting to escape through her pores. The static builds, shooting currents through her system that increase in intensity with every pulse. Her limbs jerk haphazardly in response; her legs kick up into the air and her shoulder smacks back against the wall, knocking a grunt out of her. She tries to stop, to tense her muscles so they remain in place, but it's no use. Lollipop stems go flying in every direction.

Pressure swells behind her eyes. Her teeth grind together—she can hear the grating in her skull. Her jaw clicks open like a mousetrap. She tries to slide it back into place but her face reacts in protest, the hinges refusing to rotate shut. Her tongue brushes across her enamel, outlining new ridges, points that descend like stalactites and ascend like sharpened knives. Sour iron suddenly swamps her mouth, washing over her taste buds. Air flows in and out of her throat, rushing across her palate. A sting emits from the center of her tongue, a feeling of split flesh, an open wound, exposed nerves touching the world they should be well concealed from, then instantly vanishing along with the sour taste.

She reaches her hands inside her mouth. Although painless,

she can feel her fingers being punctured. A dull sense of her skin popping open, sliced into raw ribbons. When she pulls her hands out of her mouth, her palms are covered in blood that collects and travels down her wrists.

"Daddy, Daddy! I have teeth like you!"

Yes, Vanilla. On this day, you do.

But there are no wounds to show for the damage.

Blood flings off her fingertips, splattering across the mattress and wall: a fresh coat of sinful paint against a dull surface. She gawks at it, horrified, but before she can react further, her body begins to convulse.

The pain floods in.

Her muscles harden, strained and stiff down to her fingertips and toes, as her body jumps around like a fallen plank of metal. The towel barely hangs on to her as it's smeared with streaks of red. The back of her head smacks into the wall repeatedly, pushing the rest of her body forward until she is supine on the mattress. There, she kicks and punches against soft foam, but the hurt is inside of her. The static in her skin ignites into flames. Her eyes burn and her insides melt into soup, sloshing around in the pit of her belly. Her jaws stretch wide as if to shriek, though she is unable to make a sound, the cords in her throat frozen. Her tongue twists and curls, a frenzied snake in her mouth jutting in and out from between her lips. Her teeth slice through the bubbly flesh so that her own sour blood drains down her throat.

But it won't satiate her.

All the while her mind screams out; the cry for her daddy

rattles around in her brain, bouncing against tender walls that absorb the blow and shoot the torment back into her.

A single tear drools from her eye.

Right when she feels the brink of her skin's capacity to hold it all in, right when she feels her bones about to burst through her muscles so that her skeleton can run around the room screaming for release, something creaks downstairs. Her heightened senses pick up the noise, ears perked at attention. Her body snaps and seizes, lying still in anticipation.

A map created from echolocation forms in her head as the main entrance door downstairs opens. She can hear the squeaks it makes with every inch as if the hinges are right beside her ear. The proximity of the sound is irritating, but still a weak smile breaks across her face at the thought of her daddy returning to her.

Finally. In this perfectly horrible moment.

But with one whiff, she can tell it's not him.

Her muscles release, allowing her to claw her way off the mattress. She gets to the floor and plants her feet into the concrete. Her joints crack like a broken toy as she stands upright, bones falling back into place, sockets refilling. With each crack, she feels a deepening sense of control—a broken will pieced back together. Her body emits a final snap, fully realigned. She tightens the towel around her chest.

There are footsteps downstairs. She can hear each one so clearly, see them walking toward the staircase and climbing up. She senses the weight of the mass that makes them—bigger than her but not as big as her daddy. Her fingers tense and her mouth drools from the scent of whatever has just reached the top of the staircase. Shuffling feet, tentatively dragging across the concrete. Closer and closer and closer until she sees a shadow under the door.

A creature . . . but the creatures can't get in here! Not without Daddy to let them in.

The lock snaps.

But how?

The lock . . .

"Do not touch. Not unless you wish for the creatures . . ."

The door slowly creaks, introducing a shadow that grows across her wall, leading the creature into her room with two final footsteps. But the thumping continues.

No, not footsteps . . . its chest!

It stands before her: upper half covered in a thick black layer that looks tough and impenetrable, lower half sagging with black skin, feet chunks of black rubber. It has no face. No recognizable flesh that covers its bones. Only angry dark eyes and a frowning mouth with pink lips that conceal yellow teeth. The rest of its skin is featureless, black, and knitted.

It's so close, so indefinable.

At the sight of her in that towel, it grins, its eyes licking her from head to toe.

"You're not what I expected," the raspy voice says.

Male, but unfamiliar to her. Younger sounding. Not one from the group she'd met in the Outside. Not one of the four who brutalized her. Should she be thankful they didn't follow her?

Worried that a new one found her?

"Do you live here?" he continues. "Hey! I asked if you live here!"

Her hand travels to her stomach.

"Yes," she replies.

"All right." He lifts a black object. A bent piece of metal held at the bottom, the barrel with a decently sized black hole pointed at her. "Then give me the money."

"Money? There's no money here."

Beneath her palm she can feel the chaotic thrashing, the growl of her hunger.

"Don't lie. I know there's a stash in here. A fat stash. And that pretty face ain't gonna stop me."

"What is—"

"I was promised all of it if I came in here!"

Bitter saliva leaks from behind her molars.

"Listen, honey. Just get me the money that was promised me. I don't have all night and I promise I won't touch ya once we're through." His hands begin to tremble under the weight of the metal. His breathing grows harsh. "Just get me the damn money or else!"

She doesn't speak. Her hunger urges her forward one step, her curiosity a complement to her desire.

"Hey! What the fuck? Stay back! I didn't tell you to move! I didn't . . ."

His voice mutates into whomps, tuned out to make way for the sight of that barrel. The sight of that strange black shape reeling her in.

"What are you, crazy? I said don't fucking move! Don't fucking take another step or I'll shoot! Do you got a death wish or something?"

Death.

"I think I remember being dead."

"You got one last warning! One more step and I'll definitely shoot you this time! I'm not fucking playing around here! Hey! HEY! *H—*"

A loud *bang* erupts. She stumbles backward, pushed by some sharp force. A discomfort blooms in her ribs. She looks down at a smoking hole drilled right between her breasts. Right through the knot that held her towel in place. The knot bursts apart, blood sprayed across the white fabric as it falls to the floor in a red clump. Crimson liquid pours from her chest, painting her bare stomach and legs, creating a pool around her feet.

"Fuck, *fuck*! I said I'd shoot you! Such a waste!" the creature whines. "E-gracious, my ass . . . Wait, what the fuck?"

Both watch as the hole in her chest coughs out one last sputter of blood, spits out a wrinkled chunk of metal that falls to the floor with a pathetic *clink*, then cinches shut.

"What . . . ?"

Another *bang*—another hole punctured into her chest only to quickly heal.

Her knees don't buckle. Her body does not collapse.

"What the . . . ?" the creature starts before going silent.

The metal in his hands shakes. She looks up at the creature.

The barrel is still trained on her but held by an arm oscillating so violently, it threatens to jump from his grip.

"What the . . . what the hell is wrong with your face?"

She can smell something. Smoke. No. Something salty . . . yet sweet. Something that pulls the drool from the back of her molars only to sting the tip of her tongue.

She can smell his fear.

Suddenly, the hunger in her chest is untamable, unbearable. She feels it like a raging snake in her stomach, slithering through her arms and legs and neck. Her jaw clicks like the snake is in her mouth, opening its own jaws wide to release its forked tongue.

She takes another step toward him.

"Hey! Back the fuck up!"

He turns to make for the exit, but she's quicker. Like fast-moving smoke, she materializes in front of the doorway, blocking his escape. His wide eyes stare at her with disbelief, drowning in liquid fear. Petrified, his limbs lock. She can hear the *thump-thump* thumping accelerate in his chest. She wants to open him up, to crack apart his sternum and watch his insides beat for her. Watch them pucker with life!

"How the—"

His throat disappears, ripped out by her fingertips, the chunk of piping swiped away and chucked into the corner. The creature gurgles, trying to speak, but there's no passageway for the words to travel through. Instead, spurts of blood shoot out from the cavity and shower her face.

She licks the corners of her lips and tastes the sweet candy.

Red and delicious.

He teeters on his feet, stumbling back and forth in instability. She watches, her eyes shifting side to side until the temptation plunges through her.

She pounces.

His body gives in easily beneath her naked weight, crumpling to the floor without a fight. She pins the creature down and digs her face into the hole of his neck, red and ripe and open wide just for her. She drinks, filling her belly with warm liquid sugar. She burrows her face in deeper and deeper, tearing away at flesh, finally feeling heat against her skin and inside of her, glowing like a lightbulb bright in the pit of her stomach.

Something hard hits her nose, the bite of it like concrete. She lifts her head away and looks down at her nearly decapitated paramour, his eyes staring through her—those delicious brown eyes she could pluck right out of their sockets and swallow whole, elation washing through her at the thought. Her fingers brush across his face, trace his mouth with loving affection, feeling the ecstasy of his contents fry her brain, thankful in every way for the salvation. Thankful for his sacrifice to her pleasure.

The warmth . . . oh, the warmth!

With his lips parted, she could just reach down and kiss him. Those plump lips, surrounded by that dark layer . . . tracing that thick, black . . . *fabric?*

She tucks her finger under the layer, her pinky slipping beneath, and pulls. Like a sheet, it folds away, revealing a face. A face just like hers; no older than her, maybe two years at most, still free of wrinkles with a thin nose that looks frail and easy to break, a slight dent in the bridge. His hair is auburn, straight and messy, falling over his forehead in spikes. There's a caramel tinge to his skin that she can recognize despite the wash of lifelessness in his cells.

And he looks delicious.

Her stomach growls.

That warmth . . . I'm so hungry . . .

She places her hand on his stomach and tears through layers—*all of that fabric, all of that fabric and clothes and fabric, layers and layers of fabric*—until she has a pallet of bare skin under her fingertips. She brushes her hands along his chest, savoring how smooth it is to the touch. *How strong and sturdy it must have been! How nice it might have been to press my head against and feel the pulse of life!* With one finger, she stabs through, puncturing him like he did her. Blood pools into the center of his stomach. A low-pressure spout. A puddle of heat. She leans down and drinks from it like a food bowl, rubbing her arms across his exposed body. *The heat!* She drinks and drinks until she is full and even then she drinks some more, relishing in the warmth.

Through her fit of dehydrated frenzy, she has a hazy, red thought. A thought the sane part of her still holds on to with desperate curiosity. Morbid intrigue. A thought that consumes her just as she consumes he.

"Am I . . . ?"

"I think I remember . . ."

"I think I remember being . . ."

Is this death?

The silver-haired man stands in front of the building, just outside the reach of the streetlight's yellow glow. His eyes are closed, but he listens. He listens and he waits. When he no longer hears the thumping, when the space within those concrete walls no longer beats with life, he grins, opens his eyes, and turns down the street to let her finish feeding.

CHAPTER XVIII

She loses all sense of self. Her mind, starved to the edge of a precipice, suppresses all function but that of feeding. And feed she does. She feeds until she gorges herself like a glutton and grows drowsy. She abandons her feast; her arms and legs lazily inch over to her mattress, dragging her bloated belly across the floor. There she collapses onto the bedding, passing out into a deep sleep that only the dead can experience. A sleep void of dreams, for the dead cannot enjoy such a luxury.

During that time, her body expands and decompresses, working through cells and distributing nutrients to the parts of her that have been long neglected: her stomach, her skin, her nails, her teeth. No longer needed, the rage settles, ridding for her the discomfort of want, soothing that bubbling pit called hunger, fortifying her as it does so. Like a syringe filling with liquid, it expands throughout her limbs until its properties reach her every molecule. Until the container swells.

When she is well and rested, she stirs awake, revitalized and smiling. Her spine curls into a stretch and the thought of her daddy puckers in her brain—him and a lollipop and . . .

She looks to the center of her room, expecting to see her toys, a momentary flash of amnesia muddling her brain. Instead, her gaze is met with a body. Her muscles tense, anticipating movement, waiting for the creature to jump and attack her; but the body remains limp, surrounded by a thick, jellied outline of red.

The saturated memory floods in. His face. His skin. His lifeless eyes.

The way he tasted.

So sweet . . .

She retches, holding on to her stomach, hearing a squelch from the contact. Her naked body is stained with blood, clots of it stuck to her skin that squish beneath her touch. She grabs for the towel slipped halfway off her mattress—black dust and flakes of red fall from the fibers—and wipes herself down, whimpering from the rub of slime.

She pulls her dress on over her head. Encased in fabric, she feels protected. Held together by a shield of cloth. Almost invincible.

Quietly, she picks up a lollipop stem—one of dozens still scattered across the mattress. She takes aim and pelts it at the body, hitting its leg.

It doesn't respond.

VANILLA

She waits. It doesn't move.

She crawls toward it. It doesn't react to her approach.

She reaches its side and curls her legs into her chest, watching it from behind the barrier of her knees. She presses her finger into its arm and pushes. The body only wobbles momentarily on its spine.

"Hello?" she whispers.

Nothing.

She leans over to examine the gash in its throat. Pieces of flesh fan out, tubes trailing from inside split apart. She can almost see down one of them. Its stomach is spotless except for a single red-rimmed hole drilled into the center. Her fingertips graze its skin but pick up no heat, its touch dull.

But he was so warm . . .

She crawls around the body, wanting to see it from different angles, wanting to see from every possible direction that pale face—nearly yet not quite as pale as hers—with plump blue lips and impossibly dark eyes. All the while thinking:

This creature . . . it looks so much like me . . .

As she moves about, her feet kick something that sets off the sound of rolling glass. Her eyes find the syringe in its last motions before stopping against the drum of her stethoscope. The two huddle together, wanting to be used. She searches the room for the missing third—the dutiful, blue-dog patient—but to no avail. A bloody towel, stripped stems, but otherwise empty concrete. No trace of blue fabric.

She turns back to the body and frowns. Carefully, she places her hands on its arm and pushes the creature with little effort to the side, lifting its shoulder blade off the ground. The stuffed blue dog squeezes out from under the body, only now it is stained red and heavy with soaked-up weight, nothing but a bloody sponge. She picks it up, stuffing threatening to fall out of its gash, and crushes it in her hands. A few drops drip from its fabric and join the mess of blood below.

She turns and picks up the stethoscope, plugging it into her ears. She takes the drum and presses it against the dog.

Nothing.

She kneels and places it on the creature's ribcage.

Nothing.

But couldn't I hear it thump before?

She hesitates and holds the drum against her own chest.

Nothing.

. . . nothing . . .

She looks to the body, then to the dog, her face glazed over with sizzling confusion.

And then her thoughts explode.

But I'm not nothing!

She growls in frustration, squeezing the dog to a pulp before chucking it at the wall. It bounces against the concrete with a pathetic squish and falls to the floor, regaining its helpless form. She rips the stethoscope from her ears and screams, lifting her arms to pound down on the silent chest before her with agonized grunts.

I'm not nothing! I'm not nothing! I'm not! I'm not! I'm not!

I'm NOT!

There's a crunch like shattering teeth. Her fists sink and catch on something sharp. She looks down. Her hands are gone, buried beneath chest, wrists trapped between protruding branches of jagged bone. She shrieks and yanks, ripping open the body's ribcage so that it unfurls like a flower of beige spikes. Shriveled pieces of meat jump and suspend in midair before falling in clumps across the body and her thighs.

Upset at the sight—upset at how the pit of mulched flesh makes her drool—she stands and runs from the room.

She stumbles down the hallway, holding her hand to her stomach as though she could trap its contents, keep them from bursting out of her throat. But that's not the problem. That's not truly what horrifies her. It's the hunger. It's the slobbering over creatures. It's the want for more.

Always more.

She travels down the stairs and bolts toward the big wooden door, placing her hand on that golden knob.

She stops herself, or rather, a sudden wave of insight holds her back from entering the Outside.

Out there they'll do so much worse.

Slowly, she turns away on her heels, a zombie caught between emotion and instinct.

She faces now a collection of open doors on the ground floor of this concrete building, a row of mouths waiting to be entered, all except for one that remains shut, still concealing its secrets. But even the open doors—the ones that reveal their empty, seemingly innocent insides—hold secrets. Who are they for? Why are they here? What is their purpose? She frowns, suddenly indignant, suddenly enraged by the restricted knowledge, the lack of understanding that is no fault of her own but of a world wanting to keep her blind. A world that won't stop mercilessly expanding beyond her.

No . . . not Daddy.

She steps up to the locked door, places her hand on the knob, and twists. It refuses to budge. She twists harder and harder, directing all her strength into it, determined to get behind the door and see what it hides. She grits her teeth and gives it a final tug.

The knob snaps into pieces. Hunks of metal fall from the socket, leaving a gaping hole.

She hesitates, realizing that what she finds when she crosses this threshold might not be a comfort. In her room, when the world only reached so far as her concrete walls, she felt safe. She felt safe with what her daddy chose to tell her, even if her bliss was fleeting. Because he understood that knowing any more might break her.

I'm here to keep you safe. To protect you.

Knowledge is only so freeing.

"What is death?"

Nothing.

But ignorance feels worse.

She pushes against the door with the tip of her finger. It easily swings open.

She steps inside.

VANILLA

She is greeted by a crowd of metal tables lined across the expansive walls, dividing the room down the center. These high walls are made of concrete, uniform with the rest of the building, but blackboards rest on each table, covering the lower half of the walls with their white, chalky scribbles and tacked-on documents. The room looks neat and tidy at first glance, but as she circles around, she spots scattered glass bottles and tubes filled with moisture resting atop piles of loose papers stained with splotches of sweat. They tell a different story. One of mania. One of someone attempting to cover up panic with a hasty brush. The center table holds machines decorated with buttons and dials she dares not turn. Shelves are crammed into the corners, filled with old-looking books and dusty files. But regardless of the clutter and debris, it still all looks so *sterile*.

She makes her round to the other side of the room and stops in front of a perfectly lined row of silver syringes, each one empty, the needles pointed toward her. At the end of the table against the wall is a glossy white box. She opens its lid. It hisses, and when the smoke dissipates, she sees that inside are even more syringes displayed across the box's inner shelving. But these are not empty. They are pregnant with red.

She closes the box and turns back around. On the table she notices a sizeable block of gray. She steps over to it and sees the form of a lollipop engraved into the metal; the form is mirrored on a conjoined slab, as if the lollipop were split down the middle and separated into exposed halves. Next to the block are lollipop stems—but these are not stained at the ends with candy to chew and savor every last bit of flavor. She plucks one between her fingers, staring curiously at the pure whiteness of it, then sticks it in her mouth.

The blandness makes her grimace and she places the stem back down on the table.

Farther down she finds a row of three flat rectangular glasses stacked in doubles like something should be slipped between them. Each one is labeled by a piece of laminated paper taped above. Letters are scrawled on each label—*V*, *C*, and *E* respectively—and upon further inspection, she sees that the label's edges are stained pink and the glasses are not fully clear, but rather cloudy with lines of red. She leans down to take a whiff; an acrid toxicity burns her nostrils.

She walks over to the bookshelf and stares at the leather spines. Each spine has faded lines of silver forming unfamiliar symbols, and one is cracked, exposing the brown paper layers beneath. She chooses and removes this one, a black leather book with a spine of tangled cracks and deep grooves. Its weight catches her by surprise and dust floats from the cover, making her sneeze. She carries it to an empty space on a table, shoving aside some papers to make room, and lays it open. Across the pages that creak as she flips through them are hundreds of tiny words she does not understand. Words she recognizes from photographs that contained signs in their backgrounds but that she never learned how to read.

"Because there is so much more to learn, Vanilla."

Shuffling through the pages, she sees sketches of bodies—*his sketches in graphite*—and sepia photographs of these bodies surgically cut open, flaps of skin nailed down to their sides like wings of gore revealing a cage of bone. Beneath that cage: insides that beat to make the body work. She sees photographs of different knives, clamps like jagged mouths, curved spikes and syringes like her own. In one photograph, a body is covered with hundreds of needles so that surely every fiber of flesh is pierced through. Even the skull.

The pages slip from her fingertips and open on their own to a monstrous image. A body composed of unproportionate parts, parts of different skin tones, puzzled back together with thick black stitches. The arms and the legs could be that of an adult except for the face. That face . . . it's the face of a young girl. A young and innocent girl who looks nothing like a creature. Who looks peaceful, at rest, but will surely wake up screaming at the deformity of her body. A body that is not her own.

It's a photograph . . .

"I point the camera at the real thing and snap."

She slams the book shut, the force making the items across the table jump, and runs. She hurries back up the stairs, back down the hallway and into her room, and leaps over the lifeless creature, paying as little attention to its body as she can. She lands on her mattress and curls her legs into her chest, burying her face in her knees so that she can hide in the darkness.

She takes deep breaths, in and out, trying to pretend, even if just for a second, that everything is back to normal. That she'll lift her head and the creature's body will be gone, replaced by her daddy standing in the doorway with a lollipop in his hand. He'll come and sit next to her on the mattress and hold her and tell her that everything will be okay. That he will keep her safe. And she will forget everything she has seen. The world will shrink back to the size of her room.

When she lifts her head from her knees, she is still alone and there is still a body before her.

She sucks in a rancid breath and shudders. Something doesn't smell right. Something smells awful. *Filthy.* She looks at the body in horror and reluctantly crawls back to it. Hovering, she takes a whiff. Decay fills her nostrils and she jerks away, one hand over her mouth, trying not to gag. The flesh looks sick, putrefying to gray at the edges of the neck and chest cavity, the skin a gray-blue hue, nearly translucent now. The smell is unbearable and she is worried it will stain her room, slip into the cracks between the concrete, and remain there forever.

She gets up and drags the body by what she now recognizes as its thick rubber shoes, out the door and down the hallway. The fabric on the body's back shushes against the concrete. But even as she returns to her room, the smell follows her. It slithers up and taps her on the shoulder with one wicked claw.

The hairs on the back of her neck rise and she shudders again.

She tries to sit back down on her mattress and ignore it. She gets up and paces her room, hoping the breeze she creates will whisk away the rot. She covers her nose with the skirt of her dress but knows she cannot hold it there forever, all the while watching this body decompose into gray mulch just a few paces away.

Moments later, she drags the body back to the center of her

room. She gawks at it, thinking of all the stringy veins and bones that create it. How the insides on display right now look so intricate and fragile. How it looks so similar to that sketch in graphite.

"How do you know this is what we look like on the inside, Daddy?"

She takes another whiff and cringes.

She needs to get it out of here.

She wiggles her arms beneath the body and struggles to cradle it. The act is possible, but not subtle. What kind of attention would she draw out there in the Outside with a body in her arms?

Her mind shifts to the photographs of surgical knives from the black book downstairs. Quickly, she gets up and runs down to the sterile room. She finds drawers under the tables, pulls them open. Most are filled with stacks of paper, but eventually she finds one filled with metal tools. She searches through them until she finds a small knife and runs back upstairs.

She stands over the body, tapping the knife rhythmically against her chin, deciding what to separate. She remembers the lines of stitching across limbs in the photographs—a morbid guide to where to cut. But will it be the same for a creature?

Do we look the same underneath?

She pulls off its shoes, strips its pants, and cuts away at what remains of its jacket and shirt. She slides the knife beneath the white fabric covering its pelvis, hesitates, then slices it off. Her eyes scan across the body—so surprisingly similar to hers—and maps out the invisible lines, taking note of every dent and curve the muscles make, visualizing the dissections.

And then she begins.

She gets on top of the body, straddling its waist. She leans into its chest and takes the knife, pressing it into the soft underside of its shoulder. The blade slides easily into the skin. A few drops of blood spill from the wound, but otherwise there is not much blood left. She cuts away, dragging the blade back and forth. She digs deeper and deeper through fibers of muscle, feeling the slime of exposed flesh on her wrists until she hits bone. She tries to slice through but the knife is too small and although sharp, not nearly sharp enough. The harder she tries, the more the knife slips in her hand and nearly cuts her.

She growls and sets the knife down, the blade gummed up with red, shreds of skin caught between its teeth. She sticks her fingers into the gash of the shoulder and touches the bone. It has a shallow groove she drags her fingertips across. When she pulls her fingers out, they are covered in bits of muscle; she flicks them off, only to splat onto the body's chest.

She holds the body's left elbow with one hand and leverages her other hand against its ribs. With one quick and powerful tug, she amputates its arm, the joint popping out of the socket like a broken toy. The arm slumps in her hand, wrists and fingers pointing toward the ground so that the limb looks to be expressing its grief.

"Daddy, I get sad when you're away."

She wiggles the arm and the fingers dance happily, like they're presenting a live puppet show.

"Just smile through it, my sweet. I will always return."

She sets the arm down and repeats the procedure on the other side.

She hacks away at its limbs, ripping them off then cutting them into halves, surprised by how easy the task is. She skips over the chore of its chest and sits atop it, repositioning her legs on either side of the now limbless torso. Its head looks back at her with indifference, watching as she reaches toward it and places her hands on both sides of its temples. She tugs and the cavity in its neck opens up like a hungry mouth, unhinging its jaw wider and wider until, finally, it snaps apart and the stretched flesh recoils. Her fingers grip through its hair. She lifts the head to face her, a head that looks very much like her own. So much like her own that she imagines it could begin talking to her at any moment in the tongue she understands.

"How do you know?"

The sketch in graphite. That's what I look like on the inside. And so do you.

The creature's eyes, still so dark and unchanged. Glossy, once filled with such confidence and fear. Emotions she very much feels herself. Her eyes meet them.

Would I be this easy to pull apart?

"How do you know this is what we look like on the inside, Daddy?"

"Don't ask silly questions."

It turns out it wasn't such a silly question after all.

You didn't want me to know the truth. But I can handle it,

Daddy.

Because they are just like us, aren't they?

They were supposed to be deformed. Grotesque and dark and horrifying enough to chill her down to her very core until her bones turned brittle and fractured. Monsters in the shadows she'd cowered from in her thoughts and dreams. The ones that would steal her away from her daddy and take her to a bad place. A place where she would never see him again while they beat down on her with their giant fists and sticks. But that's so obvious, isn't it? Seeing monsters with their claws and horrible faces, those aren't the ones to fear. In fact, they are the best kind because they are recognizable. But the other ones ... the ones that can hide are cause for true fear ... because under those layers of black, under that ugly shell of hate, they can shed their skin and become something else. It's easy to avoid what you can see so clearly. It's easy to avoid what looks like it wants to bring harm. It's the ones you can't see. The ones with the kind faces and familiar smiles. With trusting eyes just like your own.

The worst monsters are the ones invisible to you.

The ones who can hide amongst you.

"How do you know, Daddy?"

Because they look just like you.

CHAPTER XIX

A tap on her window. She squirms within her warm sheets and furrows her brow at her book, trying to dive into another world. A world created by words lit through her fluorescent lighting. Trying so, so hard to ignore—

Another tap. Her bottom lip quivers, torn between the want to shrink into herself, to become so small he could never find her because she'd hide in the cracks, and the knowledge that she'd die if she did.

Another tap—

"What?!" she snaps, turning toward the window.

He could be a standing corpse, there on the other side of the glass with no movement or expression, his mouth a flat line. And those damn, sick blue eyes.

He lifts a boney white finger, tips his nail against the window, and slices down the glass. She drops her book and slaps her palms over her ears, teeth gritting against the horrible noise. When the screeching stops, he is as still as before, only now there is a smile across the bottom half of his face, fangs as large as knives.

She groans and stands from her bed. "I know you can get in here if you want, so *why* do you insist on making me come to the window?"

His smile grows larger as she approaches, places her fingers beneath the sash, and lifts.

The glass barrier between them is removed and he answers:

"Because, Tiffany, I like it when you let me in."

His frozen breath breaks across her face and she shivers. He reaches out to touch her cheek, his contact cold and unforgiving. She whimpers but does not dare move away from him. His fingers run down her skin, trace through her curls, and grip around her neck. She yelps as he pulls her over the windowsill so that her body balances on the hinge of her hip bone, hanging half inside and half outside. His face is so close; she can feel the heat of that blue fire in his eyes.

"Don't make me wait again."

She grunts for air and tries her best to nod in compliance.

"Good. Now, for business. She'll be outside the building soon. I expect you to be there when she is. In fact, I expect you to leave immediately and wait however long you must."

"But my shi—"

Tiffany chokes on her words as his grip tightens. His hand slithers up her shirt and bites down on her side.

"Finish that sentence and I will cut off your tongue to toss in formaldehyde."

She silences, attempting to subdue her gasps. But his hand bites down harder into her skin and she can't help but cry out.

"It's her life or yours."

He releases her and she collapses on the sill like she's stretched across a guillotine and the window could come down on her at any moment to split her in half. She wants to scream for help but knows she'd be dead before she could make a sound. His fingers hold her chin and lift her head.

"Tiffany, you defiant child. If you so much as come close to failing me, I will drag you back into your concrete cell, tear you to pieces, and stitch you back until you are unrecognizable. Do you understand?"

"Okay," she hisses, tears swamping her eyes. "Okay, okay. I won't fail." *You sick fuck.*

Pleased, he holds out his other hand. His nails are coated in her blood. He looks at the massacre, his face scrunched with repulsion, and wipes the mess away on her neck. She shivers from the feeling of a cold hand wiping warm blood.

"I can still smell the rot in your blood," he growls. "It's too bad."

She is falling backward, her arms pinwheeling to gain balance until her spine thuds against the carpeted floor. She gasps for air, sucking in breath not only to fill her lungs but to stop herself from screaming.

The glass is back in place, window closed, only empty

darkness finding its way through. On the sill is a pile of lollipops.

Her muscles collapse, sinking into the floor as her chest stutters with laughter. She can smell the iron from her blood, knows it's soaking through the side of her shirt. That it will probably get into the carpet and she'll have to spend hours laboring to clean it up.

But she doesn't care. Why should she care? She might as well revel in it. She might as well laugh at it. Because no matter what she does, this is it. This is her life.

Oh, Tiffany. You already know. You were made so aware of it, it's been carved into the flesh of your brain. You already know and it should be no surprise because you're living in it now. You already know.

That dying is pain.

CHAPTER XX

Tugging and pulling and gripping and smushing and it's all so complex. It's all so greatly complex and I'm discovering it all. Discovering it like Daddy did with his sketches in graphite. This is it. This is what I look like on the inside. This is what Daddy *looks like on the inside and it's all so fascinating. It's like peering into him—me, myself! It's like understanding something so much deeper than how we work.* Her hands are sunk, shoveling through meat and fat, yanking out organs and studying them, noting their placement, their shape and length, before tossing them onto her flattened blanket. She breaks down the creature's spine, shucking off each vertebrae from the stem, each time producing the stench of rot that she no longer notices.

Everything inside is so complex and dense. So full and endless.

There's really only one piece she's particularly interested in. She'd already found it and left it off to the side while she finished the job, as if saving the best for last, but now that there is only a chunky ball of stomach and lungs that sighs out of shape before her, she turns to it.

The creature's heart rests against her thigh, waiting for her.

She knows it is the heart. She is very much aware of its ability to thump—how it thumped before, how it is exactly what should thump within her. She remembers the sketch in graphite all too well—made a point to ask as many questions as her daddy would allow before he lost patience, and made sure to note the piece she loves to listen to.

The piece she has been trying to revive.

"What's that? In the center?"

"That is called the heart. It's a part of the cardiovascular system, which—"

"Does it thump?"

"What?"

"Does it thump?"

He had paused, as if tasting for the correct answer on the tip of his tongue.

"Not always."

She can tell this one no longer thumps. She holds it naked in her hand and can feel its cold stillness. The lack of a pulse, a throb; no *thump-thump* thumping.

Nothing.

She places her hand against her chest and pauses. Is it possible to lose a heart without having to open yourself up? Or can a heart just quiet down to nothing on its own? Grow tired and take a rest from thumping for eternity?

Is that what happened to hers?

She looks over to the blanket, at the creature who is now just a collection of parts. Once it was moving and thumping, but now it isn't.

Is that what death is?

The two thoughts have never come together before—the interlacing of a silent heart and the concept of death. But she supposes it's possible. She supposes it could be that one leads to the other.

There is nothing. And then there is death.

But there's a deviation making the problem too complex to solve. And it's her.

Because I'm not nothing. And I don't remember losing my heart.

She removes her hand from her chest and holds the disembodied heart in her palms, cradling it with great care. Slowly, she stands, walks over to the blanket where all the pieces—the body, the lollipop stems, that heavy black metal with the violent barrel—are waiting, and places the heart in the center. She brings all four corners together and ties them up tight. She lifts the makeshift sack and bounces it up and down a few times. It maintains its integrity, though some spots bleed from gray to red and then blotch her exposed upper thigh with color.

She hopes it won't be noticeable.

She slings the sack over her shoulder and rushes down the stairs, wanting to get this over with as soon as possible so she can return to her room to wait and think. The weight of the sack slams into her back as she hurries. She reaches the bottom of the stairs and runs to the wooden door. Her fingertips grip the knob.

Out there they'll do so much worse . . . just don't get caught.

Taking in a deep breath, she pushes the door open.

The air is lighter than before—instead of an infinite black ceiling, the sky is lined with yellows and reds, a color like blue but much more somber. She wants to hold her gaze, stare at the shifting sky with feathers of color that swim in swirls, but the street is bare and she doesn't want to waste time in case the creatures decide to come out from hiding. She hurries from the doorstep, remembering the alley cluttered with trash she found herself in before.

She is sure the creatures have not returned. She remembers the fear in their voices.

She walks faster and faster, each footstep landing harder and harder, until suddenly she is sprinting, trying to get rid of something on her back. Something tickling her spine and prickling her skin. Something following her.

She sprints until the alleyway comes into view and then sprints faster, not stopping until she is well inside of it. Once she feels untouched, once the static on her spine settles, she stops and turns around, gawking at the entrance of the alleyway. At that stone mouth gradually filling with light.

But nothing appears.

She lets out a sigh of relief.

Along the wall of the alley are stacks of bags and metallic bins overflowing with unwanted waste. Judging by the smell, everything rots here as well. A fitting home. She scans the different containers, looking for the perfect one. One that would house her creature with proper care and discretion. One she can trust to absorb the evidence so it never comes back to haunt her.

A single bin stands out—a dirty green plastic filled to the brim with crumpled papers that sprout out in jutting spikes. As she steps up to it, she realizes they're sticks. Sticks that have been shoved around the rim, spearing garbage on their way down. She tosses the sack on top of the trash and stares at the sticks in fascination, grazing her fingertips across the rough edges, feeling the ridges bite.

"They'll beat down on you . . ."

She pulls away, averting her gaze, and shovels through the trash, trying to bury the sack as deep inside the bin as she can. She digs, struggling to keep her eyes off the sticks. The sticks that poke out like bars to a cage.

"They'll beat down on you . . ."

She unknots the sack and sprinkles the body parts down the tunnel of waste she's just carved out. They roll off the blanket and plop into the bin, each with a wet squish. The black metal with the violent barrel rolls off and sinks with an ominous *thud*, and the lollipop stems follow in a staccato clatter. Wrapping her hand in the blanket, she punches into the garbage, compressing the damage, covering it up with more papers, and compressing again until it is a compact secret.

Until it is buried and gone. Goodbye, you fascinating pile of rot! Thank you for playing with me, but now I can return to my room and pray that the rot did not settle. That the trace of you is gone and I can wait and wait and wait and hope . . .

She pauses, staring into the trash, thinking about what it would take to wait. How long she'd be willing to sit in her room on her mattress with her toys, starved of lollipops, for everything to return to normal. If normal is even possible now. How long would she be willing to wait?

. . . until death?

Something steps up behind her. She can hear the crunch of gravel and that *thump-thump* thumping. She freezes with full certainty that she is shrouded in enough shadow to be camouflaged. That as long as she does not move, it will not sense her.

And then that something speaks: "What are you doing?"

She drops the blanket and unsheathes a stick from the garbage bin. It comes up much shorter than she'd have liked, ribbed with skewered papers, but still, she uses it to confront the voice. A dark figure about her size stands in front of her. It's backlit by a now blinding skyline that enters the alley and casts the figure in a voluptuous silhouette.

"Stay back!" she yells, but her voice cracks, so she whips the stick in an *X*.

"Hey, whoa! Calm down, will you?" The voice is pitched higher than a male's, like hers. The figure jolts back and raises its hands. "Put the damn stick down! I'm just trying to help! You look hurt. You're barely wearing any clothes and it's *freezing* out. Where are your shoes? You're covered in fucking blood for Christ's sake!"

The figure hesitates, that *thump-thump* thumping accelerating in its chest. The sound of its thumping pounds in her ears and she squints at the discomfort but holds her ground. The figure takes a step forward, halting when she whips the stick at it again. It inhales and she can see its shoulders sink with its exhale.

"Come on. Stop that. Let me help you."

"What do you want from me?" she demands. "Please, I don't wish to fight, just let me be." She squints, trying to make out the figure's features, but the light is flooding in and blinding her.

"Fight? Who said anything about fighting?"

The figure takes another wagered step forward. She whips the stick again and it makes a noise of frustration.

"Goddamn—okay, come on. This is a little ridiculous, don't you think?"

"No."

The figure stops, processing the matter-of-fact answer, then throws its head back and laughs. She can see its chest throbbing, filling the air with misplaced emotion. Each laugh accents the now rhythmic *thump-thump* in its chest, and she thinks it sounds so lovely. So *warm* in this damp place.

So void of nothing.

Hypnotized, she takes her own step toward the figure—toward that gushing thump. It notices and suddenly its hand is on her wrist, but she doesn't flinch away because even though she can't feel the warmth, she can sense it. She can sense the pulse of carefree laughter emanating through its skin and into hers. Somehow filling her with a different kind of heat that replaces the tug that has yanked so mercilessly in her pit for far too long. Replacing it with a soft glow.

The figure hums, a drone encompassing her mind and filling it with a brilliance like the most high-powered lightbulb is tucked away within her brain.

And it's so warm.

"I'm not going to hurt you," the figure says. "Let's just put the stick down and start over, shall we?"

She can feel her grip on the stick loosen in obedience. She can feel the stick being pulled from her grasp. She almost reaches for it again but hears it clatter to the ground before she can make a defensive decision. But better on the ground than in either of their hands.

"Good," the figure says.

Yes, good, she thinks, entranced by the soothing wave of words. *Good is good.*

The hand tugs at her wrist and she lets it guide her out of the alley, perhaps because she trusts that warmth and perhaps because she is simply tired of fighting.

But that warmth is everything.

The light swells as they step out together and then it engulfs them both. It's the sun. She's been told about the sun. Like a rising lightbulb in the sky. She flinches at the searing power of it; her arm tenses with the thought of retreating back into the shadow, but the figure only holds on tighter.

"Hey, hey, that's okay," the figure soothes her with a hush, grabbing onto her other wrist in an act of connectivity, a circle created by their limbs. Only it's not a figure. It's a creature, basking in the golden glow of the breaking dawn. A female with brown hair that curls in delicious rings down the length of her back, tossed to one side of her head as if the weight would be too much to carry on both shoulders. With skin as silky and dark as that infinitely black ceiling, missing only the twinkle of dots but compensated by the lick of the sunrise. She wears a red skirt and a yellow shirt with a collar that hides beneath a puffy beige jacket. Her lips are thick and pink and her eyes are dark and endless pools of *warmth*.

It's everything and it's so beautiful.

The creature smiles at her as if she too can feel the power channeling between them. The intensity of being totally consumed by first sight.

The creature speaks: "My name is Tiffany."

CHAPTER XXI

Let's just start over, shall we? Please, let's just start over. Because otherwise, if we don't and if you run away, I'm going to be in big trouble.

"My name is Tiffany," she says to the girl with the blond pigtails she just watched slink out of the alley behind her. The girl with the easily tamable behavior. That makes sense. Going through hell would make anyone submissive. *I'll bet he made sure of that.* "What's your name?"

The girl doesn't respond, only flinches against the sun, her skin so pale like a newly formed membrane.

"That's okay, that's okay," Tiffany assures her again. She leans back and gives the girl a good look from head to toe. "But, *fuck*, what happened to you?" she asks, maintaining her grip around the girl, afraid of letting her go. Afraid she'll bolt and afraid of her own blue-eyed reaper coming for punishment. She pulls the girl in close for inspection. "You look like you've been through a garbage compactor." She takes a whiff. "Sheesh! You smell like it, too. Have you been in that alley all night? Were you alone this whole time? Did someone touch you or hurt you? Is that why you're bleeding? Why were you digging through garbage? Are you hungry? When was the last time you had something to eat? Or a clean shower? Do you have a place to stay? And once again, *where* are your *shoes*?"

The girl stares at her, her expression paved over with thought, digesting the questions one at a time. Tiffany waits patiently as the girl tenses then settles. She can feel the tendons in her wrist pulsate in rhythm to some unheard tune. Tiffany loosens her grip, but immediately the girl grabs her hands before they collapse to her side.

"Tiffany," the girl says, slowly, as if saying the name for the first time. Her fingers curl around Tiffany's, feeling smooth against her tough skin.

Tiffany's eyes search the girl's, finding nothing but genuine curiosity. She smiles, her exhale shooting out steam from her nostrils like a dragon. "Yes . . . yes, that's my name. Tiffany. Can you tell me yours?"

"Vanilla."

"Oh! Vanilla? Okay, well. Interesting name. But I guess I can't really judge."

Tiffany is rambling; the girl watches her with indifference.

It feels like I'm fucking trying to pick her up. And failing miserably.

"Aren't you cold? It's freezing out and at least I'm in a jacket."

"No."

"You're not even shivering." *She feels cold.* "Well, do you have anywhere to go?" *But I already know she doesn't.*

Vanilla's brow creases as though the answer brings her painful confusion. She breaks eye contact to look down the road. Her body starts swaying in slow-motion toward that direction, like some gigantic magnet in the distance is reeling her in. Her fingers loosen their hold. As she is about to step away, Tiffany pulls her back in.

"Hey!" *You're not going back there, that's for sure. Concrete jail, my ass.*

Vanilla returns her attention to her, her face filled with shock from the yank. But it quickly settles into a smile. "Tiffany," she repeats. She reaches out and grazes her fingers across Tiffany's cheek.

The touch is like having ice dragged down her skin. Tiffany shivers beneath it and places her hands around Vanilla's, removing them from her face. She cups the delicate white fingers between hers and breathes hot air onto them.

Her skin is still so cold.

"I don't know how you're not shivering, but you are freezing to the touch. The sun's coming up but it won't help much, and when it does, you don't want people seeing you looking like the aftermath of a three-car pileup. They'll crowd you. So come on, now. Let's get out of the cold."

VANILLA

She pulls on Vanilla, hoping she will just follow. Hoping she will make this easy. *But of course it's not. How could it be? Nothing about this is fucking easy.*

Vanilla resists with a frown.

"Look, I would feel terrible just leaving you out here like this all by yourself," Tiffany reasons, glancing around nervously. Seeking the lurker. "A pretty girl like you." *A gorgeous girl, in fact. And I'll bet he loved that about you. I'll bet he loved having a perfect doll like you around.* "You're bound to get harassed. I don't want that on my conscience if I walk away." Tiffany flashes her a smile then tugs on her wrist. "Come on. You'll be my good deed for life."

When Vanilla still resists, Tiffany holds her breath, feeling the ice sting her throat, and sighs it out in a turbulence of regret and reluctance. A cloud of self-hatred from having to pull a card she wishes she could keep tucked so deep within her sleeve it might never see the light of day. But the power it holds is too great. Its usage is inevitable.

"Tiffany. Listen carefully. If she doesn't follow you, tell her this."

Tiffany bites down on her tongue, the dots across her arm lighting up beneath her sleeve, the want to itch paired with the refusal to acknowledge. But still she persists.

Above all, she persists.

"Vanilla . . . Vanilla, if you come with me, I'll give you a lollipop."

CHAPTER XXII

Vanilla listens to the girl's reasoning, but she's thinking about her room. Thinking about her gray walls. Thinking about stepping into that building, walking those stairs, and locking the door behind her—that delicious *snap*. Thinking about sitting on her mattress, gathering her toys around her, and waiting.

Just waiting.

For what?

For Daddy, of course.

For that press, *nothing,* inject, press, *nothing.*

For that *thump-thump* thumping that will never come.

"I'll give you a lollipop," Tiffany says, her voice breaking through.

Lollipops?

That sweet bite!

Vanilla lights up with recognition. She looks at Tiffany as though seeing her for the first time. Not seeing her as a creature but as a provider. Someone to mend the hunger. To retrieve normalcy. Someone whose presence is so sugary to the senses.

"Would you want a lollipop, Vanilla?" Tiffany asks again.

Vanilla can almost smell them. The sweet candy. She takes a step closer and inhales, her mouth drooling. She can hear the thumping in Tiffany's chest, the rhythm so wonderfully intense.

"Where?" Vanilla asks.

"Where? Oh! The lollipops. They're in my room."

"Your room?"

"Yeah. Like, where I live and sleep. You know, a room. With a bed and a window and a mirror to get dressed in front of." Tiffany bites her tongue when she sees Vanilla's face scrunch.

"And toys?"

"Toys? Sure! And toys! All the toys and lollipops you could want!"

"I had a room like that," Vanilla responds, her expression deadpan.

Tiffany hesitates, then forces a grin and whispers, "I'll bet you my room is better."

Vanilla leans in and looks around the slowly brightening but empty street. She whispers back, "Is it safe?"

Tiffany's jaw nearly drops. "Of course it's safe . . . safer than out here. Let me show you, and if you don't like it you can leave. But I promise I'll keep you safe. I'll protect you. How about that?"

The corners of Vanilla's mouth crack upward.

"I'm here to protect you, my sweet."
But he lied about ever returning.

So Vanilla follows, her feet stepping in line behind Tiffany, who she is tethered to by nothing but a weak grip that is somehow so strong, all the while thinking about the lie. Thinking about the lie and the empty promises and how the creature got into her room and her daddy wasn't there to keep her safe. How she lost control of her body and how her daddy wasn't there to take care of her. How she now follows a creature that claims to be pulling her toward safety and lollipops and how she is so willing to follow because this creature is the closest thing right now to her daddy. To the comfort he brings—despite the lie. And she doesn't think she can wait for him in that room all by herself until he returns. *Until death.*

Tiffany walks ahead, dragging this complete stranger behind her who is only so obedient to follow because she is filled with lies. Because of the lie she is forced to participate in for the sake of her own life. A life that is only so valuable. *After all, beneath our sleeves, we both have those dotted scars to show. That damn itch. But one step at a time.* One step at a time because she has to entertain the man. To show that silver snake she'll listen to his orders now, but in the end, in the end she has free will. Even if the consequence of using that will is a life.

And as she walks, Tiffany sees those piercing eyes and that dead smile greet her from the corner of her eye. Her heart leaps and she can feel Vanilla squeeze her hand as if in knowing. Tiffany's walk stutters, but not long enough to alert Vanilla to what she's looking at. Just long enough to pull the posted flyer off its staple on a telephone pole they pass by before Vanilla can notice. She crumples the flyer up into a ball with her free hand and lets it fall to the street. She turns back to check on Vanilla, who smiles at her through oblivion and whose pale skin looks so fragile against the rising sun.

I have fucking free will, Tiffany thinks. She turns back ahead and continues their journey into Hell.

As the two girls travel away, the flyer slowly uncurls from the damp morning mist. A man's face, a man with sharp features and a jaw like a diamond, is hand-painted in black and white, confined to the size of a square portrait. Beneath this image, the flyer reads:

DOCTOR VICTOR CROHN

PEDIATRICIAN AND IDIOPATHIC SPECIALIST

ARE YOU OR A LOVED ONE SUFFERING

FROM AN UNKNOWN AILMENT?

NEED A CURE?

CONTACT THE OFFICE TODAY!

CHAPTER XXIII

Some-odd-decades ago in the 1920s, Victor Crohn befriended a patient named John Lloyd.

John Lloyd lived alone in the outskirts of their small town and visited Victor's medical practice frequently due to a serious case of the tics—tics he explained would often climax into full-blown seizures. During these tics, John claimed to lose consciousness; he possessed a deep fear that one day he might unknowingly knock his head against a sharp object and soon after die of a concussion. Victor would laugh at his concerns but entertain them nonetheless, giving John weekly and then biweekly checkups pro bono, never seeing a tic or issue of any kind for himself but enjoying John's lighthearted presence in his otherwise clinical office.

Their friendship flourished and checkups expanded to outings at parties and pubs and nights across many towns over. The two men became somewhat of local celebrities in their community, invited to any and every event and gathering to be oohed and aahed at for their preternatural looks. One was never seen without the other. Jokes abounded about them being attached at the hip.

On June 6th, 1922—a date that will forever be ingrained in Victor's memory—the hinge of fate swung. Victor and John were attending a mansion soirée they'd been invited to by some mysterious mogul. The mansion was beautiful, the drink was abundant, and the masses were positively enraptured. The evening was filled with grasping hands and prodding questions that made the drink escalate from a trickling stream to a raging torrent. When John found himself too drunk to stand with Victor (who faked inebriation), they escaped into an isolated room, shut the door, and collapsed onto the bed in giddy foolishness. John stood, making a show for Victor in mockery of all the women who approached them that night.

"Oh, hello, Mister Crohn! How nice to see you again. It seems that fate keeps trying to push us together, wouldn't you say?"

In the unlit room, Victor could see John so vividly: the crooked turn of his smile, the twinkle of life in his eye. He sat on the bed and clapped with hushed laughter, encouraging John to continue as he danced about the room, hopping from one foot to the other. The laughter between them grew and grew until it could no longer be contained in this room alone.

Sure enough, others noticed.

John slipped, his sole, sliding in a sideways twirl, losing traction with the carpet so that he nearly fell. Victor tensed, ready to catch him, but John seemed to take no notice and continued with his merry dancing. Victor relaxed, paying less attention to each micro slip as John bounced around. But the air in the room began to compress, John's merriment began to decrease, and every hop seemed more and more mechanical. That twinkle of light vanished from John's eye and suddenly he was only a twirling puppet on a loose string, his mind seemingly vacant, his mouth slack, allowing for drool to spill off his lips.

Victor stood to pounce, sensing the short current, but was too far to grab John by the shirt collar. He missed by a mere hair and John fell like a domino, eyes rolled into the back of his head, which crashed into the corner of a vanity table and split wide open. Victor fell on top of him in his failed rescue and watched the blood pool around his dear friend's head. The red rushed beneath Victor's fingertips—

And his hunger ignited.

The door opened and ladies' giggles entered, hesitated, then screamed at what Victor could only imagine was the sight of a crazed-looking monster crouched atop an unconscious man leaking red fluid onto a cream carpet. Victor glared at the ladies—their mouths were contorted in such hideous horror!—then took action, lifting John's body, laying him across his shoulders, and charging out the mansion.

He rested John in his Bentley parked out front and sped home before the blood filling the passenger seat could truly trigger his rage. Once in his home office, Victor placed John on the couch and paced about the room, knowing that if he did not act quickly, his dearest friend—and closest thing to family for centuries—would perish.

John's heartbeat was slowing. Still, Victor refused to share in the spoils of his immortality. Instead, through a hazy, insane thought about the healing properties of his blood, he reached into his desk drawer, pulled out a syringe, and emptied himself into John.

Victor waited. John did not respond.

Victor waited further, watching over the body, unable to do anything about the bleeding without risking an insatiable appetite, until the gurgle in his stomach forced him to leave. He retired to his bedroom, snuffed out the scent of blood by inhaling chemicals, and fell asleep along with his hunger.

The next morning John was gone, but the stain of blood on the couch arm had grown swollen and dense, the spot staring at him like an empty eye socket. Victor searched the house for John or signs of him with desperate curiosity until his phone rang. He answered and John's voice blasted through the receiver:

"Hello, Victor, ol' boy! I don't know what you did to me last night but I feel right as rain! Some real magic you've got in that office of yours!"

Victor laughed with relief, welcomed his good friend, John, and told him he'd see him soon but to be sure to rest up.

"You gave your head quite the bang, after all."

The next day, John was knocking on his front door, yelling about how his tics were back and demanding more of the magic that made him feel right as rain. After an explosive argument,

Victor finally agreed. He escorted John to the couch—any trace of blood cleaned off the arm by now—and slipped into his bathroom with a syringe. When he stepped out, Victor told John to close his eyes. Only when John did so did Victor press the needle into John's vein, slowly injecting the contents into his dear friend.

"My god, Victor. Is that blood?"

Victor looked up to see John's eyes wide open in disobedience, directed at the procedure as the last few drops were pumped into him. Victor scowled and told him not to worry the slightest bit about it, for it was just medicine in its clinical phase, and quickly shooed him out the house, watching covetously as John skittered down the driveway.

A flurry of calls came to Victor's home office line that night—calls not from John but from acquaintances and strangers demanding the magic for any sum of money. Before Victor could scream *"What the bloody devil do you mean?!"* John came knocking on his front door, a huge grin plastered across his guileless face.

"Victor, my dear friend! We are both about to be wealthier than god!"

And Victor, seeing John's crooked smile and wonderful twinkle that brought him so much joy, obliged.

John managed the appointments and accounts, kept the secret he dared not discuss, and tamed the masses, while Victor tended to people's ailments, ridding them of their torment for a period of time. During that time, he slowly began to realize what injecting his blood truly did. The drug he had become. The stain of dotted arms from injections spreading across the town. The happy, deluded faces of those who wore those scars proudly.

The *God* he had become.

Weeks later, as he and John were having drinks in Victor's newly furnished dining room to celebrate their success, Victor stood with the eerie ease of someone in complete control, stepped over to John, who sat so unsuspectingly in his chair with a nice single malt scotch sloshing around his crystal glass, and loomed. John looked up at Victor, grimaced at the ice-cold gaze of his piercing blue eyes, and said:

"Why, Victor, you look as murderous as the Devil himself!"

Victor responded in a mocking tone, thick with resolution:

"Why, John, I think that's enough of you."

And slashed John's throat.

John's body froze, then twitched, then began to convulse in its seat as blood drooled from the smiling wound in his neck. Victor placed his emptied glass under John's throat, collected his drink, and sipped the red liquid, sweet with sin, as he watched John suffocate on his own thirst. No one asked about John's whereabouts in the coming days, and as Victor cleaned up the mess, he knew that those who did would be immediately silenced, held hostage by his magic.

Victor continued the practice in John's absence, learning more and more about what his blood could do as the rumors spread like wildfire, growing crueler and crueler as the demand grew ravenous and the exploitation so laughably advantageous.

And as he sits at his desk, in his penthouse apartment in

present day, he still remembers looking into John's lifeless eyes and thinking:

There can only be one god, my dear John. And God is immortal.

"Hello, this is Doctor Victor Crohn. Ah! Yes. Hello, Mrs. Goldman. How nice it is to hear from you again. And so soon, might I add . . . Yes? I see. Well, I think I made myself very clear from our last conversation that I am not taking appointments at this time. Yes, Mrs. Goldman. I understand the state of your son's— Yes, I understand that he is very sick, however— Yes, I know what the signs say. Flyers grow outdated and I've taken down all of the ones that were in their original postings. However, I simply do not have the labor force to search around the city and clear them up. Yes, I understand the amount of money you are willing to pay, but it is not a matter of money, Mrs. Goldman. You must understand, it is simply— Raising it will do no good. I will . . . You don't seem to grasp what I am telling you."

Victor takes his pause, allowing Mrs. Goldman to shriek until she feels sufficiently heard. And when that is done, his answer will be the same.

Hopefully she grows tired of arguing. This persistence is exhausting.

He supposes he could hang up the phone, cut off that voice, and maybe she'll continue speaking into the line without noticing the dial tone. A yapping bird with an empty skull. But that wouldn't be good for business. When things calm down again, he'll want to reopen. Let the floodgates flow. But for now, he is too busy to be taking care of the sick. Hopelessly ill children thrown at him like Mardi Gras beads.

This is a first for the practice, shutting it down. Denying aid to those in need—in almost seventy years! John would have disagreed.

"We must always keep the masses happy, Victor, ol' boy!"

The blowback from temporarily locking the practice is both amusing and pestering. But it must be done. Because he has something more important to invest his resources into.

Victor's voice slides off his tongue in waves of feigned sympathy. "That does sound terrible indeed, Mrs. Goldman."

Terrible, indeed. Poor, poor mother. All the money in the world and she can't buy her son a cure. It's too bad you can't buy what doesn't exist. A terrible ailment. From the details he's been given, her son has an estimated seven months to live as his organs shut down—curl and shrivel into brittle flesh, killing him from the inside out. A year at best, and that with a miracle.

Just not his miracle.

They had better make the most of it, damn fools, instead of spending their time and energy arguing with me.

And that's all it really is, isn't it—human life? Time and energy.

"Don't you care about the masses, ol' boy? Doesn't your heart just swoon for the people? To be a devoted servant to your brethren?"

VANILLA

Oh, John. How Victor tires of his constant voice.

We both loved the money—this is very true. But, ahhh, my dear, John. That's the one thing you never understood. I have no brethren. And how could you have understood? You weren't the one with the power.

Yes, the practice used to be for the masses, but since John and his interests of servitude have been fired from the business, he's focused on the children of the masses—*that* is where true desperation lies. Where the thread of rationality can be so easily manipulated and the game of life and death becomes interesting. Because the younger players are so fresh, so new to the rules, which makes their lives more valuable to the preexisting. Which makes them all the more willing to play. And pay.

So he accepts all players' places on his board and cycles them into the game. *His* game, where he is the merciless dealer. The sole permanent player. But the temporary players don't see him. He isn't the obstacle or the goal. He is just the invisible hand. The sublime giver of the potential goal. No, the masses don't see him, because the masses only see the child. The most important piece. The key to perpetuating the game forever despite the deluded concept. And that is fine—the less they notice him, the more influence he has.

"Yes, Mrs. Goldman. I've already understood what you mean."

The game perpetuates regardless of a player's participation. That's what egotism makes them blind to. As long as he exists, the game runs. And the players don't have to be active for the game to keep going. But they want to be active for as long as they possibly can. And that's how he'll play. That's the challenge for which they battle and he moderates. The goal to achieve at the end of an endless board.

So, they step up to plate, they set their figurines on Go, and to advance, to receive the extra lives he possesses and they desire, they have to sacrifice. For every dollar, for every moment of time and energy spent from themselves or stolen from other players, he hands to them that extra life and they get to move up one measly space. From an overhead view, it doesn't look like much—maybe an inch or two. But to them, it's miles. So they'll keep sacrificing and inching forward and he'll keep handing life over to them with a dark smile, knowing that they don't realize to take is to lose so much more.

And once the game is ready to remove a player, no amount of money or care in the world can force the player to continue. To buy into just one more round.

And everyone loses, one way or another. Everyone gets knocked off the board.

It always comes to an end. And in the end, there are no winners.

Well, except for me, of course. And that's another thing you never understood, John.

I'm the only one who can win.

Victor stands and paces back and forth along the length of his mahogany desk, his fingers gliding across the luxurious wood. The receiver continues to spit out Mrs. Goldman's now grating voice.

VANILLA

He can almost feel her saliva splatter across his cheek. He tries not to explode in turn.

"Yes, yes, Mrs. Goldman. I'm listening."

He stops, loops his finger through a drawer ring, and pulls it open. Inside are four syringes, all pregnant with his blood.

The extra lives.

He picks each one up and turns to his fireplace. He points the needles toward the yellow flames and presses down on the plungers, emptying them. The fire licks the sides of the brick in a fit, curls and blooms into an unnatural shade of neon red.

"Once again, Mrs. Goldman, I understand your situation. However, I simply do not have the resources to help you at this time. I am afraid I am truly of no good use to you in your current predicament. I really do hope the best for you and your little Mr. Goldman. I suggest you attend to him with what time you have left. Now, have a good day."

He hangs up the phone and empties the last syringe into the fireplace. The last glow of red bursts before the flames return to a pale yellow.

Benevolently denying was a fun exercise at first, but now this is growing tiresome.

He picks back up the receiver and dials into his voicemail.

"Hello. This is Doctor Victor Crohn. I am currently out of office. I will answer pressing inquiries upon my return."

He ends the message and saves it.

That'll be enough.

He sits back down on his throne, sighing into the silence, and places his hand atop the other on his chest. He happily ignores the pile of little sick faces staring at him from his desk. An audience of watery eyes pleading for an encore. Children from all corners of the continent who are sick with no cure or sick with no root. Whose parents have sent chart after file after chart from past doctors who couldn't find an answer, doctors who stood there with their clipboards and lightboxes without words. He recognizes a few of the conditions: MRSA, Kuru, Von Hippel-Lindau, cancers of all kinds. Some of the conditions have an unknown cause or a strange combination of symptoms.

But the cure is always the same.

As long as the parent signs the contract, he takes the child in for a few weeks of blood injections, drawn from his arm to theirs, and returns them better than ever with nothing but a few dots to show for it. He doesn't have to feed them or clean them because the blood does its work, freezing the essential systems of the body so that the healing process can take over. So that his blood can easily slither through them as it mends the destruction in its path. The child feels no hunger or thirst, no internal movement, and very little pain. And when they are sent home, their functions kick back into gear. The symptoms abate and rarely return.

No one ever asks how he does his work and no one cares enough to investigate. Because without him, they'd lose the game. Because he keeps them in play.

And how they love to play.

A soft grin sits on his lips. He gives in, sifting through the pile of two-dimensional children to relish in their helplessness. Each picture, a card in a deck of useless plays. One young girl with blond pigtails, blue eyes, and gray skin, her mouth clenched around what is about to be a painfully raspy cough, lands atop the pile. The resemblance isn't exact, but it's there, present enough to pull his mind toward Vanilla, and for a moment his heart aches. He's been shoving thoughts of her into the back of his mind, trying to avoid micromanaging, to let the process unfold. *As it naturally will.* But it has been ninety-six hours, and it makes him irritable to be away from her for so long. As if she is the cure to his rage. Or to his withdrawals.

What sweet irony.

If it weren't for this practice, he would never have been given Vanilla. Been offered money and fake gold by a tweaked-out grin that sparkled with decay, in exchange for the rotting corpse of a baby soon to become his one and only sweet. Her body wrapped in a pink blanket and handed to him like a delicious gift to cradle in his cold arms. That blanket he would have handed back if not for that thin mouth that, despite the pain, struggled into an upturned crescent at the sight of him and sang to him like a muffled song from a closed music box. That little skeleton hand, so translucent and emaciated, from beneath the blanket, reaching out for him. Her sweet brown eyes—the only life-filled part of her—staring right at him. Right into him.

As if seeing him for the truth they would both come to share.

He would never have experienced taking her home, reading every inch of her brittle skin and eventually finding a space tucked between the tendons of her wrist that wouldn't burst with pain upon injection. How she remained obedient, letting him distract her with fluttering fingers, her big brown eyes lethargically following his movements as he pressed down on the plunger. She instantly inflated with life and started to giggle as though his blood were made for her. As though she'd been waiting since her birth for a taste of him. How she lifted both of her arms to be picked up and held by him. She smiled with her little pink gums, a twinkle in her eyes, her laughter filling up the cold concrete room making the walls warm to the touch.

The realization that he, too, had been waiting for her.

He would've never experienced her. How she grew and grew; grew healthy and strong. Threw tantrums and jumped about the room to play as any normally developing child would. How she grew and never stopped despite the blood within her. Despite the lack of hunger or thirst. The longest withstanding treatment on the most befitting patient.

His child.

My little Vanilla. My sweet.

He tosses the deck and glances at the framed photograph of Vanilla on the edge of his desk, pushed as far away as possible without falling off the edge, her smiling face outlined in a ring of laced gold. The only thing that has been keeping him sane these past days: a printed substitute for something much stronger. He grabs the frame, brushing his thumb across her glazed cheeks, and whimpers.

This photograph was taken sixteen years after she became his.

"Daddy? What is that?" she'd asked when he took out the

camera.

"This, my sweet, captures memories so that we can keep them forever."

Taken over by confusion at first, the gears turning in her skull, her eyebrows eventually shot up in recognition. "It makes the photographs!"

"That's my smart girl."

He chuckles at the memory of her reaction to the flash. After the photograph was taken, she squinted in horror, her mouth stretched back to release a yelp. But he assured her before she could scream that it was all right. That her vision would return to normal. Her apprehension settled into rapid blinks before she agreed.

"You're always right, Daddy!"

They sat together, blossoming in each other's company while he fed her lollipops and hummed happy birthday.

How perfect she was. How her mind was filled to the brim with pure bliss, ready to spill over like a gushing dam. Safe from the Outside, from all that could harm her . . .

Until that dreadful night she grew ill. Until he realized it wasn't only the Outside he needed to protect her from. The danger was within her, too.

Was it me? Was it truly my blood?

No, it couldn't have been. But the unprecedented nature of it all lingers in the back of his mind nonetheless, prodding the fault toward himself. He's been siphoning his blood into her for years. It was making her healthier. It was making her stronger.

What made her so damn sick?!

He slams his hand down on the desk, the pile of cards jumping from the force. Children quivering at his might. The question will haunt him forever. A floating diagnosis he will never reach.

He sets the picture back and stands from his throne. He walks past his desk and up to the penthouse windows—a wall made of transparent glass. The reflection of the glass reveals the inside of his apartment: leather furniture, expensive arts of all kinds, statues and paintings decorating the spaces that still feel empty. He stares down at the expanse of the city from his ivory tower as the reflection of that pale yellow fire crackles and pops behind him. The sun has just started to peek out from the building tops and the streets are still empty because the ants have just begun to wake in their beds. But there is still a little activity. He can see a poorly lit street where a group of boys advance behind a lone girl, approaching closer and closer . . .

A sinking feeling, a thick lump of worry, hits his stomach.

He exits his penthouse, and a few minutes later he is on the pavement, walking down the sidewalk and sniffing the air like a bloodhound. A sweet scent carries into his nostrils. He speeds up, following it, turning corners and taking shortcuts until they're in his sight.

Two girls, hand in hand, cut from different cloth but sewn into the same fabric. He watches as they walk down the street, Tiffany in her usual work uniform she seems to live in and Vanilla looking as disheveled as ever. He makes mental notes at the sight of her. Of how she's covered in that boy's blood. *Another pawn lost to this game.* Tiffany holds on to Vanilla's wrist, tugging her down the street like dirty laundry.

He grinds his teeth.

Treat her well, you stubborn girl.

Besides the abhorrence, everything seems to be falling according to—

Hmm?

He sees a woman drenched in dirty rags slink past him and approach the two girls from behind. She looks strangely familiar, her hair unnaturally blond, as if years of trauma have bleached it nearly white, and chopped short, almost shaven . . . but if it had been any longer . . .

He eyes the quick shine of a thin, gold necklace around her neck.

Dammit! How?!

CHAPTER XXIV

In this city, there are many unfortunate souls who are tossed into the eternal damp and dark, forgotten and left to scrounge for life between the filthy cracks of society. Some of them may never get the chance to play Victor's game; some of them might not even know it exists. But a few—a very unfortunate few—know the game all too well. Have played it and learned the meaning of loss before their hand was revealed and they became a pawn. One of these few is Greta Charr, also known as Needlepoint to passing vagabonds because, similar to alchemy, she can create clothing out of anything.

Greta Charr who years ago stepped on Go.

At forty years of age, she roams the streets, heavy with regret despite the flush of drugs from her system. The flush that should have made her feel clean. Should have swept the dirt off her skin

VANILLA

and from her veins. But dirt doesn't always wash off so easily—especially when it's already rotting your core.

When Greta was twenty, she met Billy Maine, a loud, destructive, and alluring boy who passed through the city in a blaze. He pumped her full of music, love, drugs, and something a little less savory.

And when Billy Maine left, he promised to return, promised to come back to Greta with fame and fortune. He left, and he left Greta to mother a drug habit and a pregnancy.

The drug habit grew hungry, and nine months later, after Greta lost her apartment and switched to a shelter, her baby was born and grew hungry with it. But her baby never cried, even though she was born shaking, as if she knew this life was too cruel to waste a single tear on. She only ever whimpered—until, that is, the withdrawals she entered this world with took over and turned her silent and blue. An ugly contrast to the baby-pink of life, but a beautiful complement to the decay.

Greta didn't have many options. She loved her daughter, yes. But taking her to the hospital would mean losing her own freedom. Could Greta survive that? And as her baby drowsed in her arms so quietly, Greta thought of her more and more as already dead. As already passed and at peace.

But those brown, watery eyes too big for their head watched her, not accusatory but accepting. Passive to whatever her fate might be. Passive to whatever her mother chose.

So Greta marched to the hospital. Because her baby wasn't dead. She was very much alive and deserved a chance—even if that meant Greta's being taken away. Because of those weak, innocent eyes.

Greta marched and marched and marched.

But not before seeing the face of God.

He was stamped on a telephone pole, regal and stoic, somehow so present even in a simple black-and-white print. She pulled down the sign, read the fine print, thought it was a message from above, and kept it tucked away in her pocket, pulling it out every once in a while to memorize his features.

Doctor Victor Crohn.

Her baby angel could last a couple more days, sure! She's a strong one, Greta believed. After all, she'd lasted this long. And when Greta finally saw Doctor Victor Crohn in the flesh, she felt that salvation was so close. That the burden of her troubles would soon be lifted off her and placed into someone else's capable hands.

She memorized the doctor's route and on the night of confrontation, snuck back into her estranged mother's apartment, stole seventy-three dollars and a thin necklace she hoped was made of gold from her nightstand, and waited on the street. When the doctor came ambling by, Greta stepped out from the shadows of the alleyway and stood her ground before him. The sensation of this man felt immediate and all-consuming, as if she might choke on his aura.

She was foolish enough to mistake it for divinity.

"Can I help you?" he asked, the corner of his mouth turned upward but his gaze dead.

"My child—"

"Ah, let me stop you there. All inquiries can be phoned in—"

"But she doesn't have much time!" Greta shrieked, interrupting the doctor into silence. She bit her tongue, afraid she'd angered him with her blasphemy.

But he just stood there, one eyebrow arched. "Well?" he said. "You've come this far. Make your case."

She gasped, nearly choking on the sudden intake of air as she argued for the stand. "Please, *please*, Doctor," she begged. "I've seen your flyer, I've heard the miracles you can do. Please, just hold her in your hands. See how sick she is! I have nothing else!"

She held out her angel and, to her surprise, the doctor took her in his arms. She watched as he brought her, the sweet little bundle of pink, to his face, inhaled . . . and grimaced. Her heart sank.

"Please," she continued. "I have one hundred dollars and a gold necklace. It's all I have. I'll give you the clothes off my back if I must. I'll—I'll do anything you want me to do!"

The doctor frowned at her comment, nearly stuck out his tongue in disgust, but she persisted. She got down on her knees, the gravel crunching beneath her skin, digging spots into her flesh. She lifted her hands to him, the payment in her palms, and prayed for him to accept.

"Please . . . you are my only hope. I have nothing else. I'm begging."

But despite her prayers, he bent down, ready to return the bundle without a hint of remorse as Greta's heart picked up speed in her chest.

And then, after days of silence, her baby spoke.

Greta's heart stopped. She looked to the bundle, amazed, as a tiny pale hand reached out from the pink blanket, fingers twitching to grab for the doctor's nose. The bundle sang a weak note that pulled the doctor's attention. Now he was looking at her—not as before, at a bundle of whatever stink he had sensed, but truly looking at the sick baby in his arms. The thing of such potential life suffering from decay.

The ice-cold aura filled with abrasive power Greta had sensed around him seemed to melt away.

"Keep your things," he said. "I will save her."

Greta's fingers gripped tightly around the money and necklace, tears bursting from her eyes as she cried out in gratitude. The doctor vanished before she could weep her first thank-you.

She was free.

Days passed and the loneliness began to feel like iron clamps, squeezing her of breath. The isolation like black walls surrounding her, but really they were just open mouths shouting laughter at her from the pits of their dark throats as they inched closer and closer. She paced back and forth across the same alleyway for days, waiting for the doctor to return, but he never came, and as the anxiety built up within her brick by brick, she ruined her system to deal with the edge. Incapacitated against a dark wall, her mind became a mush that those open mouths of laughter relished. Her head felt like it was sinking into the brick and she could hear her once-beautiful blond hair crunch against the back of her skull.

Blue eyes appeared before her. The eyes of God. Swirls of

silver and teeth. She smiled—or at least she thinks she smiled—her face dripping upward as she reached out toward God.

But he pulled away. "I'm sorry. Your baby didn't make it."

She struggled to sit up, breathe forward and ask "Why?" But he was already gone, the darkness stretching until she was swimming in it. Until she could see Death approach, those swirls of silver morphed into a crescent moon.

And that's when she realized it wasn't God she found.

She climbed out of the black pit, scaled that mountain in an avalanche of sludge as Death followed, and somehow survived. Somehow outwitted both evils. All for those big brown eyes.

Because my angel never gave up.

Now, her hair is cut short in a ritual of rebirth. Her skin is cracked with age and trauma, her joints worn, and she feels forty years older than her true age. She lives in that alleyway and does nothing but sew. A punishment of and for her memory. She sits between warm garbage with a needle and fabric and skillfully avoids any pricks without the aid of a thimble, although her hands tremble.

The *pitter-patter* of feet pulls her attention at this odd hour of morning. She looks up from her handiwork to see two girls hurrying down the street.

And then she sees him following behind.

She places the fabric on the dirty ground, stands as though an invisible hand leads her, and exits the alleyway. When she looks down the street, he's not there. Just the two girls, their backs facing her as they skip away. But that one girl . . . that girl to the left with the unnaturally blond hair ... she feels so familiar. A palpable echo of a memory.

Greta takes a step forward, then another step, until she's nearly sprinting. They seem to sense her; the one leading pulls the blonde ahead, but Greta doesn't let up.

Finally she calls out, not realizing what she is saying or intending to say until the words fall out of her mouth: "Baby angel? Angel, is that you?"

The girls turn to face her and Greta is struck with recognition. This quiet child with bleached pigtails. This child who squints, shielding her eyes with a pale hand like the sight of her own mother might be too painful to bear.

"Can I help you, lady?" the leader asks, taking a defensive step in front of those pigtails. "Look, we don't have any money."

"Angel? Oh, my baby angel!" Greta cries out. She reaches her dusty hand toward her daughter, her fingers jerking out of control.

Those pigtails flinch away, lids squeezing over those huge brown eyes.

But, baby ... baby, baby. Don't you recognize me?

"I think you've got the wrong people, lady," the leader remarks, moving to swat Greta's hand away.

"My baby," Greta continues. She can't stop. She stares into those brown eyes. "I would recognize that look. I would recognize her anywhere. Even with all of that dirt covering her face. Even after all these years!" Her wet gaze drifts off then twitches back into focus. "Oh, angel! What's happened to you? You look like you've been hurt!"

She reaches her hand out again and her baby lets her touch her, even if it's just the fabric separating their skins. Greta thinks she can feel the vibration of blood beneath her fingertips. Rivers of red bound to her, a link so distinct she can taste it like sweet iron on her tongue.

"Are you hurt? Did someone do this to you? Why aren't you speaking to me? That's all right. This must be very confusing for you! But now that I found you, we can be together! Oh, baby angel! Baby, baby, baby angel—"

Her words end on a strangled choke, her excited rambling cutting short her breath. She kneels over and gasps, water droplets falling from her face to the tar below. She hasn't cried in years.

Those big brown eyes simply watch her.

"Let me take you away." Greta tightens her grip and begins to tug. "Let me take you somewhere where it can be just you and me! Just us, together forever! The way it was supposed to be! I'll never leave you. Not ever! Never again!"

"Hey, hold it right there!" the leader growls, and this time she does smack Greta's hand away. "Do us all a favor and let's keep our hands to ourselves!"

"But, my baby . . ." Greta tries to reach out again. Something in her chest vacates when her hand is smacked away a second time.

"I said, hands to ourselves! Don't you understand, lady?" the leader says, but Greta notes she shakes with fear. This leader, filled with so much bravery and confidence, in the end is nothing but a child herself. An innocent showcase for what lurks around. A puppet on strings. The leader turns to those blond pigtails while

Greta stutters to tell her that she understands, that she's been there too. *I've met the Devil as well.* "C'mon, let's get away from this quack."

Greta tries to speak but the words won't come. Those blond pigtails travel away. She lets them. She collapses to her knees. *I never deserved her.* But when Greta looks up, those big brown eyes are still watching her, wet with reflection. Shallow fogs of breath escape her mouth as they maintain eye contact.

"Angel . . ." Greta exhales, adding her pain to the rays of the rising sun.

Those eyes squint until they are mere strips of white and brown. Squint as the distance between mother and daughter increases, two magnets of the same pole destined to be apart. Forever separated by a decision made before their time.

And then they are gone. Lost to the sunrise. They are gone and Greta never even got to hear her daughter speak. Never got to see her twitch around words as she expressed affection, pain, sorrow, resentment. Never got to apologize, to beg for forgiveness against all of her regrets.

Greta will never get to hold her angel again, that pink bundle lost long, long ago.

Because he is here to reclaim her now.

His presence is unmistakable—cold and evil, a sting in her spine, just as the day they first met. Just as the day she lost everything because she didn't care enough to think twice about that presence. About the pact she was making. But she knows now—is a veteran of sin. Is aware that she escaped by the skin of her teeth, but not really, because now he has returned for what is rightfully his. She doesn't know if her daughter recognized her, but she knows *he* does. And he is here.

Because she made a bet with the Devil. Gambled against the odds. Threw her die. And lost.

CHAPTER XXV

The rising sun itches Vanilla's skin just as did the creature who approached them. The static energy between them felt agonizing. There were no sticks or black metal to harm her, but the energy was all wrong. So strong and electric, like staring at a lightbulb for too long and burning her eyes down to the very core.

Tiffany seemed desperate to get away. Vanilla didn't mind. Tiffany's energy feels warm, like curling up with a blanket in the space her daddy left.

"There are a lot of crazy people on the street. I don't like to be rude, but you still always have to protect yourself first."

"Why do you call them homeless?"

"Because they have no homes to sleep in."

"But isn't their home the Outside?"

"Yes . . . I guess so. I guess for some of them."

A few turns later Tiffany pipes up again: "Speaking of homes, this one's mine."

They step up to a small red door embedded in the face of a brown building.

"My place is pretty small, just so you know. Although, any place for you is probably . . ." Tiffany stops herself, glancing at Vanilla guiltily as she reaches into her purse. There is a muffled jingle from her bag that she pulls out in the form of a keychain. Hanging from the metal ring are two silver keys that glint as if to wink at a secret, their teeth chattering against each other with gossip.

Tiffany uses one of the keys to open the front door. The lock snaps, shocking Vanilla deeper into the trance she isn't cognizant of being in. Deeper into the parallels of her world and this one. The question of reality swells and contracts in her mind and she follows that warmth. That comfortable substitute for what used to be.

The door swings and Tiffany steps inside. But Vanilla doesn't. Tiffany watches her attempt to take a step forward only to stop as if something in the empty doorway blocks her path. Some magnetic field she can't see. Vanilla reaches her finger out and pokes at the threshold, feeling the invisible barrier like dense rubber.

"What are you doing?" Tiffany asks, reaching out for Vanilla's arm. She holds on and pulls, but something stops the motion and she assumes it's Vanilla digging in her heels. "Okay, enough of that. Come in already. It's cold."

The next tug brings Vanilla collapsing in. She stumbles over the doorframe, eyes wide in shock, and Tiffany watches her rebalance her body. Watches her stand and wipe down her dress like there's muck dripping from her shoulders and thighs. Vanilla shudders, looks back at the doorway, and refocuses on Tiffany.

Tiffany clears her throat. "Anyway ... the one nice thing about my place is that I don't have to walk up all these stairs. There's no elevator in this building, but I live on the first floor. I guess you could say I got lucky."

Tiffany uses the second key to open the door immediately to her left. The lock snaps and the door opens to a single room with a single mattress elevated by brown logs shoved into a corner. The walls are white, pristine—no blemishes for someone who has better things to stare at—and the floor is white carpet, the texture of towels stained in a few places by dust. Pushed up against the back wall is a wooden vanity with a stool. The vanity is cluttered with harmless sticks too small for damage and powdered colors of all kinds. Some she's never seen. A glass jar is stuffed to the point of bursting with lollipops, a few having toppled over onto the vanity counter.

And that is where Vanilla's eyes land. Tiffany notices her unrelenting gaze at the glass jar. Vanilla swallows hard.

"Be a good girl and I'll give you one. Just make yourself comfortable. Sit wherever you'd like."

Vanilla takes a moment, the parallels of this reality and her former one eroding into canyon-level depths, before she steps inside. The feeling of discomfort that was clogging her pores is instantly washed away. The door snaps shut behind her and she shudders. To her right are strange machines not unlike the ones with dials on steel countertops. A portion of the wall is covered by black fabric. There's another door that Vanilla can see leads to a bathtub and the peeking-out edge of a toilet. Tiffany walks into this smaller room and for a while only her backside is visible through the doorway. Vanilla can hear her turn on a faucet and shuffle things around.

"Don't you go fucking around with stuff and leave! I know where you live!" Tiffany calls out, a painful tinge of laughter in her voice.

But Vanilla won't leave. She's already locked in.

She walks around the room, placing a footstep on every square inch of carpet, feeling her toes dig into the hairs. Her trail is muddy, marking her past. Marking a different universe where a different her is walking in her room that has slipped into another reality. A reality filled with cushion rather than concrete.

She steps up to the vanity and pulls the stool out from under it. She sits, like how her daddy would sometimes have her sit on his lap, feeling the comfort of cushion under her seat rather than rods of bone. She looks at herself in the mirror.

Only when she sits head-on does she see the crack splitting her face in diagonal. A diffracted line separating her horrifying image.

"You are so beautiful, Vanilla."

But not now. Not in this moment. She can feel his fingers retract from her in disgust: her pale skin, covered in streaks of red and brown; her hair, falling out of its ties and knotted into nasty chunks; and her dress, torn and crusted with grime. She reaches out to touch her reflection, feeling hard glass rather than soft skin. Her fingertips leave a red smudge on the mirror.

She looks like a creature. No—that's not it.

I look filthy.

She flinches and turns away. Her eyes find the jar of lollipops, one rolling closer and closer to her across the counter. She starts to drool, but obedience holds her down.

"I'm drawing a bath for you," Tiffany says from behind her. "It's filling up as I speak and should be ready soon. I hope you like boiling-hot water. I know I do." She steps up behind Vanilla and touches her skin. "You feel warm now. Do you feel warm?" Tiffany looks at her in the mirror. Vanilla can see their reflection: Tiffany hovering over her, the glow of golden light in her eyes, the skin of her arms now that her jacket has been removed.

Tiffany smiles in the mirror and Vanilla smiles back.

"Do you want one? You can take if you'd like," Tiffany says, pointing to the jar.

Vanilla nods and drops her jaw wide open.

Tiffany hesitates, staring at the pink muscle inside Vanilla's mouth, the roll of its movement like a bloated worm. Her ivory teeth that she imagines could break a finger in half like a carrot with one unforgiving *snap*—but she shakes the thought from her mind, pulling herself away from the conspiracy.

Tiffany rotates Vanilla to face her, then plucks a lollipop from the counter and unwraps it. Her fingers tremble around the white paper until the candy is bare, exposed to her senses. She places the red ball on the center of Vanilla's tongue, props her fingers under

Vanilla's chin, and guides her jaw closed.

"You've been a good girl," Tiffany says. "You deserve this."

Vanilla releases a deep sigh in satisfaction, her skeleton settling back to comfort within the caves of her muscles.

"Have as many as you'd like," Tiffany says. "They'll be right there if you want them." She looks over to the bathroom. "That bath should be ready."

Tiffany holds out her hand and Vanilla takes it. She lifts Vanilla to her feet and leads her to the bathroom, where a thick cloud of steam greets them, wetting Vanilla's skin. She wiggles her nose. Droplets of water grow plump until they cannot sustain their weight and glide down Vanilla's cheeks off the precipice of her jaw.

Tiffany rushes over to the tub and turns off the faucet, taking a seat on the lip.

"There. Perfect," Tiffany says, her eyes landing on Vanilla at the word *perfect*. "You can get in now."

Her curly hair has expanded, strands twisting for release. Vanilla wants to dig her fingers into them to see where her hair ends and her neck begins. Tiffany motions for Vanilla to come to her and she obeys, stopping when there's an inch between them. Their dark eyes stare at each other in expectation until Vanilla lifts her hands up like she's about to dive into the abyss. Tiffany leans in, fingering the hem of her dress with caution. She looks up to meet Vanilla's stare—a stare that tells her *It's all right*—grabs the bottom of her dress, and stands, yanking the dress up and over her head.

Vanilla is bare. Nothing underneath the dress to cover her. But she stands in her naked skin like it's the most natural thing in the world. Tiffany tries to divert her gaze, but as Vanilla steps into the tub, she can't help but glimpse at Vanilla's perfectly smooth complexion. Like a river of milk streaked with dirt.

Vanilla slips into the water. She does not react to the change in temperature, despite the scorching heat that would be just barely tolerable to any normal person. She simply sinks into the boiling vat like she has found her natural temperature. Like she isn't a tea bag of dirt steeped into a freshly brewed pot.

As Vanilla rests her head back against the porcelain and closes her eyes, Tiffany's mind churns with rusted gears. Gears old and tired, processing and protesting over and over again as she hovers her hands over Vanilla's neck. Her fingers twitch, reaching out toward that pale throat and retracting with such defiance. She draws near but the gears catch on a chipped surface and her movement diverts to grab for a nearby brush.

She bites down hard on her lip and silently winces.

Tiffany pulls a chunk of Vanilla's hair, stretches out her fist, and runs the strands through her fingers, feeling how soft they are to the touch despite the blood and gunk stuck in chaotic patches. The bands snap off with ease and Vanilla's hair rushes down, unraveling gold across bare collarbone. Tiffany dips her cupped hand into the tub and pours hot water over Vanilla's head. She runs the brush from scalp to end, grazing the bristles across milky shoulders, traveling across mountains of muscle and bone. Vanilla nuzzles up to the touch like a well-groomed pet. Like a perfectly manicured pure breed. *She just got lost from her owner,* Tiffany thinks. *An owner who doesn't want her anymore. Who's grown tired of her.* Vanilla's legs, thrown out before her under the water like a mermaids' tail, gyrate in glee as she tries to help smooth out the clumps. Tiffany reaches for a sponge from a nearby ledge and plunges it into the water, scrubbing the surface of Vanilla's skin. Dislodging mud and blood from unblemished porcelain.

There are no wounds . . .

"Why are you doing this?" Vanilla whispers, interrupting her thoughts.

Tiffany turns to meet her question, steam evaporating into her lungs. "What do you mean? Why am I helping you?"

Vanilla nods. Tiffany runs the sponge up and down her legs. She reaches for the distant parts of her body, her core trembling. The sponge travels up Vanilla's chest and across her back before Tiffany forces herself to stop.

"Well, because I was like you once. I know what it's like and I know what I wish someone did for me."

In a matter of minutes, the plug is pulled and the bathwater is drained. Tiffany helps Vanilla out of the tub, averting her eyes, and wraps her in a towel. She leads her to the bedroom.

"All right. Now to get you that dress," Tiffany says. She turns to a door by the bed guarding a recessed closet. "Your old one will probably have to be thrown out. Actually, scratch that. It most definitely will. It's way, way beyond repair."

She shuffles through a rack of clothing, each item screeching against the metal bar as she shoves it deep into the pit of the closet.

Rejected. After a few items, she stops and pulls out a dress.

"I'm sure it's nicer for you to wear something you're already comfortable in. This dress is the same but just a tad different with the white detailing. You might look like a nun, but at least it'll be a sexy nun."

Tiffany winks, and this time her laugh sounds genuine. Not strained or screechy, like the sound of hangers grating against rusty metal. She holds the dress out to Vanilla, who touches the fabric with satisfaction, the pads of her fingers grazing down laceless black. Her lips curve into a smile.

A beautiful dress.

"You like it? All right, good. Lift up your arms."

Tiffany slides the dress on over her head, removing the towel out from under as she does. This time she doesn't avert her gaze, looking for marks crusting with red. Something to explain all that blood that is now staining her white porcelain. But she finds nothing.

Once the dress is secured, Tiffany claps her hands together. "There! Done."

Familiar tight creases splayed across dark skin curl into contentment. Vanilla loves the way they look on Tiffany. She steps in front of the vanity and looks at herself in the mirror.

"You look, so, so beautiful, Vanilla."

Her smile grows.

A brush glides through her hair.

"You know, maybe you could try wearing your hair down for a bit. Those pigtails don't look very comfortable. I don't even know how you kept them so well and tidy for all this time outside. Must've been real fucking hard. But I guess it's like they say: beauty is torture . . . or was it 'pain'?"

Vanilla takes a seat at the vanity as Tiffany continues to brush her hair. As she does, Vanilla grabs a chunk of her own blond locks and twirls it between her fingers, rotating the lollipop between her lips in a matching rhythm. Thick droplets of water fall off the stem and land onto her lap. Her skin is sensitive enough to feel each drip on her bare thighs. She watches this unreactive stranger in the mirror, so familiar yet so distant. Her—but a version of her that's been placed in a new setting so the elements have changed. A her that exists in a new room in the Outside with the creatures. A her that has been taken away, or is perhaps following them.

She shifts her eyes to Tiffany's reflection. *You are so beautiful. Maybe you are not a creature at all. Maybe the creatures finally got you and took you to a bad place. Maybe you are like me but never had a daddy to save you. Maybe you are just lost.*

Maybe that's what is happening to me.

Maybe I'm lost.

A glimpse of Tiffany's skin, caught under the perfect lighting as she is about to bring the brush down on the top of Vanilla's head, illuminates dark dots. A splatter of stains. Vanilla instantly snatches her wrist. Tiffany gasps as Vanilla jerks her arm in.

"Fuck! What's that for?!" she yelps.

Vanilla ignores her surprise and twists her wrist so that the underside of her arm is facing upright. Scattered across her skin are tiny dots. She looks back up at Tiffany, who can see the delight form across her face.

"Those things?" Tiffany chuckles in embarrassment. "They've been there for a while now. From a bad habit I've already kicked." *More lies. Does she know? Does she have them too?* A bead of sweat breaks out on her forehead as the itching sensation ignites in her arm. "It might have killed me if I hadn't."

Vanilla twists her own arm upward and places it next to Tiffany's, tugging her dress sleeve up. Untouched, pale skin looks back at them, but Vanilla can remember the dots before they vanished. Tiffany's lips press into a tight line.

"Happy freckles," Vanilla whispers. She thinks they look beautiful across Tiffany's skin. A dot for each joy.

"Yeah," Tiffany mutters. "Happy freckles."

CHAPTER XXVI

This should be done, Tiffany thinks.

But Vanilla won't stop staring at her arm and she can't stop thinking about why Vanilla's skin is so perfectly sealed. Like it never once split open—*was* split open by someone else to see what's inside.

It should be done soon. It should be done right now. She stares at Vanilla, the anticipation of murder vibrating down her arms, spreading out her fingertips. *Just grab her head. Just grab her head and—*

But she knows it's not that simple. A *snap* never is. And she's too scared to pull back the curtains to give herself the motivation. Even with daylight rising behind those dark shields, his presence is bone-chilling, like being caught outside on a winter's midnight. She knows the light is painful but easy for him to navigate.

"I used to have happy freckles," Vanilla comments. "I don't know where they went."

As Vanilla scrambles to find an explanation, Tiffany's body lurches and pulls. Her mind swarms with all the moves she could make. *Just yank your arm away. Yank it and use it to knock her out. Or push her to the ground. Get on top of her. Her neck is thin. Get on top of her and straddle her so she can't move and just put your hands over her neck. That's it. And lean in. Just lean in with your weight and press down until . . . until . . .*

Until that snap.

Tiffany looks at herself in the mirror. Her body looms over this frail girl. How easy it is to imagine such violence. To bounce bloodshed off the walls of her skull like her thoughts are nothing more than an innocent pinball.

Is this what fear does to me?

Aw, keep your chin up, dear! How many times do we have to go through this, my good little puppet? My sick little child! You think you're hurting now? Oh, ha, ha! You think you're hurting now?! You know, you've known, you'll always know! So why stop now? Why stop here? When you've already come so far? Why not prolong the hurt a little longer? Because the alternative is worse!

Because dying is pain!

"Listen!" Tiffany says abruptly. She pauses, shocked by her outburst. "Listen," she repeats. "I have to go to bed."

Vanilla looks up at her, her eyes large and understanding. She nods and slowly removes each finger from Tiffany's arm in succession, relinquishing her grasp. Tiffany brings her arm back to her side, willing herself to keep her nails from digging into the dots and connecting them with a scratch.

"You can sleep on the bed," Tiffany says. "I don't mind sleeping on the floor."

Vanilla watches Tiffany shake and Tiffany can feel her body grow numb. "I have work tonight," Tiffany thinks aloud. "I should get some sleep. I should go to bed . . . I-I have work."

Without changing, she clicks off the light and crawls to the ground. Insanity wraps around her system like a hot string. She just wants the cool dark. To rest, to slip away into sleep where she can no longer exist.

The top of her head is inches away from the bottom of the wall. She lifts her arm up and digs a nail into the plaster, shoveling back white paint. *Scritch-scratch, scritch-scratch.* A habit she'd broken out of a year ago, but suddenly all of those awful tics are flooding back in. *The dots, the itching, the scratching.*

There's a pressure on her back. The feeling of another body. A plush stomach pressed against her hard spine. She can smell the soap from Vanilla's skin as the scent lifts off that pale body and into her nostrils.

Another hand joins hers against the wall.

Scritch-scritch, scratch-scratch.

They both dig into the plaster now, torturing the wall as they echo each other's patterns.

"Do you need to be fixed?" Vanilla innocently pours the question into the dark.

Tiffany shudders like frozen steel is being pressed against the most sensitive parts of her. Her answer carries the pain of years of disobedience. Of pleas for cessation. Of torturous healing:

"No."

"I should go to bed . . . I-I have work."

Vanilla watches Tiffany break. She knows Tiffany's breaking because she knows what breaking looks like. She's broken before.

She watches Tiffany struggle to move, to speak rationally before shutting down entirely. Unable to stand upright because breaking, although mental, manifests into the physical. She watches Tiffany turn off the light and sink to the floor like a weight she can no longer carry.

Do you need to be fixed?

It's an innocent question because she's needed to be fixed many times before when she'd break. Those mini fractures that occurred because her daddy came and went without explanation—sometimes after showing her a photograph of something she couldn't make sense of, like a disembodied shoe fallen to its side on a concrete sidewalk.

Do you need to be fixed?

But she doesn't know what broke Tiffany. Only that when she broke, she enjoyed the comfort of her daddy. But how disheartening it was to always break and need fixing but never be the one to fix.

They are both inside the room, the lock snapped, the Outside out. There are no snakes, no photographs, and no Daddy. So when she hears the *scratch* greet her like a soft whisper and sees Tiffany through the darkness curled up like a poor, bleeding dog, Vanilla crawls onto the ground. She presses her body against Tiffany's, against her warmth she can sense but cannot feel, and joins in. She presses her body close because she wants to hear it. She wants to feel it.

Thump-thump. Thump-thump.

That splendid thumping.

"Do you need to be fixed?" But even as she asks it, she knows what the answer is. Broken things never admit to needing to be fixed.

"No."

They lie in thumping, scratching silence.

Vanilla inhales, smelling something familiar. "I feel like I know you," she whispers as she exhales the intoxication.

The scratching stops and Vanilla can tell by the increasingly lethargic *thumps* that Tiffany is no longer awake. That she has fallen asleep with the scratch. So she stops scratching, too.

Maybe they are the same. Maybe Tiffany is a creature or maybe she is simply lost. But something doesn't feel right. Because, as Tiffany's body freely falls into unconsciousness, as she eventually plummets without a single twitch in her muscles, Vanilla remains wide awake, her lollipop long having dissolved, trying her hardest to keep back the lust inside of her begging to rip into Tiffany's chest.

Tiffany can't sleep. She can fake it. She's learned very well how to fake it. How to relax her body so that her internal clock ticks at a low threshold. Low enough to fool a predator. Or a reality she simply wants to avoid.

So she fakes it because she can no longer face Vanilla. Can no longer find the words in her arsenal to pull out in response to this confused girl. Can no longer accept the fact that she scratched *and she scratched, too*. The bad tics and the déjà vu.

She senses Vanilla awake for a couple more hours, and when she shifts around, she can see the whites of her eyes. How they gradually sink behind her thin lids. And finally, when Vanilla falls asleep, it's no different from watching a body die. Her eyes shut, her chest stills, and her skin radiates ice.

So Tiffany lies there, her body touching this body that is arguably a corpse, feeling her own skin turn to ice, wishing for her thoughts to be snuffed out by sleep when all she can do is fake it.

With laughable suffering, she thinks: *Well, better fake it till I make it.*

… PART THREE

CHAPTER XXVII

"Tonight, on Shell City Local: The burnt body of a middle-aged woman was found early this morning at approximately oh nine hundred hours in a secluded alleyway between Colorado Avenue and Fifty-seventh Street. The victim fell prey to the 'wick' effect, burning for approximately one and a half to two hours. There was no trace of accelerant and no evidence of foul play at the scene, concluded forensic experts. Neighbors to the alleyway did not notice the fire and no other witnesses came forward. The woman has been identified as thirty-seven-year-old Greta Charr and today we are interviewing forensic expert—"

The television is muted, but Vanilla continues watching. She attempts to read the passing characters across the bottom of the screen, but they move too quickly for her untrained eyes. Instead she watches the reporter's mouth change shapes, like an excitable

VANILLA

black hole; his expression surrounding his mouth remains perfectly stern.

The reporter isn't actually here. The reporter can't see them, even though she can see him. He isn't shrunk down to size and locked up in that television box, where he'll remain for the rest of eternity—where he'll remain talking or not talking or gesturing information to you for your benefit and your benefit alone.

"No," Tiffany had said when she asked. "He's recorded somewhere else and then that recording is broadcast for the TV."

"Like a moving photograph?"

"Sure. Yeah, exactly."

The reporter isn't here in this dingy neon diner, but Vanilla is—even though Tiffany tried to leave her in the room. She had one foot out the door and it didn't look like she was going to turn back. Vanilla grew anxious watching her, hoping she would tell her to follow along. Tiffany's hand trembled against the edge of the door and it looked like she was about to leave. She was muttering something under her breath. Vanilla was pretty sure she was repeating, "Just go," over and over again. But no one moved.

"All right. You want to come with me? Fine. But there are a few people you gotta know about first. I don't want you getting spooked."

The reporter is replaced with the face of a woman. Her choppy blond hair flashes onscreen, caged within a two-dimensional box. A photograph of a memory. Vanilla's muscles tighten.

"Hey! Why'd you mute it?" the big man behind the counter asks.

"First thing's first, there's Tony. He may look a little scary, but he's as harmless as a teddy bear."

Vanilla turns her attention to Tiffany, who stands in front of the counter holding the remote. She refuses to make eye contact, but Vanilla can see her jaw bulge while Tony stares at her with raw confusion.

"I don't want to hear that crap," Tiffany says.

"Ah! Miss Brave, Miss *Courage* over here suddenly doesn't wanna hear it!" another waitress says with a cackle.

"Then there's Vanessa—or Ness for those who really know her. She's a loud mouth, will probably screech until your ears bleed the color of her hair, but she's a good one. Just don't engage too much and you'll spare your hearing."

"Ness, I think you watch too much news," Tiffany bites back. "It's not good for that little brain—"

The bell chimes, slicing through the conversation. All three of them grow stiff, hairs standing on end like a static balloon just floated between them, before breaking into action as two new bodies enter.

"Finally, we have our customers. I work night shifts, so sometimes the customers aren't as nice as they'd be in the daytime. As long as I do my job and don't talk back, there aren't any problems."

Tiffany grabs two menus from behind the counter, Tony fumbles back into the kitchen, and Ness haphazardly presses buttons on the register. The whole movement is one coordinated performance. A chaotic dance on strings for order.

"And if I do my job and don't talk back, that means you got to sit there quietly and do the same. Understood?"

"Understood."

"Hello!" Tiffany sings in greeting. Her knuckles turn pale from her grip around the menus. "Welcome to Big Daddy's Burger where we always feed you right! Will that be a table for two?"

Vanilla's ears perk up as the two heads nod.

"But, 'customers'? As in other creatures?"

"Why do you keep calling them creatures? I mean, I guess you could. They ain't exactly gentlemen."

Vanilla twirls her thumbs together. The creatures—one large and one thin—look hungry. They step away from the door, which shuts with a second chime, and the wind on their backs that blew their short hair this way and that ceases. Something in the kitchen begins to sizzle and the creatures lick their lips.

"Follow me right this way!" Tiffany says.

She turns with a leading smile but the moment she makes eye contact with Vanilla, her smile fades. Her eyes dart to a space behind her head and Vanilla follows them back to the television, where the screen is changing.

The woman's picture shrinks to the corner of the screen to allow space for the reporter to return. His lips move and Vanilla tries to read them, but she can only understand pieces of a monologue that otherwise remains lost to her.

The woman from the photograph is the same woman from early this morning. She is certain of it. Although she looks different in this image. Younger, but still falling apart. She stands in front of a white wall with black stripes painted across. Her skin looks paler, almost purple, with dark splotches by the base of her neck and cheeks. The bags under her eyes drag her expression downward so she looks sad and tired and altogether darkly wicked rather than animatedly crazed.

Vanilla's torso hovers over the table, her face magnetized to the TV. She's on the verge of deciphering that derelict expression when the screen changes again and the photograph disappears. Characters in flashing yellow pop up onscreen and dance around a line of black. She falls back into her chair with a sigh. Tiffany's voice recaptures her attention.

"Go ahead and take a seat at the booth by the window. It's the best seat in the house."

The creatures follow obediently and take their seats. Vanilla watches as they each take a turn gazing at Tiffany from head to toe. They lick their chapped lips again and Vanilla shudders.

"Can I start you off with any drinks, gentlemen?"

"Yeah, lemme get a chocolate milkshake." The large creature has a voice like concrete. Rough and abrasive. "And your juiciest burger, honey."

Tiffany, unfazed, turns to the other creature. "And for you, sir?"

But this creature isn't paying attention to her pad and pen. His attention is on Vanilla, and he does not flinch when Vanilla meets his stare. In fact, his grin widens; she can see his baby pink gums from beneath his lips.

"I'll take a malted shake," he says. "With some fries. Warm

like an oven."

"Will that be all, sir?" Tiffany sidesteps in front of his view.

He blinks a few times, refocusing from the broken eye contact, and looks up at Tiffany. "Yeah, that'll be all," he snarls.

"Great! I'll be right back with your orders then." She spins and walks into the kitchen, but not before clicking on the machine atop the back counter, which sputters to life with a low whirr, leaving Vanilla alone with the two creatures and Ness at the register.

The thin creature tries to reconnect with Vanilla, who quickly turns away to eye the wall. She wants to follow Tiffany into the back but was specifically ordered to stay in her seat. Still, her spine begs to stand and skitter away. Her thumbs dig one into the other as she chews on the inside of her mouth. A series of pops comes crackling from the kitchen followed by the *pop!* of gum from behind the register. Ness stops clicking buttons and shifts her concerned expression to the blond girl in pigtails.

A wide, toothy grin takes the seat in front of Vanilla. The thin creature exhales, so close now, his sour breath slamming into her nostrils as they stare at each other. Her eyes flicker across his amused expression until he finally speaks.

"What's your name, doll?"

His pale skin against his jet-black hair makes him look like a skull, the ones with sharp jawlines sketched in graphite. But the flesh stretched across those bones gives him an awful expression no matter how dead. Only now does Vanilla notice how that happy smile doesn't reach his eyes.

"Don't feel like talking? Well, that's all right, honey. I can do all the talking for you. My name's Dick. Dick Marcus. And I'd like to take you out on the town. You should be so lucky, too! Girls beg and plead to get a single night with Dicky and here I am offering it up to you like it weren't rare!"

Vanilla stares, dumbstruck, brow furrowed. She can hear his friend snicker in the booth behind him and can see Ness in her periphery watching them, her jaw hanging open like a swing.

"What's the matter? Nobody taken you out before? Nobody ever shown you a good time? That's surprising! I mean, look at you!" He leans over the side of the table to stare down at her legs and drags his eyes up her body. "A hot thing like you? I could do a line off that porcelain skin. Damn, does it look good! In fact, I'll bet you taste just like my shake! I'll bet you taste just like vanilla—"

Vanilla grabs him by the collar and yanks him toward her. He's silenced by the rest of his backed-up words. The snickering stops and Ness quickly turns away to the back counter. The whirr from the machine picks up speed and is accompanied by the metallic screech of chairs against dirty linoleum and the distant sizzling of meat.

"What the—?" Dick breathlessly exclaims, trying his hardest not to choke on his own collar as his upper body struggles against the tabletop.

"Vanilla?" is all she can mutter in answer, her head tilted to the side. The reaction was involuntary, a mix between innocent curiosity and bubbling hunger. But the question remains the same.

How does it know my name?

"Hey! What's the big idea? Let go of me, you freak!"

He starts to sweat. Vanilla watches his collarbones pucker with dew. She feels him writhe against her grip, but her muscles are like concrete. Unmoving and unforgiving. Her stomach speaks up in low growls. She pulls Dick in closer and takes a whiff.

"Hey! Hey, hey, *hey*! Someone get this psycho off me! Buster! Get off your fucking ass and do something!"

Dick flails his arms about, pulling and tugging, but Vanilla doesn't lessen her grip and Buster doesn't move from the booth. He remains frozen and faint from the shock. Spit flies off Dick's tongue and lands on Vanilla's neck. Drool pools in the back of her throat in response to his scent. Between the two of them, they hear a soft tear come from Dick's collar. A slight give from the tug-of-war strength. Dick pauses in shock before all of the blood surges to his face, turning his skin a bright red.

"Let *go* of me!"

Tiffany shuffles out from the kitchen, two plates balanced on her arms with two shakes and a cup she picks up from the back counter held in her hands. Immediately she hustles over to the booth where Dick's friend sits in paralyzed confusion, sets the servings down, and turns toward the scene.

"All right, we're gonna let the nice man go," she says with cool certainty. "C'mon, c'mon. Loosen your grip now." She places her fingers on Vanilla's and gently pries them off.

Dick falls back in his seat, his face wrinkled with anger.

Tiffany wipes down her uniform and turns to him. "Now, sir," she starts, and gestures Dick toward his booth. "Your food is ready, if you wouldn't mind returning to your table."

Dick's expression transforms into disbelief. His mouth opens and closes. Paired with his hunched shoulders, messy shirt, and overall look of defeat, he resembles a small child who has just been blamed for something he did not do. Slowly, he regains his bearings and burrows his glare into the perpetrator, who is staring up at Tiffany in awe. He scoffs and stands abruptly from the table, making the chair screech once again across the floor. Incredulous, he grabs the bottom of his stretched shirt and tugs, puffing out his chest with inflated pride like he wasn't just locked in an inescapable chokehold by a waif of a girl. He turns to Tiffany and begins: "This is unbelievable! Is this the type of people you host in this establishment?"

He allows Tiffany to escort him back to his booth but not without spitting complaints along the way. Tiffany smiles and nods her head in feigned agreement as Vanilla watches on.

Tiffany's smile doesn't reach her eyes either.

"I just don't see how I could give money, no matter the amount, to a place that allows for this kind of assault! I demand my meal be free! Furthermore—"

"Yes, yes. Of course, sir."

Dick slumps back in his booth, a returned gift to his useless friend, and continues his rant. Vanilla turns away from them and tunes out their words. Instead, she pays attention only to their tones and stares at the TV.

The lady never did return to the screen. Her memory is already old news to the public and she is already fading from Vanilla's mind. The reporter now has to share the screen with a picture of a broken building. He seems to struggle for space, as if he might shoulder away the second half of the image.

"Hey, are you okay?" Tiffany appears by her side and places her hand on her shoulder.

Vanilla looks at her and nods.

"Well . . ." Tiffany's lips purse into a line. She shakes her head, replacing her frown with a slight smile, and sets a paper cup down on the table. "I got you a treat. The machine made too much, so I brought you the extra." Her hand slides up Vanilla's neck into her hair, where her fingertips fall in cascading strokes. There's a twinkle in her eye where the warmth swells.

"Thank you."

"Of course." Tiffany pats her head a final two times then returns to the kitchen.

Vanilla watches her leave then looks to the cup. She grips her fingers around the flimsy wet paper and pulls it toward her. She peers inside and moves the cup in circular motions so that the white, lumpy liquid swirls in smacking chunks. She brings the cup to her nostrils and inhales. Her face curls with disgust, but she doesn't allow herself to set the cup down, thinking about Tiffany's warm smile. She forces herself to take a sip. The contents taste like soot spreading across her tongue. She slams the cup down on the table and scrunches her mouth into a horrible pucker, forcing herself to swallow the single sip. Burning grime slides down her throat and singes her stomach. She runs her tongue across her teeth just so she can mask the taste with her own sour saliva and tries not to gag.

She pushes the drink away and shoves her fingers into her sleeve. Frantically, she pulls out a lollipop she snuck from Tiffany's vanity and wedged into hiding between her skin and dress. She knows it was a bad thing to do, that if Tiffany were to find out she might call her a bad girl and not let her have any more lollipops, but the act seems perfectly rational—necessary, in fact, in a case like this. She unwraps the candy and shoves it into her mouth, feeling relieved by the sweet taste. She would throw the stem in a heap of trash later. She lets out a deep sigh and slumps, resting her forehead on the table to stare at her feet.

Meanwhile, Dick has not stopped watching. He's arrested in his booth, his temperature heating up to dangerous levels as he stews in humiliation.

"Hey, Dicky. Just forget about her," Buster whispers after noticing his friend's unwavering glare. "The girl's a quack. Just leave her be. A girl like that don't deserve you, anyway. C'mon. Eat your food and let's get outta here. There're a lot more fish out there in this big city."

"Yeah . . ." Dick mutters. "A lot more fish . . ." He looks over to the register. "Hey, what about you, doll face?"

Ness looks up from where she discreetly hides her phone and smacks her gum, her face shining with bewilderment. "Who? Me?"

Vanilla looks up from her feet to observe.

"Yeah, you." Dick grins, relishing in what he believes is newfound jealousy from the little blonde at the table. *She'll regret denying me. That's right! She'll regret denying good ol' Dicky!*

"What about me?" Ness says.

Dick's face falls blank. His eyebrows knit together. "Well . . . I dunno," he finally concludes. "What's your name?"

Ness snaps her gum, a flash of fear striking her eyes but just as quickly disappearing. "Name's none of ya business, *doll face*."

Dick looks mortified. Ness glances over at Vanilla with a wink.

Vanilla lights up at Ness, whose attention is already directed back at her phone. When she realizes Ness won't be turning her way again, she looks to Dick, whose eyes are burrowing into her in a way she recognizes.

In the way her daddy's did the night she ran away.

CHAPTER XXVIII

Pop.

"Hey, Tiffany?"

Pop.

"Tiff?"

Pop.

"Tiiiiiiifff!"

Vanilla listens to the *thump-thump* thumping pick up speed a few feet away. It explodes.

"Jesus Christ, Ness, *what?*" Tiffany shouts from her place in front of a glass display case.

Dick and his friend, the lustrous creatures who seemed to stick like gum under a table, have left and forty-three other tables have already been served. The sky outside is still dark and it will be hours and hours before the sun peeks out to say *hello*.

"I see ya cleaning up pretty fast. That glass ain't gonna clean itself, don't I know it. But ya seem in quite a nervous rush right now." *Pop.* "I hope it's because you're tryna get home quick for the—"

"Oh, shit! Ness . . ." Tiffany groans, tilting her head back to strike puppy eyes at her coworker.

"No. No, no, *no*, Tiff! C'mon! You promised!"

"I know, Ness, but—"

Ness pops her gum, only this time it sounds like a gunshot.

"'Ey! I don't wanna hear no 'buts'! A promise is a promise, unless you wanna get a load of me!" Ness picks up her fists, shifting into a fraudulent battle stance that's comical at best. But her glare and the way her lips purse to reveal high cheekbones show how serious she is.

Pop!

Tiffany flinches and turns to Vanilla, chewing on her lip. Sizeable elevens crowd between her dark eyebrows. "I had plans tonight," Tiffany whispers under her breath as her eyes flutter to the floor.

"No, no, no! You had plans with me for this party a long, long time ago, Tiff. And ya know that! Ain't no other plans more important than this! I swear, Tiff, if you ditch me again, I will flip! I will flip and you'll never hear the end of it, Tiff—"

"Okay, okay!" Tiffany interrupts before Ness tumbles into a meltdown. "I'll go, I'll go. But I'm bringing her," she concludes, pointing at Vanilla like a child would point at a puppy.

"That's fine! All the merrier! In fact, I was hoping ya would!"

Ness throws her hands up into the air. She drops her thin sticks for limbs back down to her sides and walks over to Vanilla, who has been watching with innocent fascination. The *thump* that comes from Ness's chest seems to grow heavier with every step she takes in her direction. When Ness reaches her, she sets her elbows down on the table and props her head up on her hands. "This little miss will be more than welcomed. Such a beautiful thing, it's hard to believe ya related to Tiff, even if it's distant enough to put ya's on different ends of the spectrum!" Ness reels her head back and laughs. "Ya gorgeous, you know that, babe?"

Vanilla notes how Ness's lips shine like they're layered by a thick gloss of drool. She nods her head in agreement with whatever Ness says. Ness, who is another one of those creatures that seems to fall into the category of "exceptionally pleasant."

"*Oh!* Not so *humble* now, are we? That's fine," Ness continues. "In this day and age, a girl's gotta know her worth. Otherwise these men out there will swallow you whole, like ya another ol' piece a candy."

Vanilla cringes at the thought of a creature shoving her down its gullet. A flashing image of her legs kicking and thrashing just outside of Tiffany's unhinged jaw makes her teeth hurt.

"It's a man-eat-woman world out there. You can't just be pretty and strong like you is. Like how you showed us earlier!" Ness reaches her hand out and strokes Vanilla's face. "And lemme tell ya, babes, you as pretty as they come. But ya gotta be smart as well. Like Tiffany over there! But for how beautiful, smart, and strong she is, Lord knows she has her own problems!" Ness laughs again, the pitch of her cackle increasing.

"All right, Ness. That's enough."

"Aw, don't be all grumpy like that, Tiff." She looks over at a frowning Tiffany standing by the counter with hitched shoulders. "I'm only warning the girl. Ain't no harm in that. Probably the best thing someone'll ever do for her." She turns back to Vanilla. "Ya gonna have so much fun at this party. We'll show you a real witching-hour disco! What's ya name, babes? Gotta call you something other than 'Tiffany's distant cousin.'"

Vanilla stares at Ness in awe, listening to the strangely accented words as they pour out of her lips.

"C'mon. Ya gotta have a name."

Ness brushes her thumb across Vanilla's cheek, her eyes glimmering as they shift like they're reading one of Daddy's books.

"Vanilla," she whispers.

"Vanilla?!" Ness squeals as she removes her hand from Vanilla's face and slams it down on the table. "Oh, sweet thing, ya name's Vanilla? Oh, *har-har*, did ya daddy name ya after what you is! He set you up to be a star, didn't he?"

Vanilla's mouth curls uncontrollably, enjoying Ness's voice as it rolls out her name.

"Vanilla, Vanilla! Oh, sweet, sweet thing, Vanilla!" she sings.

Ness dances around the table, clapping her hands. Vanilla mimics the claps with a giggle. She likes the way her skin smacking together makes a celebratory *slap!* and how it falls in rhythm with Ness's thumping. *Sweet, dancing, giggling Ness.*

Vanilla's stomach growls.

"All right, I think it's time to go," Tiffany interrupts, walking between Ness and the table. She's already visited the kitchen stealthily to retrieve her things and now stands with her purse and jacket in hand, her body shifting with nerves. "We have to go home and get ready. We'll see you there then, Ness." She grabs Vanilla by the hand. "Let's go," she orders, yanking her up from her seat and walking her out the door.

"Can't wait to see ya there, you two!" Ness calls from behind.

"Why are you upset?" Vanilla asks when they enter the Outside and Ness's laughter is cut off by the door.

"What?" Tiffany answers, only half paying attention. "Oh . . . no, I'm not." She searches the dark street, turning her head over each shoulder.

"Are you looking for something?" Vanilla asks.

"No." She grabs Vanilla, who knows Tiffany is lying, by the arm and quickly pulls her down the sidewalk. "Let's hurry up," she says, addressing Vanilla but looking elsewhere. "We have a damn, fucking party to get ready for."

CHAPTER XXIX

The night is exceptionally freezing, but Vanilla doesn't gasp with salvation when they enter Tiffany's room. She doesn't cry out, thankful for the heat. She simply steps inside, delicately removes her shoes—the shoes she seems to strongly dislike, though she won't willingly show any sign of it—and sits down at the vanity. Her freezing skin, protected only by a thin dress since she never asked for a jacket, gradually rises to match the room's temperature.

Tiffany stands behind her, staring at her blond-blanketed back, knowing that Vanilla is staring at the pile of lollipops on the counter. The ones given to her by a monster. There's an overflowing cauldron of questions she tries to shove down the gullet of her brain, but the bubbles keep rising. Rising and rising until they burn the skin up to her wrists and she has no other choice but to flinch and let them rise higher.

"Tiffany?"

"Yes?"

"What's a 'party'?"

Tiffany nearly bursts out with laughter, in part because the question is so obvious and in part because her sanity is slowly breaking. She sucks the tremors back down.

"It's when people get together to have fun. Ness likes to throw them—"

"So a party is an object you throw? At others? To have fun?"

Tiffany clenches her lips together. Her mouth trembles as it barricades more incoming laughter. A sudden desire to scoop Vanilla up in her arms, to hold her with all the love in the world she was never afforded, overcomes her, but she stands her ground.

"Why would people get together to have things thrown at them?"

That desire molts into despair. Into the immediate realization that this girl might have never been free. Might have never tasted real air until recently. A sucker punch of pity charges into her gut.

"No. A party is like what you call a gathering of people. *Throwing* a party is just how you say it."

"Oh. An expression?"

"Yes," Tiffany says with surprise. "You're pretty quick. Yes, it's an expression."

Vanilla smiles, pleased with herself. Like how a child might be happy after making their father proud. Only Tiffany wishes she weren't about to ruin it. To turn that happiness sour.

"It doesn't matter anyway," she grumbles, the need to vomit

now washing over her. The lack of conviction fights against her will. "We aren't going."

"What? Why not?" Vanilla whips around in her seat and stares pleadingly at Tiffany. The dim light casts ugly shadows about the blonde's face and Tiffany nearly falls back in fear. But she stops herself, knowing she isn't the one of the two who should be afraid.

She wants to hurl. Maybe her vomit will spew and burn Vanilla into ashes so she won't have to consciously commit the crime herself. Or maybe she'll gag so strongly that the force will empty her of all her organs and she can die peacefully on a pile of her innards.

But you already know . . .

She's trapped.

. . . that dying is pain!

"If it's fun, why wouldn't you go?"

Acrid saliva builds in the back of Tiffany's jaw. Her skin, only moments ago so cold, now prickles with sweat. A voice, so small, screams inside her head: *You're not ready! Buy time! Buy time! Buytimebuytimebuytimebuy—*

The oxygen leaves her system, and she knows that if she moves now she'll only stumble and fall. And what a nightmare that would be. *To lunge forward with a knife only to trip on my own weak body and impale myself.*

"Tiffany . . . if something is fun, why wouldn't you want to go?"

I can see this going two ways: I buy time and get dismembered for it, or I do this now and most likely still get dismembered for it.

A million other scenarios zoom through Tiffany's mind: reasons why she should go—to avoid suspicion, to avoid Vanessa's rage; reasons why she should just lock the door and board up the window—to avoid a monster, to not die herself. But in the end, she knows what she is capable of.

"You're right," she wheezes. "You're right. You do go. *We* will go. Okay?"

"Okay!" Vanilla's teeth gleam and the shadows lift about her face.

"We will go. But if we're going to—" Tiffany chokes on hot mucus. "If we're going to do this, we are going to do this right." The nerves slowly ascend from Tiffany's body, bubbles unlatching from skin and innocuously rising to the surface. But her gut still churns, even if only a little. It reminds her of when she was no more than four feet tall, standing by her mother's vanity, watching her with tears in her eyes after a whooping because she spilled her cereal carelessly all over the new carpet. Watching her mother smile in the mirror, telling her it would be all right, *it's just so you can learn, my love, because you know how Daddy gets*, while she plucked and painted what she called "artwork on skin." How the tears dried up from her face and her chest stopped palpitating with snotty cries while her mother smeared rainbows across her lids.

How those brush strokes and colors were replaced with needles and nothing but red.

Tiffany gulps and turns to the mirror, seeing the bags under her tired, sunken eyes. The ashen quality to her petrified skin and the patches of red that are slowly lifting to the surface like an

VANILLA

allergic reaction to fear. Like a reaction to memories that haven't dared to cross her thoughts since they were formed. She turns back to Vanilla and with a clenched throat manages to ask the girl with the perfect face, unblemished by fright:

"Have you ever worn makeup?"

Vanilla turns back toward the vanity, too, and meets her gaze through the mirror. "What is 'makeup'?" she asks, flopping her tongue around the word.

"Welp, that answers my question." Tiffany steps over, leaving her frozen terror behind and embracing distraction. She leans against the vanity to face Vanilla. "A little mascara, some lipstick . . . blush to liven up that pale face." She can feel her voice wanting to crack with screams, the little girl inside of her saying, *It's not the same!* "It's like paint and pencils . . . artwork for your skin."

She pinches Vanilla's cheeks to get some color into them, but they remain white. She can't feel the temperature of that pale skin. Like it matches her own exactly, camouflaging into her touch.

Vanilla looks up at her. "Like graphite?"

"Like what? Graph— *Sure* . . . sure. Like graphite."

Vanilla nods, but her bottom lip is pulled in between her teeth.

"Here—" Tiffany grabs a lollipop and unwraps it mechanically, automatically, staving off the trembling in her wrists. "It's no big deal. Suck on this while I do it."

Vanilla's tongue drops from her mouth and Tiffany pastes the candy to her flesh. There they hesitate: two girls cut from different cloth, yet here, stapled to the same moment, on opposite ends of receiving.

Then Tiffany begins. Just as her mother once did while the little girl fell and fell endlessly into the trance. Vanilla's skin is freshly blown glass. An unblemished canvas; a still pool of water. Dipping sticks into her eyes and brushes across her face disturbs that water, flushing droplets from her lids. But the body still never moves, partially because it is landlocked and partially because it is happy to be where it is. Partially because it smells something in the river across from it that makes it feel at home. Tiffany's skin is that raging river of concrete. Faded scars, sun marks, and streaks that look like permanent tear trails. Texture—a montage of a life in the Outside blended with expressions from generations old. A picture only a hand's width away from Vanilla's face as Tiffany's breath washes over the tip of her nose. *A beautiful sketch.* Another pencil dips into that pool and Vanilla can't help but wonder why anyone would sit through this torture. Why *she* is sitting through this torture.

"This is eyeliner. It'll make your eyes pop."

It's because Tiffany asked me to. It's because she wants to sketch me in things other than graphite.

"Pop?! I want them to stay where they are!"

"No, no! It's okay! *Pop* just means 'attention grabbing.' Your eyes aren't leaving your face, I promise you."

When the sketch is complete, the sticks are put away.

"There. Done." Tiffany smiles, a short sigh escaping her lips. She stands and moves away from the mirror, her body visibly shaking now, whereas during the procedure it was wound tight with focus.

Vanilla doesn't need to gravitate much closer to her reflection for the shock to ensue. The image staring back at her—the image that is supposed to be her—looks very different yet the same. Like some foreign entity is attempting to be her. To devour her and regurgitate a picture of her onto its own flesh.

"Do you like it?" Tiffany asks when she notices Vanilla's delayed response. Her hands unlatch from each other in front of her chest and fall to her sides, fingers twitching and shoulders slumped. "Do you . . . do you like it?"

Vanilla hates the frown growing on Tiffany's face. She wants to turn around and scratch it away. Scratch it into a smile. So when she turns and says, "It is beautiful," and Tiffany lights up, she feels she is doing just that.

"All right . . ." Tiffany starts, ready for the next task, but then her mind flashes to Vanilla's shoes. How she tumbles over her own legs like she's wearing bricks of magnets and can't navigate her own body away from the pull. How uncomfortable she seems but still carries on. *Because she knows I want her to. Because she thinks it'll make me happy.* "You wouldn't want to try on something other than that dress, would you?"

Vanilla tenses. Her eyes grow wide and her jaw tightens, clamping teeth together like an iron maiden so that Tiffany is answered with a sharp *crunch*. The lollipop shatters to pieces across Vanilla's tongue. Her shock ignites, but Tiffany doesn't yell. She doesn't scream and thrash her arms in the air, calling Vanilla a filthy little girl, nor does she threaten to leave the room.

To leave Vanilla all by her lonesome. Instead, she looks down upon her with eyes identical to her own, if only for the sorrow that fills them, and lifts the palm of her hand to her cheek. Her thumb brushes across the bones below her sockets.

"I'll wear something else if you'd like," Vanilla says. "I'll wear whatever you'd like me to."

Tiffany removes the naked stem from Vanilla's mouth. "No. That's okay. You don't have to try anything else if you don't want to."

She turns to her vanity and plucks a lollipop from the glass jar. When she turns back, Vanilla's tongue is already hanging down her chin. Tiffany hesitates for a moment, staring at her plump lips and long tongue. Those teeth that sparkle and the two that jut out almost as if . . .

As if replacing love and rainbows with hate and steel.

Her heart picks up—she can feel it in her chest and Vanilla can hear it in her skull. Vanilla inches to the edge of her chair, toward that *thump*, although Tiffany doesn't understand that this is why. She thinks something else incites this attraction. Incites the proximity. The touch of Vanilla's inner thighs on her hips. Her mouth just beneath her chest.

Tiffany is motioning the candy to Vanilla when she makes eye contact with those wet, desperate eyes and decides to redirect, like an adult stealing from a baby. She takes the candy and holds it up to her own mouth, in front of her breath, trying to detect a scent but smelling only her own hot air. Wanting to know, wanting to be pushed out of the dark yet not daring to touch the thing directly to her tongue, she gives the lollipop a kiss.

Her mouth peels away and she returns the lollipop to Vanilla, who slowly bites down, crunching it softly between her teeth. Vanilla tilts her head to the side, feeling something within her flutter. Tiffany can't help but smile, spreading her mouth from ear to ear with the hope that this innocent-seeming moment could last. That they could remain frozen in time with no course of action forever. No monsters to get them. But her tongue curdles as she licks her lips, tasting stale iron. The shadow of the lollipop leaves a bitter knowledge. She opens her mouth, wanting to blow away the taste, wanting to understand why a flavor so cursed is stuck to her tongue—

Before she can try, there's a knock on the window.

Then another.

It begins quietly at first, like the soft tapping of a twig on a windy night. Something easily unnoticed. But soon the knocks increase in frequency, banging against the glass, until the slamming grows so violent it screams and screams for attention, threatening to shatter the window to pieces.

Startled, the girls both turn toward the sound. Tiffany, who stands in front of Vanilla, blocking her view, is the only one to see the large, pale fist torturing the glass through the slit of curtains. As soon as her eyes make contact with it, it disappears.

"Was that a creature?" Vanilla whispers.

Tiffany can't find the strength to remove her eyes from the window. Her heart clogs her throat.

"Tiffany?" Vanilla taps her on her shoulder. She can feel her body shaking. "Tiffany, it's fine," she says, holding her arms at both sides and turning her back around. "I'm here and you're safe," she assures.

Tiffany stares at her. At this sweet, innocent thing in front of her, her skin painted with her mother's artwork. She bows to the return of guilt. Guilt that keeps her in this moment from obeying the monster that just threatened her within the confines of her own room. Guilt that makes her feel sick to her core. So sick she could keel over and collapse into Vanilla's lap.

Guilt that makes her want to disappear.

That makes her want to curl up. Shrink until there's nothing left.

She returns from the infinite trance of submission and forces a smile.

"Yeah. I already know."

CHAPTER XXX

"I already know. There's no point."

The girls are walking down the centerline of the street. The sun is hours from waking and the streetlamps struggle to keep alight. Their flickering makes Vanilla nauseated, but she follows them nonetheless. Because Tiffany follows them. Tiffany, who is vibrating by her side like she's cold, though Vanilla herself can't feel if there is a chill.

Tiffany's eyes are deadlocked, glued to the ground in front of her, and it's as if they might just fall out of her head and stick, and Tiffany would just keep walking, her mind lost somewhere far, far away from these present pavement footsteps. Far, far away from Vanilla, who wishes Tiffany were warm. Warm like Tiffany was before she stared at herself in the mirror in her room, her beautiful face ruined with concentration. Before her chest collapsed and she turned to her to say: *"There's no point. I already know. There's no point."* She laughed like the seams that stitched her smile together might break without warning and then she walked out the door. *Skipped* out, in fact.

Before she could break any further. *And isn't it that the more Tiffany breaks, the hungrier I feel?*

The street is empty as they make their way, but still there are whispers. Soft whispers coming from the dark cracks between buildings. Vanilla looks over into the alleyways, where she finds rows of strange eyes staring back at her. Strange eyes made up of all shades of brown. Ones that look vibrant and thirsty. Ones that might belong to snakes waiting to slither out from their homes for a fresh meal, their mouths unhinged and tongues jutting out like forks ready to feast. Inching and slithering closer and closer. A hand gropes for hers and constricts. She looks over to see Tiffany staring at her, her mind unhappily back in this world. Her plump lips mouth around the word *Don't*.

"Nice night out, isn't it, ladies?" the whispers say. The eyes twitch as they speak and Vanilla imagines their spiked tongues darting in and out between their jaws. Tiffany tightens her grip, squeezing Vanilla's hand as though she is trying to squeeze the blood out from her fingertips to create spurting fountains. "Are you ladies looking to go for a spin?" Off-key laughter and wheezing. "*A spin* . . . and we can show you a good time. *A grand ol' time.* How about you join us? It'll be fun." Harsh whispers, too low to register. "There's only two of you . . . only two and so many of us to go around." Throat clicks and slurping, the sucking of saliva as it drips off open lips. "C'mon, what do ya say, ladies?"

Vanilla stops. Tiffany tries to tug on her arm but Vanilla refuses to move, a stone statue fixed toward the dark alleyway. Toward a particular set of eyes that have not spoken. Piercingly bright blue ones that lay deep within the shadows and have been watching her with intense focus.

"Yes. That's right, my sweet," the eyes speak, the subtle melody in their depth so familiar, drowning out everything else. "That's right . . . come closer . . ."

Vanilla stiffens her hand, forcing Tiffany off. Tiffany tries gravely to hold on tighter, but Vanilla is stronger and pries the fingers away like petals. Because suddenly her brain feels like it's melting. Like that voice has infiltrated her skull, reminding her of something she has been so bad to have forgotten. *You foolish, foolish girl! Don't you remember?* And she needs so desperately to remember.

"Hey!" Tiffany snarls. But her attempts are useless. She stands by helplessly as Vanilla drifts away toward the black. Her feet are planted on the ground, keeping her from chasing that blond hair back to safety. Still she tries, knowing that losing her will sprout millions of roots in the directions of both Heaven and Hell. "Hey, what do you think you're doing? *Get back here!*"

But Vanilla isn't listening. Each step brings her closer and closer until her foot, covered in stiff rubber that she cannot desensitize from, passes the threshold, and the inky cave engulfs her. But no matter how many steps she takes, the blue eyes seem to be traveling away, like an optical illusion, always five steps ahead in endless night.

"Such a beautiful sight. Come closer, you sweet thing . . . come closer so that I can admire you . . ."

Vanilla obeys. She obeys and obeys until the eyes stop traveling and are mere inches from her own. Until her sight adjusts and she can see that they are truly somehow floating amidst the bricks and garbage—the only vibrancy in a sea of stillness. They curve into a smile and whisper:

"Oh . . . how I've missed you."

Vanilla sighs into them, wanting to fall into that blue. Wanting to be wrapped around the cords of that voice. Wanting to feel them touch her skin. And these eyes are happy to charm her—elated indeed!—to offer a distraction while a scent creeps out from under her unsuspecting chin. A strong, pungent smell that would make others keel over with tears of disgust but explodes vivaciously within Vanilla's nostrils. There is no delay in her body's reaction, a short moment for the back of her throat to taste the scent before her stomach abruptly wakes and screams out for it. Her jaw clicks. Her muscles force her bones into stiff patterns that make her hunch over and grunt. Her tongue blossoms out from between the pink flesh of her inner mouth as her body yearns to find the source of that sweet scent. And all the while, she can't stop looking at those eyes.

"That's right, my sweet . . . closer . . ."

Vanilla's head jerks forward, her mouth longing to bite down on the taste. Her teeth miss and painfully clack against each other. She sniffs, nostrils flaring to relocate the smell, her head gyrating so fast that it just might snap off. But she can't help it—the pain in her stomach is begging for it. *Pleading* for it. A bitter hole in her crying out to be filled. To be whole once again.

From beneath those electric blues comes a deep chuckle. A hair-raising sound that Vanilla wishes she could fall into if only her body weren't reacting so immensely. Like a wire, snapped, disconnecting her extremities from her mind.

The laughter stops, fades to whispers. The blue blends to black and the scent slowly dies. Vanilla cries out, reaches for it, lunging like her arm is an extension of her hunger. But the blue shuts like a solid metal door slammed into its frame and does not reopen. Her hand smashes into a wall, fingers breaking upon impact then snapping back into place with a wail.

The eyes are gone. Only now does she see the cinder blocks in front of her. Only now does she question whether the eyes were there at all or if she was just projecting them onto this backdrop. But the click in her jaw and the hunger dissolving her insides make her feel otherwise.

Her stomach lurches. Again all thought extinguishes from her mind. She continues searching for the scent like a fiending animal. She twists around herself, whimpering for the answer to her discomfort. But there is only silence and the smell of wet garbage.

A hand clamps down on her shoulder. Her muscles react with a twitch, every fiber tensing in a ripple effect. She spins around, grabbing the hand and slipping her fingers between the spaces of its digits, and yanks it toward her. A body, soft yet firm like a heavy blanket, falls against hers with a delicate harumph.

"Fuckin' A! It's only me!" Tiffany yells. "Why'd you leave me alone out there?" Her complaints light up Vanilla's senses. "Where the hell did you go?"

Vanilla inhales, watching Tiffany's eyes search for her in the dark, bottom lip quivering as her sight pulls in nothing but the pitch black. Nothing that lurks within it. Vanilla inches closer, her nose a breath away from Tiffany's mouth, and inhales again. The back of her jaw bursts with sweet acid.

Thump-thump. Thump-thump.

Vanilla wants to take her hand, fingers curved into a spade, and hold that thump in her palm. Dig into Tiffany's chest, breaking through muscle and rib to feel that pulsing warmth. Her eyes hurt, bursting inside her head, morphing and churning into an unbearable headache like gears grinding at the dead gray matter. Tiffany's aroma is immense, her proximity titillating. Palpable and magnetic. Her tongue might as well be touching Tiffany's skin if she were to let it loose from behind her teeth. If she were to only just lean in a little closer . . .

Vanilla's mouth drops into a slit—no more, no less—her top lip lifting. She tightens her grip around Tiffany's trembling hand while a hidden part of her keeps from crunching down on bone. Breaking skin, each web between fingers splitting so that everything wonderful, *everything beautiful and hidden inside pours out in a glorious wave of—*

"Fuck! That hurts!" Tiffany yelps. "I didn't mean to frighten you, I'm sorry, but let's calm down and get out of here, okay? It's creepy and no one should be lingering in dark alleyways, especially us. It's like a damn snake pit in here."

Tiffany twists Vanilla's arm and grabs her wrist. The sudden shift in power stops Vanilla in her tracks. She's dragged out of the alley. Out of that innate black. The blue eyes have already fallen from her mind. So has the scent and her reaction to it. Only the agitation remains, small magnets on endless charge vibrating between her fibers.

The lights from the streetlamps seem brighter than before. Too bright. They pierce her pupils like molecular needles. And even when she closes her eyes, the lights penetrate through her lids. Through her skin. Now the thumping is in her skull. It's pulsating, it's burning, *it's on fire!*

She stares at the concrete. Glues her eyes to the sidewalk. Watches her feet trample before her as Tiffany nearly sprints down the road. She holds her breath in an attempt to lessen her sensory strain. All the while, she can't get that thought out of her head:

It's like a damn snake pit in here.

CHAPTER XXXI

The wind is vicious. Either that or they're moving so fast the still air smacks them with its backhand. Vanilla can feel the smacks against her skin but she refuses to look up and greet the wind. She wants to remain with her head down, watching her feet move, rather than look up and see all the buildings and lights as they rush past her. All the shining pain she can't look at, all the air that won't fill her lungs. A few turns, a few steps, three over and two up—

And they stop. Vanilla hears something. A tangled mess of noise on a loop. Something like humming, only inhuman and more pronounced. Metallic, like scratching a syringe against a metal door. It bleeds into the ground and roots through the soles of her feet. She can feel her muscles thump against it.

Is this supposed to be music?

A knock. A door creaks. The string of sound grows louder.

"Tiff! Ya finally here!"

"I told you I'd come."

Tiffany releases her grip and Vanilla reacts to the loss of contact, finally looking up. A doorway looms in front of her. Ness is in it wearing a strange yellow-and-brown-speckled dress, arms wide open and welcoming. She looks excited, smiling from ear to ear, but her eyes move constantly as if searching for something that isn't there.

"Oh, shush with ya attitude!" Ness envelops Tiffany like her arms are jaws snapping down on fresh prey. Her blush-ridden face burrows into the curve of Tiffany's neck, leers up, and spots Vanilla. Her eyes adjust to the new sight and her smile shifts into a grin. "And look! It's sweet, sweet Vanilla!" she sings out, letting go of Tiffany and latching onto the new prey. "Oh, hug me back, ya silly girl! What? Ya don't know what a hug is? Ya so stiff!"

Vanilla lifts her arms and wraps them noncommittally around the redhead's waist. A perfume of sweet iron escapes from her skin and Vanilla wants to lick it from her neck. To dig her tongue into the curve like Ness dug her face into Tiffany's. Instead, some of her fire-red hair gets caught between Vanilla's lips. She chews on it for a moment before spitting it out with disinterest.

Ness pulls back without releasing her hold. In fact, it tightens. She visually takes in the little blonde, absorbing her from crown to toe.

"I see ya haven't changed since the diner..." Ness looks momentarily disappointed. "That's all fine, babe. The outfit suits ya. And I like the makeup!" She gestures to Tiffany's outfit with contempt. "I see *neither* of ya changed. What the hell, Tiff? Ya living in your work clothes now? All right, all right. No need to look guilty. I know ya tried and I'm just happy ya came. Well? Shall we join the party? Welcome, welcome! Come on in!"

Vanilla's skin crawls when she steps toward the door, but Ness pulls her in with welcoming eyes and lips that bid her access. A second step crosses the threshold and immediately the atmosphere changes. Those tenebrous pricks that ailed her pores are washed away. There is no wind here—no air, nor much space. They're suffocated by loud, awful sounds and lights, bodies of creatures clustered together in tight packs of raging motion, heads of all hues bobbing like a wave, smells of iron and smoke, steaming adrenaline, and the touch of Ness's fingers gliding across Vanilla's hips.

"Everyone! Look who's here! It's Tiffany!"

Ness's shout is so loud it stings Vanilla's eardrum, and she hisses under her breath. But that voice carries across the crowd and scattered individuals pop out like rats from sewers in search of food. After confirming Tiffany's presence, they squeeze out from their grates to greet her.

"Tiffany, my love!"

"It's been so long!"

"We've missed you!"

Shouts volley from this way and that, trying to overcome each other and be heard against the cacophony. The creatures grab at Tiffany, covering her body with hooked hands. She squirms against them. Vanilla takes a step toward her, trying to ask why she's suddenly surrounded by all of these raging creatures, but she's snatched away before she can reach.

"Where do ya think *you're* going?" Ness whispers. She smiles at Vanilla, purses her lips, and lifts her chin to shout, "Don't worry, Tiff! I've got her!"

The layers of hands grow, covering more and more of Tiffany until she flashes Vanilla one last look and mouths *It's okay . . . you're safe.* Tiffany forces a smile and gives in, vanishing into the storm of bodies.

"Tiffany?" Vanilla whispers when she can no longer see her. Her eyebrows furrow; her eyes dart from side to side. Her body tenses and she wants to scream, but she holds the sound tight in her throat like a knot.

"Oh, don't worry, babe. Tiffany'll be back soon. She's just saying hello to some old friends for now. Come on now, sweet Vanilla!"

Vanilla follows with hesitation. *It's like a damn snake pit in here.* But Tiffany led them to it. Tiffany, with her face carved in discomfort. A topography of anxiety. Vanilla tries to understand why she would take them to something so awful. Away from the comforting black and into this madness.

Ness leads her to the edge of the large room. The extra space and distance from loud noises makes Vanilla relax, like settling into a bath after a breathtaking tantrum. From her periphery, she sees Ness conjure up a large glass bottle of water from between two doors in the wall, then grab a bright red cup and tip the nozzle over. The bottle spills, gulping with vigor as it empties into the cup.

"Here, drink," Ness orders as she shoves the cup into Vanilla's chest.

Ness's voice is commanding but her face kind. Vanilla brings the cup to her lips in incremental steps, cautious about the water inside and those demanding eyes staring her down. The first step makes her stomach curdle because the stench from the cup has misted into her face. The second step makes her wonder why this water smells so awful. The third step burns her eyes. She blinks a few times, trying to soothe them, but the discomfort only grows. A tear leaks and drips into the cup. She doesn't remember the last time she cried.

"Go ahead, honey! It's not gonna kill ya! Drink!" Ness places her fingertips under the cup and tilts it upward, forcing a stream of whatever this is to pour down Vanilla's throat.

And it tastes like fire.

Vanilla coughs and sputters, nearly dropping the cup, but Ness snatches it from her hands before it can fall. A dizziness overwhelms her and she grips onto a nearby counter to center her bleeding vision.

"What's wrong? Can't hold ya liquor?" Ness cackles.

Vanilla tries to get the sting out of her mouth. Tries to push the terrible taste and the lurching in her stomach away. She drops her tongue from her jaw and pants, saliva dripping off the tip and onto the floor.

"Hey, hey! You okay? Sheesh, sorry. I didn't think you'd react like that . . ." Ness's face strangles with concern then relaxes into something hungry. "But my, my . . . what a long tongue you have." A groan escapes her throat and she takes a step closer. "Do ya want another sip? Just another taste? The pain grows mighty addictive." She holds the cup back up to Vanilla's lips and her smile drips with temptation.

Vanilla shakes her head, pleading no. She holds her breath, desperate to avoid another inhalation of that liquid fire.

"All right, honey. That's no problem." Ness sets the cup down on the counter and grabs Vanilla's hand. "Come."

Vanilla doesn't want to go any farther, but she'd already decided she would agree. In Tiffany's absence, she would agree with Ness. *Because Ness is pleasant, isn't she?* She's pulled away from the counter and from the doors holding fire water and is forced through the crowd of creatures. Her skin tightens as she is digested between jumping, slithering bodies in rhythm with blaring sounds and beating lights. Her senses swell, but there's a sweet aroma, unique for each individual in the room, that soothes her, and although the scents are hidden behind odors, she can discern each one like pins on a grid.

But one scent is missing.

She pulls back against Ness, forcing her to jerk and face her with surprise.

"Where is Tiffany?" she asks.

Ness smiles and strokes the back of her hand against Vanilla's cheek, brushing her hair behind her ear. "Tiffany is talking with some friends right now. She hasn't seen 'em in a while and we want to give her space to say hello. Right?"

Vanilla nods, pressing her lips together in a tight line. Her stomach rumbles.

"What? Don'tcha like my company? I thought maybe we could—"

"My *god*, you are beautiful."

A deep voice licks at Vanilla's spine. Ness's face drains of color. Her teeth clench and she stares daggers at whatever spoke from behind. Vanilla's ears perk up as something taps her shoulder, egging her to turn around. She does so and confronts the face connected with the voice.

A tall creature, blond hair like hers and a coy glint in his dark eyes, stands in front of her. He holds out his cup and says, "I see you don't have a drink in your hand. Could I offer to fix you one? I make them real—"

"Excuse me, but we ain't accepting dick tonight," Ness hisses, taking a defensive step in front of Vanilla.

"All right, Ness. I wasn't talking to you, I was talking to—"

"Well, tonight I'm speaking for her! And like I said, we ain't accepting dick!"

"Jesus Christ, Ness. I dunno why you always have to be such a bossy—"

Ness yanks Vanilla away, forcing them both back into the chaos, cutting off the creature's response with a barrier of bodies. Swallowed into the fray once more. Ness has summoned extra brute strength from the interaction to pull them through, and Vanilla tenses her tendons around that grip and against that rip.

Fingers graze her skin. She tries to nudge them off, but more take their place. Her vision, still dizzy from the drink, swamps with dirty colors and ghostlike motions, a shutter of silhouetted movement. She turns her head to chomp at the extended limbs, nostrils flaring as her agitation blooms. Her mouth leaks and she comes close to ripping off an entire arm. But these creatures are quick enough to unknowingly avoid her. When the two finally squeeze out from the crowd, Vanilla's senses cool down. She turns back and watches the creatures, all clustered in the center of the space, clinging to one another like parasites.

Ness's fingertips tiptoe across Vanilla's palm until they unite with her fingers. She takes them up a set of wooden stairs that creak with each step—feeble and unreliable, not stairs built from concrete. Ness looks down at her every two steps and Vanilla attempts to return her smile. They come to the top of the staircase, where Vanilla expects to see an extended hallway with rows of metal doors. But this image is overexposed against the reality of beige carpet splitting down two short hallways to the left and right. There are only three doors made of glazed wood, not several lined up like iron soldiers.

Ness turns right and opens the door at the far end of the hallway. She motions for Vanilla to enter first.

The room is huge, massive, in fact, centered by a colossal mattress that seems to be the room's only want or need. A huge cloud floating on glass blocks. On either side of the mattress are closet doors filed neatly yet bursting with bright and colorful clothing. Paintings in black and white hang across the beige walls and discarded items are tossed about the floor.

"I like your room," Vanilla says, a hint of jealousy seeding within her.

"Thank you."

Vanilla hears the door behind her shut. The noise running around her eardrums since they arrived is mercifully muffled. Snuffed out by a wooden click. When she spins around, Ness is standing right in front of her with a deep grin and thirsty eyes. She places her hands on Vanilla's shoulders and shoves. The backs of Vanilla's legs hit the bedframe and her knees buckle, collapsing her onto the bed.

Vanilla tries to prop herself back up, startled, but Ness climbs on top and settles her down with the crushing weight of her body. "*Shhhhhh* . . . there, there, sweet Vanilla."

"What are you . . . what are you doing?"

"I'm doing what I want . . . what *we* want." Ness brushes her fingertips across Vanilla's lips. The taste of Ness's skin makes the backs of her eyes light up with effervescence. "There, see? Don't ya like it? I can hear ya purring." Ness smiles and nuzzles herself into the cavity that is an incapacitated Vanilla. The girl who can't help her taste for creatures. "Let me tell ya a story, little Vanilla." Ness's thigh travels up the bed. The sheets whine from the friction. "When I was a little girl, I was the prettiest little girl in the schoolyard. It's true! All the boys chased after me. They gave me flowers and crappy poetry. They tugged on my hair and tried to hold my hand. But I ran from 'em. Each and every one of 'em. They all disgusted me, the savages. And I did everything I could to get away.

"One girl, who looked just like you, sweet blond hair and pale skin, would hide me away and keep back all of those savage little boys. Fight them off! 'Cause she knew how much they bugged me. And they probably bugged her, too. She became my best friend. I brought her over to my house and we would play and play and play all day and deep into the night.

"One night, we played a little too close and my daddy found us in the middle of it all . . ." Ness clicks her tongue and shakes her head, rubbing her nose against Vanilla's. "Oh, my daddy did not like that. Not—one—bit.

"I begged and cried for him to leave her alone, to let her go, that it was all my fault. But, you see, my daddy had a temper. Didn't matter that she was just a little girl, that she didn't know what she was doing, or that maybe she was only trying something new with a close friend. Maybe that close friend convinced her first. But no, to him, she was the devil! And what do we do with devils?"

Ness pauses, then continues for her audience of one.

"We strike 'em and toss 'em out! Which is exactly what my daddy did. Exactly what he did to my poor, beautiful friend. 'Ya coulda had any boy ya want—beautiful, ugly, smart, dumb, Black, white, goddamn *old* if ya'd like! But ain't no daughter of mine gonna be a whore with the other girls like some kinda homosexual prostitute!' And he did everything in his power to make sure of it. He grabbed my dear, beautiful friend by the arm, dragged her across the living room, didn't stop no matter how hard she cried or how much I screamed, and threw her out on the street. Just like that. No calling her parents, no making sure she got home safe, no nothin'.

"The next day, she wasn't in the schoolyard. In fact, she never came back to school after that. She never came back to save me from all of those savage little boys. She never came back to hide me away. So they got me. Just like my daddy wanted . . . they got me."

Ness chokes up. A silence sweeps between them as Vanilla reads her sorrowful eyes. Eyes filled with repulsed, melancholic pain.

"Your daddy . . . he sounds like an awful man," Vanilla whispers.

Ness regards her with a newly enlightened smirk. "He was. A very—awful—bad—man."

With considerate care, Ness lowers her head. Her wet mouth becomes a shot in the dark for this pale girl's beacon. The space between them gets smaller and smaller until it does not exist and their lips are pressed together. The connection surges down Vanilla's throat and into her stomach, where it detonates. An explosion of salt and saliva keeps the burning alive.

Ness's lips force hers open. Her tongue finds Vanilla's hiding inside her mouth and pushes against it. It's hot and drenched and it cascades down her throat. Ness's hands slide over the curvature of this porcelain figure. Her fingers dip beneath the skirt of her black dress and enter freely with drunken giggles as she realizes there is no barrier to reach her sweet Vanilla. The fuel burns hotter.

Vanilla shuts her eyes and dissolves into the light show

projected across the backs of her lids. She loses herself slowly, happily, dripping in flames as Ness melts into her, swallowing every drop.

"Ow!" Ness pulls back. She takes her finger and brushes it against her lip. It stains with blood. Ness looks at it and Vanilla thinks she might scream. Thinks that look of shock will sour into hatred and she'll yell.

But no. She smiles.

Ness returns to her, her high heels loosening from her feet and hitting the floor with two clicks as their bodies reconnect. Sweet iron drips onto Vanilla's tongue and fills her with euphoric hunger. She sucks on Ness's bleeding lip. Giggles vibrate from Ness's mouth, shooting off bigger and brighter flares of light. Toes stretch and curl. Vanilla works around Ness until the blood reaches her stomach and, there, consumes her completely. She grabs Ness by the waist and flips her over, drinking her until her lips aren't enough.

Ness moans, her eyes closed in crescent moons of delight, her body fully responsive, twitching with energy like her hair is truly on fire.

Vanilla kisses her chin, her jaw, her ear, where she traces a river down to her neck. Her tongue rolls out from between her teeth and feels the pulse, hears the gushing. The canal of feverish life. The liquid to youth and vitality. The flow waiting to be set free, to connect force to force and giver to taker. Unite syringes with little dogs and paper with graphite. To be and not be energy, the freeing light as well as the confining glass and—

"Ow . . . *ow*, shit! It feels nice but it's starting to hurt. Do ya hear me? Are ya listening? Ow, ow, *ow*! Vanilla! *Va—*"

Vanilla gives a guttural growl, like water sloshing around rusted pipes. The neck swells like a gaseous ball then bursts. Blood spurts into the back of Vanilla's throat and she makes sure not to lose a single drop, to inhale all of Ness, because a single ounce, a single *drip*, lost would be a shame. Her stomach enlarges to make room for her. All of those lighthearted giggles. Ness struggles beneath her, trying to object, but Vanilla's hand is pressed down on her throat, squeezing the blood out of her body and constricting her vocal cords. Her other hand grabs at her wrists and pins them down above her head. Ness's body flails. She kicks and knees Vanilla in the crotch, but the impact does not hurt her. She can barely feel a thing, her synapses busy with all too much. The body beneath her jerks then cries then grows weaker and weaker until it stops moving altogether. Until it is completely tapped out. Vanilla bites down but draws nothing. Her teeth refuse to unlatch until the emptiness is affirmed. Her jaws click open. She moves her head out from underneath Ness's face and sees bulging eyes staring at the ceiling, a petrified mouth strained open, and broken red-nailed fingers. Vanilla notices her own hand clamped around Ness's throat and her knee shoved into the small of her soft stomach. Quickly, she moves off, releasing her grip. She sits beside the body, licking her own mouth clean, and gives Ness a light shove.

"Ness?"

No response. The eyes look as though they might pop and roll down either cheek.

"Ness . . . ?"

But despite this little girl's pleas, there is still no reply.

Vanilla furrows her brow and leans down, pressing her ear to Ness's chest.

Nothing.

Vanilla gasps and jerks back upright, her mind churning on dry gears. *Nothing? Nothing! It means there is simply nothing. Doesn't it? Nothing? Like stethoscopes and cold iron.*

And death.

She rests her hand upon her own chest.

Nothing.

Is this death?

Ness is lifeless. Like the creature who entered her room, although it feels like ages since that now. She can barely recall. But she had torn him apart to get him to leave and Ness is still whole. Still in one piece.

But does that matter to Death?

Vanilla places her index and middle on the tops of Ness's eyelids and pulls them down, a final curtain, snuffing Ness in darkness. She tucks her hands beneath Ness's body, restructuring the blanket to make sure she's comfortable.

Even if she is nothing . . . even if she is *(death)* nothing, she deserves to be comfortable.

Quietly, Vanilla gets up from the bed and walks out the room, shutting the door behind her without taking a final glance. She returns downstairs. The raging rhythms find her again and scream their greetings. She squints until her sensitive eyes adjust. But she feels steady. Calm. Totally in control.

She needs to find Tiff—

"Hey! Long time no see!" a familiar voice calls to her.

She turns toward it.

"And still you have no drink!" The blond-haired face crinkles at her. "Has no one gotten you one yet? How terribly rude! And where's the oh-so-kind-and-gentle Ness? She was wrapped around you like a snake on a mouse! I'm surprised she hasn't fixed you up."

His smile looks warm and inviting, but Vanilla is already full.

It's like a damn snake pit in here.

"Ness isn't here."

"Then where is she?"

"Upstairs. In the bed."

The creature laughs. "Damn. She already did herself in, huh? Crazy Ness. You know, in public, she's such a prim and proper girl. Always saying 'Yes, ma'am,' and 'Thank ya, sir.' She doesn't raise her voice ... like, ever. I'm serious! Not once. But it's always the nice ones who are secretly the wildest behind closed doors. I hope this doesn't affect us, but ... eh, what the hell? I've tried it with her a few times, but her damn mouth always got in the way. Either she's too outspoken or not speaking at all! No in-between! Just crazy mood swings. But I'm sure you know that about her already, seeing how close you two seem to be. It's funny ... I never got your name. Maybe Ness spoke about you before and I just never put a face to the name ... ?"

Vanilla's lips don't even twitch.

"No worries. You don't gotta tell me your name. You just met me and I haven't even told you mine. I'm actually Ness's friend from SCC. Uh, that's Shell City College. Also friends with Tiff, if you know who that is? Name's Danny." He extends his hand out to her. "Nice to meet you!"

"My name is Va—"

A scream erupts. A pure, blood-curdling shriek with enough power to halt the entire room. Only the music continues to play, like an unobservant simpleton in a catastrophic nightmare. Heads turn toward the source of the scream at the staircase.

A girl, barely covered from the midsection down by a flimsy, red-drenched button-up, runs down the stairs in a panic. A man without a shirt and unbuckled pants follows, red handprints visible on his skin.

"Some—someone is d—" The girl tries to speak, but she shakes too violently to control her words.

"There's a dead body! A dead body upstairs!" the man shouts. He sticks out his hand to show the proof. That it's covered in blood, red droplets falling from the palm.

There is a moment of paralysis. A rest in a split second of time where the fact sinks in, for something so incredulous needs raw processing power to settle. After this short moment has passed, the entire room shifts into a violent electricity.

"Someone's dead?! Oh, dear god!"

"Who did it?!"

"There's a killer in this house!"

"A murderer!"

"A monster!"

Women shriek and men push against each other with concrete force, all desperate to get out of a single narrow doorway. A tumbleweed of limbs trying to fit through the tiniest of openings. Vanilla bears witness as creatures collapse to the floor, unable to stand back up, and fall victim to stampeding feet. Their faces smash into the ground with a meaty *crunch* that is perfectly audible over the music. Fingernails dig into skin, catching a hold of thighs to propel themselves forward. Knees drive up between legs, causing torsos to double over in pleading pain only to be pushed to the ground. Two creatures attempt to bust through the frame at the same time. Their colossal bodies get stuck. Fists punch and prod at them from behind until plaster cracks and they break through, widening the horrified mouth of this house.

"What the—?" Danny questions as he takes in the storm. He's shouldered by escaping bodies one, two, five times before he drops his drink and bolts toward the doorway himself.

Vanilla can't turn her eyes away from the savagery. From the complete and utter self-ruination of creatures.

The snake pit is no longer just a snake pit but a colosseum.

A hand clasps around Vanilla's arm. Tiffany emerges from out of the chaos and pulls Vanilla toward her. She grabs her face with both of her hands and brings her close.

"Hey! *Hey!* Snap out of it! We have to get out of here!" Tiffany yells.

"What?" Her eyes shift, wanting to witness more.

"We have to leave! *Now!* Come on!"

Tiffany pulls her upstream, fighting to pass the creatures traveling in the other direction. Some of them stop to observe the two, wondering why they move in opposite ways, why they aren't following, but then allow themselves to be pulled downstream with the rest of the crowd.

Tiffany gets them to the back wall. She makes a right and opens a small window behind the staircase. She grabs Vanilla and pushes her through, then follows. They collapse onto the grass outside, their hard limbs landing with soft thuds. Tiffany scrambles to her feet and tries to pull Vanilla off the ground.

"C'mon! Move faster! We can't be caught here! If it's true, we can't be here!"

Vanilla gets on her feet and they run into the darkness of the backyard, escaping through the slim line of trees and through the alleyways between apartments. As they run along the road, the screams from behind begin to hush.

In the distance, sirens wail.

CHAPTER XXXII

Victor scales the side of the house, his body light as a feather. The music and terror beat from within against his knuckled paws. The frantic teenagers below do not notice the apparition crawling up the walls at impossible angles to reach the second-story window. They are all too busy, all too consumed with clambering on top of each other to save their own skins. A reaction like electricity in water, spreading in the blink of an eye. Tearing apart its own path. Victor is not surprised. Human nature dictates such things.

Fight-or-flight and all that.

It's what he relies on to make it inside undetected.

He reaches the top window and snarls, realizing it might be locked and therefore impossible to get into should law enforcement be tipped off by broken glass. Hopeful, he places his fingers against the bottom ledge and leverages upward. The window catches, squeaks, then slides freely. Victor's lungs evacuate in relief.

No one would lock a window that's impossible to reach.

Victor peers inside, the stench of death assaulting his senses. The room is vacant except for the lifeless body. The last stragglers below funnel out of the house with a final cry. Their screams run to meet the sirens, still miles out.

He prods the inside like he's testing the water at a public pool. At first, he's unable to pass the windowsill. There's tension—a pushing, like when two magnets of the same polarity try to come together. Extreme repulsion. Something that makes his stomach curdle with unease. With some patience, he's able to enter the length of his fingers. Pressure, a great fist, clenches around the digits. He groans at his predicted discomfort but delays no longer.

Unlike me, time is finite.

He thrusts himself inside. To anyone viewing from below, he is a large black bat breaking and entering. He lands on the floor of this uninviting room, unstable, wobbling, as if gravity just shifted beneath him and he can't find equilibrium. All of his muscles tense, trying to maintain their position without being ejected back outside. His core vibrates and it takes a moment before he can stabilize, his body swallowing the discomfort.

He stretches, cracks his bones, and walks over to the bed where the dead girl lies. His nose scrunches as he smells the excrement. Her dress is sodden with sweat and piss; dark blotches stain the animal print. On closer inspection, he notes that the girl's skin isn't translucent, rather tinged pink like a newborn baby. He reaches down and fingers her hair, thick strands of fire; he rather enjoys the color. His fingers skim down her neck to where the wound is, unhealed, and move on toward her shoulder. He presses down. The skin turns a bright pink then fades to white, and he notes the dried-up puddle of blood nearby.

Not empty. The virus can still take hold.

Victor pulls out a glass candle holder with three wicks inside and a matchbox from his jacket pocket. He sets the glass down on the nightstand and strikes a match, lighting the wicks. They pop and crackle at their birth, dancing side to side like performers. He rips a strip of fabric from the mattress, the force emitting a loud tear that might have been heard if people were still below, and holds it over the light. It catches, the flame chewing up the strip until it licks his fingers and sets the tips on fire, burning up like a fuse to a bomb. His knuckles cycle between black charcoal and pale white, withering and healing over and over again.

"If only fresh skin burned so easily," he contemplates aloud.

He sets the fire-consumed fabric down on the bed. It bleeds out, little soldiers of flame marching in haphazard directions, building and dividing rapidly to conquer their path. Meanwhile, the fire left behind travels up to his wrist. He does not flinch. The warmth he cannot feel does not bother him, but the dryness he will feel afterward does. How his skin will be riddled with canyons of flakes and crust, cracked like a long-dehydrated desert. Those older cracks have only just begun to stitch back together, turning soft with some semblance of human skin, since the previous incident.

All of that time to be molted and reborn.

Victor grunts and stares at the girl, analyzing her for any twitch or slight movement. But she is still. He places his burning hand across her face like his fingers are teeth and his palm a poorly situated throat. His skin continues to cycle, healing properties battling against the external force. One fighting to dominate and the other fighting to devour. Realizing that it can't win the fight, the fire spreads to new territory, gorging on her hair first, bleeding sparks until there is nothing but black, sinuous threads of dust. Victor feels the skin melting under his palm. He can feel all that muscle and tissue give way to bone. The eyeballs sink into their sockets, the nose inverts—pools of gelatin and cartilage.

The girl does not put up a fight. Thankfully, she is not regenerating. Thankfully, she is truly just dead.

He lifts his hand and makes eye contact with the burnt skull of what used to be a rather attractive young lady. Someone he might have actually given a second glance to walking down the street. Maybe have even found appetizing. Pre-sodden, of course.

But now, it's too late. He admires the casualties and gives one final respectful glance to the discarded pawn. Then he commences the incineration. He places his hand on her ribcage, gives a little *harumph* and a thrust, and cracks through bone, entering her chest cavity. He feels around for that lump of dead muscle and clutches it in his hand. It shrivels in his grip.

She begins to melt from the inside out.

"Death can have her."

Her heart is reduced to ashes.

Thirty minutes from now, Victor Crohn will be gone. The body on the bed that used to be a vibrant girl named Ness will be nothing but bubbling fat and cooked bone. A mess of unidentifiable crisps. A husk of what used to be full of life.

Ness will never have a chance at eternity. But Victor will get his.

CHAPTER XXXIII

"C'mon, c'mon," Tiffany whispers.

Their shoes scuff the ground like tittering mice. Tiffany's breath is heavy, her lungs working in overtime, while Vanilla moves like she's meant to be in motion. The two run until they're several blocks away from the house—from the containment of desperation and clawing. The chaos is inaudible, those awful screams blessedly out of ear's reach. From here, behind rows and rows of city avenues, they can't even see the house. The construct of already-dead memories collapsing to ashes.

Tiffany and Vanilla will never know that the house is now on fire.

Without realizing it, Tiffany has led them a block away from the diner, an instinct she did not know she had. Her nerves settle when she sees the broken neon sign, the glowing capital *D* winking pink at her. Even though the windows are black, her mind finds Tony in his poor excuse for a kitchen flipping burgers and Ness— *Oh god, where's Ness?*—tapping buttons between the register and her cellphone. She wants to crawl inside. To hide from the Outside. From all these eyes staring out of windows, drilling into her skin. But it's Sunday morning and she knows the door will be locked. That she won't be able to get in.

Tiffany stops and bends over, placing her hands on her knees while she tries to control her breathing.

"Fucking, shit! What the hell was that?" Tiffany huffs out.

She looks up at Vanilla, who stands tall and watches her in turn. The sun isn't out yet. Close, but the moon still hangs in the dark blue air, dangling just over the blonde like a crown. Her stone-cold face is tinged with something . . . something like confusion. Yet still so frigid and unfeeling.

"Do you think it's true?" Tiffany continues. "Is someone really *dead* in there?" *Why doesn't she understand?! Why isn't she reacting?!* "Oh, man . . . oh, *fuck*! I wonder who the hell it could be . . ."

Finally, Vanilla flinches. Her fingers twitch within the fist at her side.

"What kind of monster would do such a thing? Just sneak into a party uninvited and—and *kill* someone?!" Tiffany wants to hurl. To unblock the lump of confusion in her chest and scream even louder. To ask Vanilla why she isn't exploding with gooseflesh. To give her a reason to be out of breath and in tears.

And then she realizes the harsh reality of the situation. The ice-cold irony. It almost makes her laugh.

That Tiffany is a monster, too.

Vanilla wants to speak. To explain that she isn't a monster. That it isn't her fault the other creatures curl up so easily and let go of life.

But her words seize in her throat.

As both girls contemplate their guilt, they are met with laughter. Foreign croaks that travel to their ears from down the street, wrenching their attention. Vanilla sees two figures approaching. Black silhouettes at first, but as her vision focuses, she sees the creatures who stuck like gum. The ones from the diner in the early night who reeked of hunger.

"Well, whaddya know, Buster?" the creature named Dick says. His words come out like a thick malt. "We swam across the same fish in this big, open sea."

Tiffany's eyes roll in her skull like marbles, something Ness always hated about her—*"how loose those eyes are."* She grumbles under her breath, "Oh, great. Fuck us," and straightens. The recent panic is placed on hold and she turns to Vanilla. "Looks like we're not done running yet. Let's get out of here."

"Hey! Where do you little fishies think you're going?" Dick calls out.

"Yeah! Where do ya think you're going?" the short, puggy worm named Buster echoes.

Tiffany tries to focus on the crunch of loose gravel beneath her feet.

Vanilla bobs along, wishing she could lick the air and make it sweet for Tiffany.

"Helloooo? Do ya hear me? Excuse me?! Take one more step an' I'll make sure you little fishies drown. No? You're not gonna listen? All right then, little miss waitress. You work at this diner, eh? Every night? I'm sure I could pay you a visit some other time when you're not so busy. Maybe even follow you home for a nightcap."

Tiffany stops. Vanilla mimics, wondering why the air is suddenly so stale.

"Yup. That's what I thought," Dick says, satisfied.

Footsteps grow behind them until the two creatures are by their sides. Vanilla can see their grinning faces from her periphery. They look hungry.

"Well, well, well," Buster clucks as he circles around the two, reeking like sweat and dirt. "Dicky, what's that saying? 'If ya let something go and it comes back, it's yours'?"

"Yeah," Dick responds. His throat gurgles. "Yeah, yeah, that sounds about right. So, I guess if we're following that logic correctly, it means . . . *we own them.*"

The two erupt into hiccups of laughter. Vanilla can smell the acid on their breath. That scent from red plastic cups she can't forget the taste of. Particles of putrescine sailing on a hot breeze, making her gag.

Tiffany opens her mouth. "All right, boys. Fun little game, but I think it's time—"

A sharp crack silences her. It reverberates down hollow streets. There's a moment to process the shock before Vanilla can understand where it came from. Then she sees Buster's thick hand and Tiffany's body slumped over, spine heaving up and down.

"I don't wanna hear a fuckin' word outta your mouth," Buster says, his wrist cocked at the ready to fire another slap.

Tears blossom in Tiffany's eyes as she rights herself. Her hand is cupped around her swollen cheek, trying to hide the pain, but Vanilla can see it in the spaces between her fingers. She watches her. Watches her break further, trying to stop the water escaping from her newfound cracks. The image of her burns a hole into the silence within Vanilla's chest, bright and red like the pulsating, fresh skin on Tiffany's face. Vanilla turns toward the creatures. A rage builds inside of her. Something that wants to eat beyond engorgement.

"Yeah, not another fuckin' word," Dick repeats.

Now both creatures circle them.

It's like a snake pit in here.

"So, what, what, *what* do we got here? Hmm?" Dick sings. "We've got a waitress at a low-end diner and another girl who looks like she works late hours. Work late hours, doll?"

Dick steps in front of Vanilla. His eyes bore into her with such intensity, he's taken aback when she does not falter.

"You know . . . you look an awful lot like one of those whores my dad used to bring home. Yeah, yeah! The one he used to take into the bedroom and fuck to make my mom miserable. I walked in on 'em once, ya know? I was just a little kid. I wanted to find Mommy, so I looked where every little kid would look. In the bedroom. But Mommy wasn't there. No, it was just Daddy and his little whore."

Dick reaches out and strokes Vanilla's face, running his fingers through her hair.

"I still remember the look on her face. So frigid and uncaring. Not a bit of shame for what she was doing to my family. Just going through the motions without emotion. You have the same look she did. That same distant, uncaring look . . ."

His hand runs to the back of Vanilla's head, fingers tightening around the roots of her hair. With a sharp motion, he yanks her head back. A snap emits from her neck and she is suddenly looking up at the sky.

"Like a fucking heartless whore!"

"Hey! Leave her alone! She's not your daddy's fucking whore, you miserable crybaby!" Tiffany shouts.

The crack comes again. Tiffany whimpers, but Vanilla can only see the endless expanse above her.

The lingering stars wink down at them.

"Keep quiet, bitch!" Buster yells. "I already said I didn't wanna hear another fuckin' word outta you. Fuckin' crack whore." He grabs Tiffany's forearm and twists so that the scars of dots stare back at her, reflecting the stars. What Vanilla calls *happy freckles*. "Ain't nothing but a junkie."

Vanilla can feel Dick's chuckles against her eardrums. "You hear that? Your friend better keep quiet or else . . . maybe you should explain to her what happens." Dick tugs down harder on her hair. Vanilla can feel some strands of gold rip from her scalp. She feels his breath against her neck. His lips press against her skin.

His tongue finds purchase on her nape and glides up to her ears. His wet drool sticks where it tracks. "No reaction, huh?" he whispers. "Not a single response. Just like I thought. Just like I remember. Cold and lifeless."

He yanks her head back up and shoves her toward Tiffany, still holding her hair so that she's heaved back under his control. Vanilla sees the new cut on Tiffany's lip. It's bleeding, a thick dark glob resting on her skin like an uninvited visitor. Her cheek is inflamed and nearly blue. Her eyes are glossy with shock. Vanilla's rage increases. Her fingers curl, wanting to shred herself apart to relieve the feeling. The horde of angry snakes coiling and lashing and whipping within her ribs.

Dick yells again, "Tell your friend! Tell your crack whore friend what'll happen! Speak, goddammit! Don't just stand there and say nothing!" Dick's hand trembles against the back of Vanilla's head. "Don't just stand there lifeless!"

Even in her fear, Tiffany blurts out, "Jesus Christ! Leave her the fuck alone! Can't you see—"

Buster's hand cocks back. Tiffany flinches, clenching her lids and turning away, hoping to dodge the punishment. A second passes. There is no slap. No crack from skin contact. Tiffany opens her eyes despite the fear, but no fist greets her. Those chunky fingers covered in hair and that thick wrist are still elevated, hanging in the brightening night pulled by the stars. Restrained.

Buster's force is held back by a pale, thin hand.

"Hey, what the fuck are you doing? Let go of him!" Dick yells.

"Fuck! Get this bitch off of me! My fucking wrist! *Ah! She's fucking breaking it!*"

The deafening sound of a *crunch* fills Tiffany's ears, jolting her skin with oozing electricity as Vanilla crushes her hand into a fist, taking Buster's bones along with it. Buster cries out in pain and collapses to his knees in front of Tiffany. She watches in horror, the fat of his body galvanized by his fall. His head hangs from his shoulders, shaking back and forth violently. His long hair looks like the shredded fabric that dangles at a carwash.

"Fucking make her stop! I'm sorry! I'm sorry! *I'm sorry!* Just fucking stop! *Fuck! Fuck! Fuck!*"

Saliva and snot pour from the holes in his face. Dick tries to yank Vanilla away by her hair, but she does not budge. Her body reminds him of those white statues carved from marble at the museums his mother used to force him to go to when he was a boy. Carvings worse than some whore.

Immortal.

As Buster continues to dissolve in anguish from her grip, Vanilla reaches behind and loops her arm around Dick's. He tenses up at the touch of this flesh-made noose beneath his shoulder. Her skin crawls up and down his arm, trying to find the perfect spot where his joints are equidistant. The movement is so slight, so quick that you wouldn't be able to see it unless you were staring at them with heightened focus. But Tiffany sees it. She sees Vanilla lift up on her toes and bring her shoulder down. She sees Dick's arm give in incorrectly at a point where a joint does not exist but where one is forcefully created. She sees him yelp and release

VANILLA

Vanilla's hair because his fingers have lost connection to his brain.

Vanilla shatters them into bits and pieces, their forms only contained by their sacks of skin. Tiffany can't look away. Her tears feel explosive, magnifying the scene. Both of them are now on the floor, pleading, begging for some relief. Yet their eyes are vacant, as though they've already dissociated. Dick's stare lolls over Tiffany, but he is not seeing her. He's staring into a dark eternity while his pores leak to make room for the extensive suffering. Tiffany rips her vision away and looks at Vanilla, who is staring into the distance. Into some introspective space that no one else can be a part of. A place where she does not show an ounce of emotion as she breaks what is left of them to dust.

Vanilla's thoughts are on fire.

They are only creatures.

It's a snake pit in here.

Is this death?

I can fix it.

She glances over at Tiffany, her mind zoning back into the present, and smiles.

"Don't worry. You're safe," she tells her. "I'll protect you."

And with that, she drags the two creatures into the alley, their bodies attempting to find leverage against the pavement that tears at their skin.

She isn't hungry, but she could eat. She could eat if it meant keeping Tiffany safe.

Darkness and hunger and steel and—and—

Tiffany gawks as their connected bodies disappear into the

black. Like a nightmare from a Cronenberg universe. She can't see it, but she can *hear*. The munching and sucking and crushing of cartilage and veins. The tearing and the shredding. The yelps and the pleas and then the silence.

You already know . . .

And then it clicks.

This is the reason there was a dead body upstairs. Why everyone trampled over one another, crushing each other to get out of that house. This is who is responsible. This is who the murderer is.

. . . that dying is pain!

This is the monster.

Her legs tremble as she stares into the dark mouth of the alley and she remembers the fangs. The blood and the fangs and the needles and the blood. His silver hair and merciless, piercing blue eyes. She stands there listening until she can't listen anymore.

And then she runs.

CHAPTER XXXIV

She isn't hungry. But she could eat. She could fill her belly once more. One more time, like a glutton. Like an insatiable predator. Like a leech curled over its food source, drinking and drinking from the host until the host's body lies limp and empty. Or, in this case, the two hosts.

A feast.

She drags the creatures across the ground. The skin on their elbows and hips split open with a scream against the gravel, seeping sweetness. They squirm, digging themselves deeper into the alley. She can see them, but they can hardly see her in the darkness, so they push themselves back with frantic kicks to get away. They try to spot her. Try to pinpoint where she is and lock eyes on her. But she can tell by their disoriented stares that they can only see a blended shadow of her. She is nearly invisible to them. Yet she is so terribly real.

They whimper to each other.

"Dicky?"

"Yeah?"

"D-do you see her?"

"No, but I can't see the light either."

"Oh, Dicky! What's *happening*?!"

"Shush! Quiet, or she might hear you!"

"Oh, Dicky . . ." A soft cry. "Dicky, I don't feel t-too good. My wrist hurts so bad and I can't feel my hand. I-I can't *move* it!"

"If you don't shut up, I'll make sure to break your other hand!" Dick hisses. "Just keep quiet. If they haven't left yet, we'll fuck 'em up. We'll fuck 'em up once I can see again."

A painful *crunch* followed by a desperate slurping vibrates through the air, replacing Buster's whimpers. There is a moment of silence, then another *slurp*, and suddenly Dick is missing those wails. He prays for the disturbing sound of consumption to end. For his ears to be filled with Buster's whining. For his throat to stop tasting wet garbage and fear.

Rats. It's just a bunch of fucking rats.

"Hey, do you see her?" Dick asks.

Slush. Gulp. Slush. Gulp. Liquid being inhaled by a hungry gullet.

"Buster? Buster, answer me, goddammit!"

Slush. Gulp.

"You stupid fucking prick! I said fucking answer—"

Dick swings his hand to grab for Buster in the dark but instead lands in a nest of maggots. A bowl of spaghetti. A rotten pie. A puddle of something unseen but horribly felt.

Rats. That's all it is. Damn rats eating garbage.

Dick lifts his hand. A heavy, thick slime drips off his fingers. It lands on the pavement with a sickening *plop* and his stomach lurches in disgust. Droplets splatter his shirt. Bleed through the fabric against his skin. It feels warm. Tacky. Not like rainwater or condensation. He brings his fingers to his nose and sniffs. Smells iron. He knows that smell. Has had it fill his nostrils many times on drunken nights filled with vodka-induced troublemaking.

It's blood.

"What in the hell?" he mutters. Groans, in fact. Cries in disbelief.

His hand is back in the puddle, finding the hot liquid then feeling for the rim of the bowl. He needs to know. Needs to know what is lying right next to him spilling gore. He moves up and past the rim. He feels fabric and skin and then a face, where his fingertips slip into a mouth and connect with moist, squishy tongue.

"Fuck!" he screams, yanking his hand away and falling back against the brick wall. "Fuck, fuck, *fuck*!" He tries to get up but is pushed back down by something he can't see. "You fucking psycho bitch! Get the hell away from me! Do you hear me? I said get the hell away!"

There is no response. The air is still.

Dick can hear his heart in his ears. He tries to hold his breath so as not to make a sound—*she can't fucking see me, not in here—*

but his chest forces him into hyperventilation. The fear is too immense. He kicks his foot out. It hits against something solid and before he can retract it, his leg is pinned down. His lips tighten and his muscles seize. An unfathomable pressure is placed on his shin. He feels the surge of affliction, then the bones breaking, and then he cries, "*AH! FFFF—*" but he cannot finish the word. The agony is more than enough to make one pass out as the *crack* travels up his leg into his femur.

"Fffff—" His lips quiver weakly, spit dribbling out.

A sharp twist and his leg snaps in his hip, rotated one hundred eighty degrees in the wrong direction. He goes limp, the pain scorching and evaporating all at once. His body is yanked from the wall by his now over-extended leg, like he is some broken ragdoll filled with too little hay. His spine slips off the bricks and onto the pavement. He looks up at the stars through the slits of his lids. They wink down at him.

Before his consciousness floats away, he feels a cold breath descend onto his mouth.

A soft whisper descends with it:

"I am not your daddy's whore."

She's right. Daddy's crack whore is an angel in comparison. And that is the last coherent thought Dick has.

Crack.

Slurp.

She wasn't hungry. But she is realizing that she is never full, either. Never satiated, her stomach, trembling with nerves, never calm. She sits between the two creatures, alternating between their bodies until there is no more of them left. Until they are mere husks of meat. When she is finished, she licks herself clean, relishing in the final drops. She was careful this time: a poised, thoughtful method of engorging that leaves her spotless except for the corners of her mouth and fingernails.

She stands, stretches, and purrs from the warmth as she savors the fraction of satisfaction that has been granted to her. It is already ensnared in a countdown of growing hunger, so she better enjoy it. She feels good. She feels happy. A stream of euphoria swims through the channels of her brain. She rotates on her heels and skips out the alleyway, drunk off elation as she rejoins the pale yellow streetlights.

But that is all she rejoins. The street is otherwise bare.

"Tiffany?" she says. "Tiffany . . . ?" Her voice turns into a pathetic whimper as she calls out one final time, "Tiffany, where are you?"

No response.

She rotates in a full circle, peers around the corners of buildings and down the road, but there is no Tiffany.

She is alone.

She roams, walking across blocks and blocks, hoping she will somehow cross Tiffany's path or that Tiffany will find her and rejoin her. Tell her that there was a mistake. She was lost from the one who was protecting her. She didn't run away. She just couldn't find her way back.

Vanilla would be fine with that.

But the world remains empty. She walks and walks down the street, an innate sensation guiding her to that warmth. It isn't until after some time of walking, roads and blocks worth, when she stands in front of the familiar gray building that she realizes her steps were guiding her somewhere much deeper in the memories of her subconscious. Somewhere vastly different.

They were taking her home.

And home is where she is safe.

How could she have allowed herself to forget?

She doesn't hesitate. An eagerness inflates her. She walks to the door and gives it a light push. It creaks open without objection, releasing the vat of old air it had been harboring before disturbed. She steps inside, but her smile falters.

Unfamiliar marks break up the walls, making her excitement halt and her stomach descend. Hundreds of painted white curves form words she cannot read. They crawl up the concrete and stick to the ceiling. Splatter like lightbulbs chucked at the roof, exploding with white-staining gore. Strokes of the same color stretch across the metal as well as the wooden door she still holds on to. The inside of her home looks hideous. Abused. Attacked.

Red paint runs up the edge of the staircase, leading like a snake reaching the second floor. She follows it to the top, where it splits and spreads down both sides of the narrow hallway. She traces the lines with her gaze, the paint slithering across the walls and doors. It trails deeper, to the end of the hall. She sees the door to her room slightly ajar, paint smeared across it like an open wound.

She sprints the short distance and throws open her door, half expecting to see a little girl sitting at its center. The yelp catches in her throat when she sees instead the sinuous colors of paint clogging up the concrete. There is barely any light in here—the rod has been painted over—yet the streaks are vibrant. They cover every inch, some overlapping each other to create ugly browns and puke greens and phlegm yellows that drip. They drip to the floor and onto her mattress, staining it an ugly shade of the vilest combination.

Her face turns red. She is stuffed with anger not caused by hunger. Pure, hateful, directed anger. She sits on her haunches, curls her upper body over her knees. She buries her face inside herself. Tears lick down her cheeks. A storm floods her ears.

They ruined my room! The one Daddy built to keep me safe! And they came in! They came inside and they ruined it! They RUINED IT! They violated it and dropped their disgustingness all over it! How could they? How could they walk into something that's not theirs and do this? It wasn't theirs to ruin! It didn't belong to them! It belonged to me and Daddy! Not to them! It wasn't theirs to destroy! And now Daddy is going to think I'm filthy! Just like a creature! He's going to come back and see my room and think, 'What a filthy little girl! Just like the creatures from the Outside!' He's not going to want me in his sight! He's going to kick me out! He's not going to let me stay in my room anymore! He won't let me stay! It won't be my room! It's not a room for a CREATURE!

She screams into her lap in a pitch so high it leaves skid marks on her lungs. And then she crumbles to the floor. She wants to lie on her mattress. She wants to fall asleep and hope that her daddy will be there when she wakes.

He will fix it. He always does.

But she knows it won't happen. Not for her.

She has lost both her daddy and now Tiffany all too quickly.

She crawls to the corner of the room, next to the mattress that kept her coddled for so many years, and curls into a ball. She shuts her eyes tight, refusing to look at the walls of the room any longer. The cool darkness behind her lids reminds her of what her room was like when it was pure and untouched. When it was bare of marks and scars and didn't smell awful.

When it was beautiful and innocent and taken care of by her daddy.

CHAPTER XXXV

Tiffany runs back to her apartment. It is the safest place she can think of. But even as she runs toward it, she knows it won't keep her hidden. After all, she's been hosting a monster inside of it. She's been letting it sleep beside her. So close to her vulnerable skin, like she was offering herself as sacrificial prey. Dumb and easy on a silver platter.

You already know!

But why is she surprised? This has been her life. Living in rooms that might as well be hunting grounds. Existing with bloodthirsty monsters that beg for affection then bite into her when it's not enough. When the affection turns bitter and the blood goes sour.

"Let me fix you, darling. Stay with me and be mine."

"Get the hell away from me!"

"Fine. Have it your way, Tiffany."

She remembers the cold concrete. His eyes and all of his needles. His smile vanishing along with her toys and any grasp of warmth.

"If you won't love me willingly, then you will fear me."

The prick of each scar that would never heal. But it was better than the sick. The cold wet that grew inside of her, shriveling her lungs and aching her bones.

"I can choose to keep what I fix."

Her gray skin regaining pigment and her lungs inflating once again.

"And you, I will keep."

But he let her go. Over a decade later, he let her go. And she didn't understand what he meant by his promise to control her until she was free of that concrete place. Until she realized she was free but with nowhere to run.

The headlines in the city newspaper on the week of her veiled freedom read:

MYSTERIOUS FIRE TAKES THE LIVES OF COUPLE

WHILE THEY SLEEP IN RUNDOWN APARTMENT COMPLEX

The cost of her life. There was no mystery about it.

What the newspaper didn't mention was that the couple had a daughter. A daughter they gave everything they had to be healed. A daughter they'd never see again, would never know if she made it out of that clinic alive or in a body bag.

All the sacrifices . . .

The newspaper mentioned none of this. But it didn't hide the truth.

She understood then, immediately, who was behind it all. Behind the crumbling foundation of her life. A puppeteer who holds her strings. Ties them to his knuckles and tightens the knots until she is connected beneath his skin. A puppeteer who can snap her wooden neck whenever he so pleases.

"I fixed you. I can break you."

She has her freedom, sure. But now she realizes freedom isn't so black-and-white. It can be earned in increments. So as she runs to the apartment, she knows she might as well be running back into that concrete. Because the dream of freedom is only fabricated and concrete can be painted many colors.

Her legs pump hard. They feel as though they are running ahead of her. Her heart is in her throat and she swears if she were to cough, she would hack up the lump of an organ still beating outside of her body. Her stomach cramps up. She winces and falters, leaning to the side as her leg nearly twists and trips the other, but she forces herself upright and runs harder.

"Fuck!" she screams as the cramp coils up her gut and into her throat. She turns a corner and the pain shoots down her leg, paralyzing it. She collapses to the floor. "Fuck, crap, fuck!"

She turns around, half expecting to see a blond head darting in her direction, but the street is empty. Black pavement and yellow lights. She's surprised by the feeling of disappointment.

She gets back up and jogs the rest of the few blocks home,

fighting against her body's plea to curl over and give in to the cramp. When she arrives at her building, she rams through the apartment door, slams it shut behind her, snaps the lock, and collapses onto her bed.

She sighs, the force expelling a slight scream. The cramp throbs. She curls up, nestling her stomach. "Fuck, it hurts! Please," she whimpers. "Make it stop!"

She begs an empty room.

Her body teeters, leading her to different positions that might alleviate the discomfort. She turns onto her stomach and shoves her face into her mattress. Each breath is forcefully shallow. Too sharp and it'll sting.

When the pain subsides and she can't stand the hot air fed back to her from the foam, she rotates her head, peeking at the floor with one eye. The floor where she let it sleep beside her.

It was so close.

Was it a patient? Someone he kept in that building? An experiment gone wrong? She was all too aware of the sick things he liked to do inside locked rooms. Things he spared her from. She could hear the screams from the hallway whenever he opened the door. She could hear the screams when he walked in with that sick, twisted smile.

Is that why he wants it killed? Because it mutated beyond his expectation? And if so, why doesn't he just do it himself instead of dragging her into this? Is he really just trying to get rid of his mistake, like how he got rid of her parents?

Or does he just want to prove that he's the one in control?

And the girl. It. It seemed so sweet and innocent. So naïve and pure.

But the tearing and the ripping and the blood . . .

No. It's a monster. Just like him.

Her gut wrenches into tight knots and she screams, "FUCK! IT HURTS! MAKE IT STOP!" She whimpers and cries into her mattress, soaking the sheets in her salty tears. "Make it stop . . ."

She hears the shift but does not move. She knew this was coming. A hand presses down on her spine, followed by a voice from above.

"If you ask nicely, then perhaps I will."

The Devil is easy to recognize when you've already danced.

She tenses, suffocating against her sheets as she holds still and quiet.

"I said, ask *nicely*," he hisses, pressing down harder.

"Please . . ."

"You'll have to speak louder than that, darling. I can't hear you through the bedding."

"PLEASE!"

"Now, was that so hard?"

She can hear the grin in his voice.

For a moment, she believes he will remove his hand from her back. She tries to sit back up but is unable to. His hand remains in place, pressing down, crushing her into the mattress. The pressure on her lungs forces an agonized croak from her throat.

"Ple—" she wheezes. "Fuck!"

"That is no way for a lady to talk!" he growls, placing a

fraction more of his strength into her back, forcing her to spread out her arms and legs, flatten like a squashed bug.

She yelps. She huffs. A snap in her stomach recoils across her body.

The pain is instantly gone, and so is his hand.

She hears him step away from the bed. Cautiously, she sits up on her knees and turns over. He is standing right behind her, the exact smile she imagined smeared across his pale face, showing off his teeth like knives. She glares at him.

"No 'thank you'?" he asks, faking hurt.

"F—" Before she can stammer a syllable, he slaps her across the face, smacking her skin where it is already bruised and bleeding. She cries out.

"I told you, it is not ladylike to curse."

She holds the side of her face in her hands, feeling relief from the soothing ice against her hot skin. She regathers her courage and turns back toward him. He pouts in apology, but she can see the rage in those blue eyes. She won't fall for it. And he knows he's played this trick one too many times for her to be so foolish.

"Do you know why I'm here?" he asks.

She doesn't respond, afraid that if she opens her mouth, she will either cry or curse his name.

He observes her, flicking his eyes back and forth across her face, reading her emotion.

"I am here because I feel I am about to be betrayed. Betrayed by someone I have given so much to. Someone to whom I have given my time and resources and all the money I can spare. And after all that, when I ask for one thing in return, I am made a fool. And I do not like being made a fool. Do you think that is fair to me?"

Tiffany struggles to suck back tears. He paces across the length of her bed, one hand in his pocket and the other against his chest, like he is delivering a sermon.

But she knows better.

Monster.

"Well, I, for one, do not believe this fair," he says. "I do not believe it is fair that I have sacrificed so much for this person only to be made a fool when I ask for one thing." He stops and looks around the room, clicking his heels together. "I mean, look at this place. I have paid for and furnished it with my own money. But do I live here? No. And the food that is in the fridge? My own money! Do I eat it? No! The clothes in that closet? Once again, my own money. But do I wear them? No. These are all things I have charitably given to the person who is trying to make a fool of me." He snaps his head toward her, a murderous look in his eye as he growls, "I do not like leeches."

She looks away and whimpers. There is a harsh *thump* on her bed and when she turns back, he is inches from her face, baring his fangs. Snapping like a rabid dog.

"You were a pathetic, sick child when you were first given to me! A weak, sad little thing with insides like rotten fruit!"

She presses her lips together to keep from shrieking, but the shriek escapes her anyway. Quickly, she covers up her scream with her hand and inches away from him until her back hits the wall.

He crawls toward her, a waking nightmare, as he continues spitting words like embers onto her skin. "I could have easily left you for dead. I *should* have left you for dead, you insolent child! And after everything, you can't even half-ass this one task I ask of you! You couldn't even watch her like I told you to! You just left her out on the street by herself! For anyone to find! How stupid can you be? *How could you let her go?!*"

Tiffany's throat is clogged. Her efforts come out in a gurgle.

"Do you not hear me, you stupid little thing? I asked you, how could you let her go? ANSWER ME!"

Like a cracked dam, no longer able to hold back the tremendous force, she explodes: "Because you didn't tell me she was like you!" She bursts into screaming sobs. "I planned to kill her tonight but thank god I didn't! How am I supposed to be around her when she is like you? How am I supposed to *kill* her if she is like you? An unkillable *monster* like you!"

He snarls and bites at her, fangs a hair's breadth away from the tip of her nose. "Bite your tongue before I bite it off *for* you! You don't understand a single word that is coming out of your filthy mouth!"

Tiffany tightens her lips back up. Her sobs muffle.

"Now, listen very closely, you foolish girl. I asked one thing of you, for all that I have done for you, and you've failed me. Now, think. For once, use your impulsive brain to think before you speak. Why would I ask this task of you, such an important chore, if I didn't think it was possible? If I didn't think that even someone as pathetic as you could accomplish it? Do you think me an idiot?

Do you think I don't understand the situation?"

He pauses and waits for her to answer. She shakes her head, trembling.

"Correct. Because I am not an idiot, and I *do* understand the situation." He sighs and rubs his temples with his fingers as he shuts his eyes for a moment. The muscles in his jaw continue to throb. "This is a situation that needs to be dealt with sooner rather than later. In fact, as soon as possible. I need her disposed of before others find her. Before they realize the mistake that can be created. And I will not get my hands dirty with *your* job. I took an oath to do no harm and I am far too watched to be doing such deeds. I can't even step outside of my office without the next Nancy waving me down for an appointment. If I were caught, I would be ruined, and you don't want to ruin me, do you? No, of course you don't. You don't want to be responsible for ruining the man who saved your life. Who gives you shelter. In fact, you should be begging to do this for me. Begging to repay me for all that I have done for you," he reminds her. "But alas, you've failed me. At least for now, you have. But this is no permanent thing. You can redeem yourself." He grabs her arm, looking back at her, and pulls her toward him. She reluctantly obeys, letting him drag her body onto his lap. He curls his arm around her, petting her head with the other hand. His touch is chilling yet gentle. She wants to give in to it, but she knows better. "The chore needs to be done and you will do it. Otherwise, I will find someone else who will do it for me . . . and I will make sure that they do the same to you." His voice is calm, but the threat is viciously present.

He's zoning out now, in his own stream of thought. Tiffany can tell by the way he strokes her. She flinches as his palm slaps against the top of her head then runs carelessly down her cheekbone.

"You are responsible now, not only for killing her but for getting her back," he continues. "I made her vulnerable to you once. Made it easy for you to casually come into contact with her on the street without it being suspicious. Without her killing you first."

Tiffany winces at the thought of being immediate prey. Of her naïvely stepping back into that building to retrieve Vanilla, thinking she would come out the other side with her life, only to be mauled down. Vanilla's face attacking her with hungry rage, wearing Tiffany's blood like a trophy.

Is that what Vanilla's victims see in their final moments? A sweet little girl wearing their insides?

"I practically handed her to you without you having to lift a finger. I gave that to you. And now that you have lost her, she's returned to the building. And as I know all too well, she won't be leaving her room unless she is forced. You are responsible this time around for getting her to leave again. Or . . ." He halts in contemplation.

Tiffany musters her bravery to look up at him. She sees the underside of his jaw and his pursed lips.

"What is it?" she asks, knowing how much he enjoys his audience.

"Why scare the beast out of its corner when it has already

trapped itself?"

"What are you talking about?"

He grins, evil dripping from between his fangs. He pulls out an item from his breast pocket and holds it above Tiffany's face. It's a syringe filled with blue liquid. Glittering beneath the fluorescence like a sample of untouched water from the deepest part of the ocean.

His voice reeks with sanguine pride. "You're going to kill her in that very room."

CHAPTER XXXVI

Tiffany stands in front of the gray building just before the big wooden door.

It's been two years. Two years, and here she is now, walking back into the mouth of it. She thinks she can hear its stomach grumble. Her legs shake. Anxiety builds, making her nauseous. But she isn't thinking about Vanilla—nor about the syringe hidden behind her back.

No, she is thinking about the memories. The dark, bloody memories.

"Who are you?"

"My name is Doctor Crohn. You are here so that I can help you. So that I can fix you."

Cough. *"W-what's wrong with me?"* *Cough.*

"You are sick. You are dying."

"Oh . . . what is 'dying'?"

"Such a sweet, innocent, sad little girl you are. Dying is pain."

She shudders and pushes the front door open. It creaks, widening its mouth for her to enter into that vat of pungent breath. She steps inside and sees the chaos drawn all over the walls. The graffiti written in multicolor with white accents that meld together to create a sickly hue. Some street kids must have vandalized the place while it was abandoned.

But is it still abandoned? Is Vanilla really here?

She looks around the room and at the base of the staircase.

"Now, darling, follow me up here so that I may take you to your room."

"My room?"

"Yes."

"I'm living here?"

"Yes."

"What about my old room?"

"That room no longer exists."

"Oh . . ." Cough. *"Is it dying?"*

"Well, aren't you a funny one?"

Tiffany walks up the stairs, tracing her fingertips along the rail she could just reach when she was so young. She reaches the top of the staircase and walks down the narrow hallway of doors.

Cough. "Why do I hear people screaming behind the doors?"

"Because they are screaming."

"Oh . . ." Cough. *"Why?"*

"Because they are in pain."

"Are they dying?"

"Yes."

She reaches the end of the hallway. Her old room is on the right, perpendicular to the door at the end.

"Now, this is your room. Go ahead. Go inside."

Cough. *"What about that room?"*

"What room?"

"That one. The one right in front of us. The one at the end of this hallway."

"What about it?"

"I don't hear screaming coming from inside that room."

"That is because no one is screaming inside of that room."

Cough. *"Is someone in there?"*

"Yes."

"They aren't dying?"

"No. Let's move along."

She pushes open the door. To her room. Her old room. It's as bare as it always was, only a single mattress shoved into the corner. She walks to the center of the room. The graffiti snakes in and around her walls, but she likes it. It makes the room ugly. It reveals its truth.

Cough. *"That hurts! It pinches!" Cough.*

"Quiet, it is only an injection. You will be needing six of these a day, so you should get used to it."

"Six?!"

"For now, yes."

"That seems like a lot..." Cough. *"Are you sure you're doing it right?"*

"Yes."

"But you're putting in blood and taking out blood?"

"Yes."

"How does that help me, taking my blood out?"

"Do you wish to die?"

"No."

"Then do not ask silly questions you would not understand the answer to."

Cough. *"Okay."*

"I am done now. I will see you again tonight."

Cough. *"Goodbye..."*

She turns toward her old mattress, crouches down, and collapses onto its stiff padding. She lies there on her back and looks up. The ceiling seems so much closer to her now than it used to be.

"Child, you are in the exact same position you were when I left you."

"Well, there isn't anything else for me to do."

"This is true."

"Can't I go outside?"

"No."

"Why not?"

"Do you wish to die?"

"No."

"Then that is why."

"Okay . . . can't I have my toys back?"

"No."

"Why not?"

"Do you wish to die?"

"No!"

"Then that is why."

"Will everything make me die?"

"Yes."

"Oh . . ." Cough.

She lifts her arm so that it touches the wall behind the top of her head. She can feel the grooves in the concrete under the pads of her fingers. She digs her nails into them like she used to, scratching.

Something scratches back.

Tiffany sits up. She scratches again.

Something scratches back.

She scratches twice.

Something scratches back twice.

She giggles for a moment, making patterns of sound with her fingernails, listening to them be repeated back to her.

"What are you doing?"

"Nothing!"

"I see you scratching on that wall."

"I wasn't!"

"Don't lie to me, Tiffany!"

Cough.

"Get out of this room."

"What?"

"I said, 'Get out!'"

"But why?"

"Do not ask me questions, child."

"Please! No! I promise I won't scratch again!"

"Out and you will be moved to a room downstairs!"

"Please, please, please! I promise! I won't scr—"

"OUT!"

She stands from the mattress and steps out of the room. She turns to the door at the end of the hall, placing her palm on the cold metal as though she might be able to feel its heartbeat.

Nothing.

She takes a deep breath . . . and pushes.

It swings open to a room like hers only drenched in paint and fumes. She covers her nose, trying to block the scent as she observes the heart of the vandalism through the fluorescent dark.

She sees Vanilla lying next to the mattress. The girl is curled into a ball, her face hidden in her arms and her hand leaning against the wall, fingernails scratching into the concrete. She doesn't move when Tiffany walks in nor when she walks to the bed. She isn't even sure if Vanilla knows she's there.

"Vanilla?" Tiffany whispers.

Vanilla doesn't respond.

"Vanilla . . . ?"

Tiffany crouches and places her hand on Vanilla's body.

"Hey? Sweetie?"

Vanilla's hand reaches out and snatches Tiffany by the arm.

She throws her onto the mattress and wraps around her like a constrictor, squeezing her against her chest. Tiffany panics, thinking this is the moment she is mauled by the monster. Finally eaten alive after all these years. She pinches her eyes shut, bracing for the slashing and the eventual drainage of her life. For the mouth over her skull to deliver her to its stomach.

But she feels no pain. Only calm pressure.

It takes her a moment to realize that Vanilla is hugging her.

"Why did you leave me?" Vanilla asks.

Tiffany can see her lips move when she speaks, but the rest of her face is covered by her arm.

"What ... what do you mean?" Tiffany responds, nerves jolting her muscles.

"You left me. In the alleyway, you left me. I was only trying to protect you. To keep you safe." There are tears in her voice.

"I don't know. I was afraid."

"Afraid of what? Of me? I wouldn't hurt you."

"No, not of you."

"Then afraid of what?"

"Afraid ... of dying."

"Oh ..." There is a pause in Vanilla's voice. "I'm not sure I understand. I don't know what that is. I don't understand what dying is. I hear that word over and over again, but what is it? What is death?"

Tiffany doesn't answer. The subject is too close, too suffocating for her to offer the truth. In the silence, Tiffany looks up at the wall, sees the grooves in the concrete. She lifts her fingertips to them. Her nails fit perfectly in the indents.

She looks back at Vanilla, whose head is still shoved into the nook of her arm. She looks so sweet and vulnerable. So innocent. Little does she know she's lying next to a monster.

Maybe two monsters can cancel out and make peace.

Tiffany shuts her eyes to rest and places her hand on Vanilla's chest.

"Why don't you have a heartbeat?"

"What do you mean, child?"

"When I feel your chest or your wrist, your skin doesn't beat like my mommy's and daddy's does."

"So?"

"Well . . . why is that?"

"That is because I am dead."

She presses her palm into Vanilla's chest and holds her breath so that she can feel even the most distant of heartbeats.

Nothing.

CHAPTER XXXVII

Tiffany finds herself standing in her childhood home, in her childhood room. The walls are painted pink. A white, fluffy rug hides dark wood floorboards, saving toes from the cold. Her bed is massive, a comfortable mattress lifted on an ivory pedestal and draped in blankets soft to the touch. Stuffed animals of all species and colors ranging from real to imaginary inhabit the blankets. There are windows across her room that take on the color of the sky. They welcome in fresh sunlight. Rays shine down on her face and warm her cheeks.

There is no concrete here.

She is holding a stuffed unicorn in her hands—only her hands are not her childhood hands. They are bigger. They are the ones she has now. She is not a child anymore.

There is a knock on her door.

"Come in!" Tiffany says.

The door opens and her parents' smiling faces peek through.

"Hello, my love!" her mother sings back. She looks beautiful; a halo hovering above her head would not be out of place.

In her hand is a syringe.

"How are you doing, baby-girl?" her father asks.

His smile melts her heart.

"I'm okay," she answers as they enter. "I'm so ... I'm so happy to see you both. I miss you."

"Of course you do. But at least you're better!" her father tells her. "Look at you! All healthy and strong!"

"Yeah ... but I don't know if this was all worth it. If it was worth getting better if it meant losing you both ..."

"If we didn't do it, you would be dead." Her mother's voice is sweet like molasses, yet her words feel sharp.

"I think I'm already dead ..."

Her mother takes Tiffany's hand in her empty one. Her father steps up behind her mother and places his hand on her shoulder.

"My love, you are not dead. You have more life to live, so much more to experience," her mother says, reaching out and brushing her fingertips through Tiffany's curls. "I am so proud of you. Such a strong and beautiful woman you've become. I can hardly believe you came from your father and me. Stronger than the both of us combined."

Tiffany laughs weakly, pressing her cheek into the palm of her mother's hand. A tear runs down her face. Her mother brushes it away with one nail.

"Such a strong and beautiful woman. You are not dead. You are far from dead. You are filled with life growing from inside your heart," her mother whispers, poking Tiffany softly in the chest. "And your heart is still beating loud and proud! My dear girl, you are not dead. But when you are, come find us."

They both smile in unison and Tiffany smiles back, wiping away the pain from her face. As they smile, her mother lifts the syringe to her neck.

"Mom? What are you doing?"

Tiffany drops the unicorn and grabs for the syringe. Her mother's hand feels like hot metal, steam hissing at their touch, and she pulls away before she gets burned.

"Ow!" she exclaims, looking down at her mother's skin, seeing her fingertips turn to charcoal black, melting to bubbles. She looks at her mother's face—charcoal black to bubbles. "Mom?!"

"Remember we love you, baybwe-gurl," her father says. She turns to him just as his lips drip from his face. The top of his skull sunsets from crimson to midnight.

"Dad? What's happening?!"

"Come find us . . ."

Her mother's final words before she plunges the syringe into her neck.

Blue liquid drains beneath her flesh.

Her mother and father catch on fire. The background erupts into flames with them.

"*Mom! Da—*" Tiffany tries to call out, but her lungs seize up.

She chokes on skin-flavored smoke. She wraps her hands around her neck, trying to claw at her windpipe so she can split it open to breathe. But it's no use.

She suffocates, watching her parents burn before her.

Tiffany jolts awake. She tenses to sit up, but something holds her down, knocking a grunt out of her. Piercing blue eyes hover above her through the black, and in that moment she is convinced the color of Hell is in that glare.

This is the true meaning of control.

She attempts to yell but can't. He's pressed down around her throat. She thrashes, brings her hands to her neck, and feels the cold fingers wrapped around her. She can't even sputter a cough. Her head swells with blood.

He draws close, those eyes blinding headlights, until she feels his cheek rest against hers. "Do it soon," he whispers in her ear. "Don't make me come back."

He pulls away, but his grip does not. She struggles to breathe, trying not to make a sound as she comes to the realization that he will not let her go until she ceases struggling. She forces her body to relax despite its instinct to claw its way to survival.

Slowly, he loosens his grip around her neck. Blood rushes from her skull. Her lungs deliciously inflate and her eyes shut in gratitude.

When she opens them, he is gone. Was he even really here? All she sees is dark ceiling.

She glances over at Vanilla, rigid with the idea of her having witnessed the scene, but the girl turned away in her sleep, back facing Tiffany. Her body is still, a corpse, completely unaware.

Tiffany looks back up at the ceiling. She removes the syringe from under the mattress, where she'd been able to stash it before Vanilla embraced her. Its thick glass scrapes across the floor and she bites her lip, willing silence as she brings it to a rest on the center of her chest.

And that is how she lies for some time, her eyes on the ceiling and her monstrous fingers wrapped around a syringe of Death.

With the puppeteer nearby and watching.

"Tiffany?"

"Yes?"

A pause. Tiffany shifts the syringe to her side and Vanilla turns over. A hand extends, resting on the small of Tiffany's stomach. Tiffany flinches but does not retract from the touch.

"I can feel your heart in your stomach. Like it's hungry."

That's funny. I can't feel yours.

"I'm just . . . excited is all."

"Excited?"

"Yeah."

"Happy?"

"Sure."

"Do you have any more freckles?"

"Freck— Oh, yeah. Sure. Sure, I do."

"That's good."

Vanilla rubs her thumb down Tiffany's stomach, landing in her belly button. Her tongue rolls in her mouth, wanting to speak further but not knowing what to say. She wants to hear Tiffany's voice. To feel her warmth again. But something about her has gone cold.

"Tiffany?"

"Yes?"

"Will you stay with me?"

"Stay with you?"

"Yes, in here. We can stay together in this room. I can keep you safe and we won't ever have to go into the Outside again."

"Oh. Sure . . . I'd like that."

Vanilla smiles. She stands, accidentally using Tiffany's chest as leverage, eliciting a grunt out of her. Tiffany's heart spikes.

"Okay! But we'd have to clean up. This place is filthy." Vanilla steps off the mattress and stares at the wall. She places the tip of her finger on a streak of color and outlines the design. New stains. "I suppose I don't mind the stains. But I don't know if Daddy will feel the same. And I don't want to make him angry."

Which will it be? Tiffany thinks. *You can only have one monster. Which will you choose?*

Vanilla continues, "Maybe we can clean it with my blank— Oh. But I already used that."

Tiffany regrips the syringe and rolls onto her shins.

"We can't put the wall in the bathtub," Vanilla says, as if talking to herself.

Tiffany stands, her knees popping as she ascends, making her heart skip with every creak.

"And we can't bring the tub in here."

The syringe trembles in her fist. The muscles in her arm nearly petrify into a cramp. She takes her stance behind Vanilla, tears shedding down her cheeks.

You can only choose one.

"Maybe Daddy will know . . ."

Tiffany lifts the needle, a kinetic arch directed at Vanilla's brainstem. She hesitates.

"Tiffany?"

"Yes?" Her voice breaks. A part of her wishes Vanilla would turn around. See her for the monster she is and maul her down.

"Do you think I'm dead?"

The air between them rises in suspension. Tiffany's tremors freeze.

"Why . . . why are you asking that?"

Vanilla is silent at first. She doesn't turn around. When the hairs on Tiffany's body lift in gooseflesh, she speaks: "I think I'm dead. I think I died and I'm not in my body anymore. I think none of this is real because if it were then I would feel it. But I can't feel anything. Nothing feels hot or cold or soft to me anymore. At least, not like it used to. And no matter how much I try to fake it, I can't feel truly happy or sad. Not really. I only feel angry or hungry . . . all the time."

Tiffany's bottom lip quivers.

"But I can feel you," Vanilla adds.

"Me?"

"Yes. I don't know how to describe it, but I can feel everything about you."

Tiffany falters.

"I thought dying was supposed to be painful," Vanilla continues. "Unbearable pain. A torture you'd have to live with forever. Somehow this is worse. All this *nothing* is worse. It's like being trapped in your own body. Like asphyxiating under your own skin."

The needle undulates in Tiffany's quivering hand.

"I think I'm dead. I think I died a while ago."

Tiffany attempts to lift the syringe higher, but it's so heavy. Victor's whisperings slip down the tunnel of her ear canal.

Do it. Do it now.

"I think I died . . ."

Tiffany cocks her arm back.

". . . and I think I'm somehow living in death."

Her shoulder strains under the pressure.

"I think this is what death is."

A hand catches Tiffany's wrist. Limbs wrap around her, holding her in place. She yelps but is instantly forced to swallow the sound back down as the puppeteer's strings reattach.

As he regains control.

"Sweet, foolish child."

Tiffany's blood turns cold. Each syllable feels like a nail hammered into her ear.

Why did you stop me? She can't speak. Is unable to.

Vanilla turns around. Tiffany watches as her eyes grow wide in confusion.

"Daddy?" Vanilla huffs, the shock punching her core.

"Yes," Victor replies.

"What are you doing?"

"I told you I would keep you safe, my sweet. Did I not?"

"You did . . ."

"Well, here I am."

Victor's fingers tighten around Tiffany's wrist, making her yelp. Her bones *crunch* and she drops the syringe. It makes a threatening *thunk* when it hits the floor. Vanilla watches it roll back and forth, the liquid inside sloshing around until it finally settles.

"Tiffany . . . ?" Vanilla whispers, unable to remove her eyes from the glass.

Tiffany's vocal cords are crushed.

It's not what it looks like!

She can't move. He won't let her.

"It was trying to rid itself of you," Victor says.

"Rid of me?" Vanilla looks up at Tiffany, at her warm companion, and oh, how those brown eyes melt with sorrow.

"Yes."

"I . . . I don't understand."

I didn't want to! He made me! Can't you see?

"Are you really all that surprised, my sweet? What is there to understand? It is a creature. Not like us. It does not know any other instinct than to harm."

No . . . no, that's not true!

"But . . . but she was so nice."

"Of course it was. What else would you expect from a monster?"

You lying piece of—

"Sweet and enchanting until your back is turned. Then destroys you at the first sign of weakness. And you would be a fool to give it a second chance. To trust it again." Victor's voice drops. "Are you a fool, Vanilla?"

Not a fool!

"No! But . . ." Her eyes flick back and forth across the floor. "I still don't understand. It doesn't seem right. You . . ." she says, addressing him. Finding her ground and grappling against delusion. "Why did you leave me? Why were you not here?! If you said you would keep me safe, then why did you let me go into the Outside by myself?!"

"Because I needed you to see," he responds calmly. "I needed you to see what the Outside is like, what your life would be like without me. Only then would you trust me."

"So you let me suffer?!"

"Yes."

No! He doesn't care about you!

"Are you going to leave again?"

"My sweet, my blood runs through your veins. You are mine. The only thing I have to cherish in this world. I will never leave you."

Because he wants to control you! He's the goddamn

puppeteer!

Tiffany squirms. Victor growls. Vanilla smiles.

"But," Victor continues, "as you must trust me, I have to know I can trust you. To know that you won't leave me either."

No . . .

"You can!" Vanilla yelps, taking a step closer to her daddy. He is so close now. She can almost touch him.

"Yes. But you must prove it."

"How?"

Oh, god, no . . .

"You must rid of it."

Oh god, oh god, ohgodohgodohgod—

"Rid of it? Of . . . Tiffany?" A somber visitor returns to the pit of Vanilla's stomach, tugging ever so slightly.

Tears stain Tiffany's face in ribbons.

All that warmth.

"Yes. Rid of it. Consume the creature, my sweet. You and I will be together for all of eternity. This marks the start of our journey to make the Outside a safe place for both you and I. A safe place where you and I can exist together side by side. Ridding ourselves of it will make us safer. It will make *me* safer. Protect me."

You can only choose one.

"But I don't want to lose her . . ."

But all that warmth . . .

"Then you choose to be alone."

No. You can choose one.

VANILLA

Vanilla hesitates, reading the threat with care. She steps forward and places her hand on Tiffany's chest. Tiffany wishes she could absorb that arm into her soul. Show her everything she wants to do and say.

"Tiffany," she whispers. "I liked you."

Tiffany lurches with an inaudible sob against the restraint of the Devil.

You remind me so much of myself.

"I thought . . . you liked me too."

It hurts to see.

"I can feel your thumping. It's so loud. Like it's vibrating through my arm. Like it's my own . . ."

But I can see it now. I couldn't before, but I do now. I can see it so clearly. How silly of me. You are far from being me—

"I'll miss that thumping . . . that warmth. I'll miss you."

—because I'm the one who's been dead.

She struggles under the crushing pressure of Victor's grip. Vanilla cries and Tiffany worms to break free. Instead, the noose tightens.

Please don't cry for me.

Vanilla's touch travels up her chest as Victor simultaneously pulls Tiffany's head back to expose her neck.

If dying is pain, I'm the one who has been dead all this time. Can't you see? You, Vanilla, have been so alive, it was blinding.

Vanilla's mouth opens and daggers grow like icicles from behind her perfect lips. Tiffany's face contorts with dreadful awe as this beautiful girl transforms into a mirror.

Into a monster.

You can only choose one.

Vanilla is gone. Taken over by her hunger. Her eyes are black, soulless, sprouting red and purple veins. Her tongue is forked, rolling out from her jaw with threads of saliva like thick cobwebs.

May you never know . . .

Tiffany's vision darkens at the edges as Vanilla disappears under her chin.

May you never know what dying is . . .

There's a pinprick, a kiss from her dear friend who is consuming her warmth. Blood rushes to her neck. A draining, a weakening of soul.

. . . because dying is pain.

Fangs glisten, stomachs growl, and Tiffany blacks out.

The concrete room overflows with shredding and tearing and rivers of rotting death.

EPILOGUE

Four months later

Vanilla walks down the narrow hallway, lollipop in mouth. She holds the stem between her fingertips, twirling and tugging as the candy hits the back of her teeth with a muted *clack*. She sighs in sedation. Across her neck is a thin gold chain, a glinting addition from daddy's collection.

"I have a present for you, my sweet. Do you like it?"

"It's beautiful! Did you use money to get it?"

"No . . . I used something else."

In her other hand are a key and two syringes, one empty and the other filled with her blood. She stops and turns, unlocking a door to her left with the key, and steps into a room where a small child with yellowing skin sits, coughing into the mattress. Beads of sweat cover his skin despite his tremors beneath the cocooned blanket. The room smells like rot, though to the boy it simply smells stale.

Vanilla shuts the door. She walks to the center of the room and crouches.

"Come here," she sings to the child, beckoning him over.

The child coughs and crawls out from the bed. He shivers so violently he nearly topples over. Without being asked, he sits cross-legged and rotates his arm, exposing his pale, spotted skin. Vanilla holds him and rubs her thumb across the swollen wounds that shouldn't be there. That should already be healing. She stops at a bump and scratches the scab off. It oozes a red tear.

"Count to three for me," she tells the boy.

The boy coughs then takes in a raspy inhale. "One . . . two—*ow!* I didn't finish!"

"Oops," Vanilla giggles. "I'm sorry. But hold still, please."

She pulls the plunger and the glass fills.

The boy winces when the needle slips out. The boy winces again when she sticks another needle into the same mark. Vanilla presses the plunger and the glass empties.

"What happened to your wrist?" the boy asks, pointing to the swollen puncture wound below her palm.

Vanilla pulls out the syringe and looks at the mark.

"That? Oh . . . that's my happy freckle."

"Happy freckle?"

"Yes. They're the spots on your arm that light up when you are happy. I was so happy to see you today that mine nearly exploded."

"Oh," the boy responds, thinking. "You know, before I got sick, my sister used to be so excited to see me, something like that would happen to her too." He coughs. "I'd be out in the backyard playing in the leaves and she would see me from inside the house. She would run out of the house and run to me and so many times she'd fall and scrape her knees. I got worried at first. But then she'd laugh and I'd laugh, so I think it was all okay. But sometimes she'd scrape them real bad and even though she was laughing, I could see her eyes were wet. But I laughed with her anyway. Even when I wasn't sure if she was okay."

A silence crawls into the room.

"Is it kind of like that?" the boy asks.

"Like what?"

"Like your freckle?"

"Oh . . . yes. Yes, just like that."

The boy coughs. "Well, I must be lucky to have not one but two people who care about me that much. To be hurt over me."

"Yes, you must be very lucky," Vanilla whispers. She runs her hand through the child's patchy hair. "It is nice to have someone care for you. To protect you."

"It's better to have . . . *cough* . . . two!"

"Yes . . . yes, it is." Vanilla's thumbs twirl back in her lap.

"Hey, are you okay?" the boy asks, poking Vanilla's knee for her attention.

"Hmm? Oh! Yes. You just reminded me of someone I used to know." She smiles weakly.

"Your sister?"

When she doesn't respond, the boy reaches out and places his hand on the back of hers. Something in his eyes makes Vanilla's stomach lurch with guilt. With the remembrance of all that warmth she'll never feel again.

"I must go."

"Do you have to?"

"Yes . . . unfortunately, I do."

Vanilla collects the syringes and hurries to the door. As she walks out, she hears the boy break into a coughing fit. She hesitates, then snaps the lock and leaves.

She takes the stairs down to the first level and turns into the medical office. Victor is inside, standing over one of the metal tables, lost in his notes as he scribbles chicken scratch into a beat-up notebook. A blood-filled syringe is nearby. His lace-painted tattoo throbs, a drop of blood leaking from the fresh puncture wound at its center.

"Daddy, can I get a sketch like yours on my wrist?"

"No, my sweet."

"Why not?"

"Because . . . the woman who made this is dead."

She lightly touches her own puncture mark, feeling it throb, before approaching him.

"Here you go," she says, holding out the equipment in her hands.

His pen halts for a second in acknowledgment before continuing. "Just put it in the bank, my sweet. You already know how. And make sure you put it on the left. I can smell the rot from here."

Her lips form a tight line as she walks over to the cooling unit on the back table and opens its door. A *hiss* greets her with clouds of frost. She secures the filled syringe in the empty slot to the left with the others and tosses the empty one in a bucket nearby. After a moment of glancing at the twelve perfectly placed units, labeled by simple characters she now knows are subject details, she closes the door.

She turns back to him. His face is stern and contemplative. She steps up to the table and looks over his shoulder. She has just begun to learn how to read, but his handwriting is illegible even to a trained reader. Like it's in a language only he understands. The ink coils across the notebook like the pages are a pit of snakes.

"Daddy?" she asks.

"Yes?" he replies without looking up from his work.

"That boy upstairs . . ." she starts.

"Which one?"

"The new one. The one we received yesterday morning."

"What about it?"

"Well, I was wondering . . . he seems so sick and lonely. If I could give him one of my old toys to play with . . ."

"That is very kind of you, Vanilla, but no."

"Why not?"

Victor stops writing, places his pen down, and turns to her. "My sweet, these are patients. Not friends. We treat them and let them go. I've explained this to you."

"But you gave *me* toys."

His jaw tightens. "You were not a patient."

"But you kept me in the room just like them."

"That room was made special for you. To protect you. Do you see anyone else admitted into that room? No. The only purpose of that room was to serve you until you outgrew it. Now it remains empty should you ever need it again."

"I still don't understand why we can't just give him something to play with."

"Because *it* is a creature. *It* doesn't need anything to play with," he hisses.

"So then why take care of *it* to begin with?" she hisses back.

He takes a deep breath in. The rage that flared up in his eyes tames. "Because we need *it* to survive. Unfortunately, it has what we require to remain viable, and if we can't come to terms with a peaceful way for this exchange then we will perish. So, as I've said, we take in the sick ones, heal them, take what we need, and throw them back into the Outside. *It's* happy and so are we."

"But—"

"That is enough!" His hand slams against the tabletop. "I've given you enough explanation. Now, do as I say!"

She flinches at the sudden outbreak, then calms herself, but not without that feeling, that uncomfortable yanking feeling that likes to tug at her core. She has not felt it for a while. Not since the night she lost that warmth.

"Okay," she says. "I'm sorry."

His face softens. He reaches his hand out to playfully tug on her pigtail. "That is all right, my sweet. I only want what's best for you, even if you don't understand my reasons." His gaze hardens. "You know I only want to protect you, to keep you safe, right?"

"Yes."

"Good! Now, let me return to my work."

She nods and leaves the room. Her teeth grind and her fingers curl into her palms, but she tries to settle down the boil. Tries to rationalize with his logic, even if her thoughts want other things. She hurries up the stairs to the top, not sure of what she's going to do but allowing her body to make the decisions for her. Her footsteps guide her to the end of the hall, to her door, the entrance to her old room. An old friend. She swings open the door and sees the concrete. That same, monotonous concrete. The walls have been cleaned, stripped of impermanent paint that once lived momentarily in the room. The mattress remains tidy in its corner, waiting to welcome her in. Sitting on the mattress are her old toys. She brightens in recognition of the blue fabric that has been cleaned and stitched together, resting in dust. She walks over to the stuffed thing and picks it up. It hasn't been touched for some time now, lonely and without anyone to play with.

She frowns.

A wave of certainty overcomes her as she turns to step out of her room, stuffed blue dog in hand. She tiptoes up to the door a few feet from her own and carefully places her fingertips on the handle. She snaps the lock and takes a step inside, squeezing the stuffed blue dog in her hand from her excitement, nearly bursting its stitching wide open.

She creeps out from behind the door, jumpy in anticipation, but sees that the boy has fallen asleep, his back to her.

"Hello, child! I have a surprise for you!"

A soft scratching comes from somewhere behind the walls.

Another joins.

And then another.

She takes a step closer, her eyebrows lifting. "Are you not excited for a surprise?" She bends down to her knees and taps the child's shoulder. "Wake up, my sweet! You are going to love this surprise!"

Silence.

She frowns and adds a little force to the boy's shoulder, turning him over onto his back. His eyes are open, staring in terror at the ceiling, blotched with red veins and yellowed gloss. Vanilla waves her hand in front of his gaze, but he does not move.

Scritch-scratch.

He does not flinch when she snaps her fingers a few inches from his nose.

Scritch-scratch.

Vanilla places the dog down on the mattress and leans in. His face is stiff, disfigured from what looks like so much suffering. The happy freckles have vanished from his skin.

"That's right, my sweet. Think of it as fixing. You want to fix it, don't you?"

She leans in closer, trying to hear for the exchange of air she no longer experiences herself. But the boy's breath is silent.

"Fix it and be with me forever. I will protect you. I will keep

you safe."

She lifts one hand and places her palm on the boy's chest, pressing down ever so slightly to feel for even the faintest of heartbeats.

Do you need to be fixed?

Thousands of scratches consume the room from all corners. A symphony of grooves in the making.

I know what it's like to need to be fixed.

She searches his chest.

And never be the one to do the fixing.

She searches and she searches and she searches.

VANILLA

Nothing.

ACKNOWLEDGMENTS

This story would not be possible without the following people:

To my Teta Mona. My understanding of unconditional love is in no small part because of you. Thank you for all that you've done and do for me, and for raising me to be the woman I am today.
Je t'aime de tout mon coeur.

To Todd. You've read two different versions of this book, one far better than the other. Thank you for your patience and time in this two-year project. Your enthusiasm really helped carry this across the finish line.

To Andi. As always, you know how to motivate me when I'm feeling down. Thank you for being my number one fan and for showing me the power of my words.

To Lauren. When we first met (gosh, has it only been a year and a half?) this was the book I told you I'd been working on. And from that mutual love of books and the written word, our friendship grew. Thank you for reading and responding to my questions at random times of the day and being the strong support I need. Your advice and perspective are vital.

And last but not ever least, to Spencer. Having an editor is good. Having an editor who sees your vision is like possessing magic. What you've done to my words is inconceivable and invaluable. Your tireless and patient effort with this novel and with me did not go unnoticed and any outsider who could witness what happens to these words between us would be in absolute awe of you. Cheers to the future and to the magic in your blood.

Mona Kabbani is a horror fan, writer, and reviewer obsessed with psychology and the human condition. She emulates the conflict of the good versus the bad and all of the in between in her work while providing an entertainingly horrifying experience. She is a Lebanese immigrant living the American dream in New York City where much of her writing is inspired. You can follow her on Instagram @moralityinhorror for more and sign up to her mailing list on her website, www.moralityinhorror.com.

VANILLA